A FLASH IN TIME

J. N. FRYE

ReadersMagnet, LLC

A Flash In Time
Copyright © 2023 by J. N. Frye

Published in the United States of America

Library of Congress Control Number:	2023923343
ISBN Paperback:	979-8-89091-351-7
ISBN Hardback:	979-8-89091-352-4
ISBN eBook:	979-8-89091-353-1

All rights reserved. No part of this publication may be reproduced, stored in a retrieval system or transmitted in any way by any means, electronic, mechanical, photocopy, recording or otherwise without the prior permission of the author except as provided by USA copyright law.

The opinions expressed by the author are not necessarily those of ReadersMagnet, LLC.

ReadersMagnet, LLC
10620 Treena Street, Suite 230 | San Diego, California, 92131 USA
1.619. 354. 2643 | www.readersmagnet.com

Book design copyright © 2023 by ReadersMagnet, LLC. All rights reserved.

Cover design by Tifanny Curaza
Interior design by Dorothy Lee

An inventive and manically fast-paced thriller with the feel of a Hollywood movie, J.N. Frye's *A FLASH IN TIME* is exciting, nerdy, energetic, and engaging.

—Indie Book Review

A high-concept, action-packed, and truly explosive science fiction novel set in a recognizable if somewhat advanced version of the near present-day United States, J.N. Frye's *A Flash In Time* blends the concepts of time slips and alternative realities with the conventions of the thriller genre to provide a perplexing puzzle that hinges on the danger posed by both unchecked power, government conspiracies, and possible alien invaders.

—Seattle Book Review

This book is a winner from start to finish, a sci-fi adventure with heart.

—Portland Book Review

A Flash In Time is the perfect novel for fans of the science fiction genre, it has very possible themes and ideas that when you read it, you can envision it all come true.

—Pacific Book Review

The author skillfully crafts a narrative that delves into the themes of racial biases, personal development, and the perseverance of people overcoming adversity.

—San Diego Book review

TABLE OF CONTENTS

PROLOGUE 9

Chapter 1: Heart Attack?.. 14
Chapter 2: The Ride Begins... 38
Chapter 3: Wisdom of Age... 60
Chapter 4: The Detective and the Canary 67
Chapter 5: The Intersection of Time 86
Chapter 6: A Skeptic Converted 99
Chapter 7: Book 'em Danno... 108
Chapter 8: Where's My Car?... 123
Chapter 9: A Human Face on Nameless Tragedy 132
Chapter 10: Armageddon replay – a rewind in time 139
Chapter 11: New Visions... 153
Chapter 12: What Time is it Anyway?.............................. 163
Chapter 13: I'm from the Government and I'm here…..... 169
Chapter 14: Some Vacation 181
Chapter 15: A Pain from DC... 194
Chapter 16: Turn off the Lights When You Leave 207
Chapter 17: Got Power?... 220
Chapter 18: Okay, it's over! 227
Chapter 19: What the Hell is THAT? 235

Chapter 20: The Milton Problem Solution 247
Chapter 21: Clocks are no damned good 264
Chapter 22: Join the Crowd 279
Chapter 23: New Arrivals 284
Chapter 24: Get it and Run 306
Chapter 25: A spoken story 323
Chapter 26: The End of Time 327
Chapter 27: The Details 342

EPILOGUE 361

A FLASH IN TIME

PROLOGUE

A long government project, painstakingly "dug into" the hi-desert of New Mexico was now nearly done. After years of in-fighting to get the persons needed, and table pounding arguments for Federal money, coupled with frustrating technical setbacks. Finally, the time for the test was at hand. It was a cool, very early morning of Tuesday, May 30th, 2006.

Everyone on the team was fidgety, normally silent people were talking to others, and some mumbling to themselves as they assembled in the project conference room at 01:20 AM. The schedule on the conference room whiteboard, crossed out, erased, and adjusted a dozen times had it listed as the final meeting before that big switch was to be thrown.

Everyone could see he was pissed, more now than any time in weeks. Hell, it was the culmination of months of failed tests and questionable feedback from frontline sensors which still had "unsteady" feedback, even now after five solid weeks of 15-hour days of troubleshooting. No wonder all the forced overtime and snails paced work had everyone's nerves frazzled.

So now it was all landing here, at this last pre-dawn hour. Yes, all these factors had taken their toll on the team, and mostly it seemed on the Program Manager.

"Your concerns are duly noted," the triangle shaped well-worn pink pencil eraser tapped the midnight green Formica® conference room tabletop, then the surviving 2/3 of the Ticonderoga #2 began another series of nervous but controlled flips through stubby fingers, "but I have thirteen years in this project and I'm not about to stall the activation one damned day longer! Like all of you, I'm exhausted."

Her attractive, tired face but still alert eyes flashed after this 'Wednesday into Thursdays' 20 hours at work. She turned to look at the Program Manager three seats down at the end of the conference room table. Those eyes had been going over her printout on the table in front of her, and now faced him, "Look, Chris, this thing has taken on a life of its own with you! You know we all want to get the ENet up and running, but the data coming back from the Yagi sensors just doesn't look right. I'd like to excite the array with one-eighth power again and try to check the feed-back loops, see why they're outside the expected readings." Seeing his shaking head, "Yes…again!" Doctor Joan Rand, in a white lab coat, returned to staring at an Excel print-out full of rows of numbers, held in long, manicured fingers, the right hand with a blue Pentel P207 mechanical pencil between the index and next digit. Most of the printout numbers were in red.

"We did that five times... No." More pencil taps, flips. "Not another day, not another hour! Tonight's the night. The power companies are standing by, every generator in the Southwest at 'hot ready' and they say another delay will cost yet another $90,000.00. Look Joan, it will work, I know it, the computer models know it." The pencil-free hand and arm waved an arc at the ceiling, "the fucking cosmos knows it! ...you all know I have my career and its attached ass on the line – and damn-it that important aspect of my anatomy knows it!" A sad, mis-timed, over-loud theatrical attempt to inject geek humor...falling flat.

Back to being the controlling boss as his voice had risen. Tap-tap-flip. The voice was tension charged, but exhaling a long breath, reaching for calmer tone he looked down at the tabletop, then continued. "Look, people, I know it will work! Now stop with the delaying bullshit and set the programs to excite modulators, static 150% voltage in the main array at NLT 02:00, pre-heat current to the antenna by 02:45, power up the AM Modulators from pre-heat to hot ready by 03:55, and full on at 04:00." He looked around the table with a laser stare, pencil motionless, the clear signal that no more discussion was wanted, to most not allowed. "Got it?"

Shaking her head, and in spite of the 'poised-for-a-strike cobra' stationary pencil, she said, laying the printouts carefully on the table top smoothing them in a deliberate three second pause, and with everyone around the table looking at her, "For the record and posterity, the feed-back array is showing strange data...power levels we can't account for, and I want that in these last pre-operational event meeting minutes."

Now, as he had backed his straining chair from the table, staring down at the floor in front of him, and practically hissing through gritted teeth, he said "Very well, Joan, so noted. Now get to work on the exciting protocols... run time is just a few hours away." He leaned forward and banged the table for emphasis.

The pencil snapped.

A FLASH IN TIME

PART 1

Where have you gone if you haven't left?

CHAPTER 1

Heart Attack?

Sherriff's Corporal Ivanov Longfeather is a handsome, spiritual young man. As a half Navajo and half Russian Cusack, he occasionally had what his Native-side people called "visions." Non-believers said they were just intense dreams, but Native Americans 'knew' they were more than a dream. Problem was that, like dreams, they always needed 'some figuring out.' So here he was, with a nagging feeling from an unknown corner of his subconscious, an uneasy and troubling feeling that there was something...wrong. Not exactly a vision, well not yet anyway...but a real strong feeling.

To the right side of the truck was a rough wall of rock cut by a bulldozer probably operated by a white-knuckling operator as the machine was at any second ready to flip off the side of the mountain. Out of the front windshield the wash-board dusty gravel road disappeared into the darkness upward toward the peak, and behind down toward the valley and town. A sheer drop-off of 600 feet about a regular lane width away loomed in the darkness to the left.

Staring out of the windshield, nothing obvious appeared, well, okay, something was moving on the windshield. His 1,200-lumen mag-light illuminated a little green spider, maybe a quarter inch across, that was busy walking from the windshield wiper up toward the top of the glass, stopping every few seconds like it was reading a map. Ivey thought, "Wonder why they do that? Don't those little girls live on a web or something? Wonder how they stick to the glass? Wonder why the hell I'm thinking about this?" Tiring of tiny green spider contemplations, he began a mental checklist.

Cops do that. Some say organizing thoughts into a checklist format is a cop thing because of their regimented training – follow the rules. It's pounded into every part of their Academy schooling and ride-on instruction. Some say that it's part of what draws one to be a peace officer, attention to the law, which when boiled down to it, are lists of rules written by Lawyers so no one can understand them. Rules. Mental checklists come out, especially for cops on boring duty, late in the night-early morning of a boring shift. It's a method of keeping the mind working when every neuron fiber is tugging at unconsciousness, asking, nay, begging for sleep.

With this particular conjured "out of the blue" checklist Ivey started to answer the 'something wrong' he was looking for, something out of place, the abnormal, anything to help with the uncomfortable nagging, pebble in his cowboy boot type of uneasiness he just couldn't shake. Not the regular cop checklist, like, is that license tag obscured? Is the driver drunk? Is her seatbelt on? Is she texting? Is she hot? Okay–okay a more relevant checklist, he laughed to himself. Still...on a young healthy straight male Deputy's checklist, hot counts, well that one should be on any personal checklists anyway, as should mini-skirts, tank-tops, bright smiles, good tans, and in the winter, those high, tight knee-length boots...he stopped there, mind caught, then added yoga pants...Okay, that list was taking a pleasant but useless turn and could go on for hours.

This was no traffic stop, and so far, it was absolutely nothing... but.

He contemplated the scene out the windshield again, the grey of ¾ moon night moonlight and big sky beauty, then noticing the music that came from somewhere, some city, from across those big skies and a trillion-trillion pin-point stars, music from some place he didn't even know. Here on this high mountain, it could be anywhere on the left coast – musically pulsed dancing electron energy sent off a tower in some unknown city screaming to space at near the speed of light and "skipped" back to earth by the ions of the earth's silent protector – the ionosphere. In this case the skip brought Loreena Isabel Irene McKennit, who was singing a classic ballad of a highwayman and the inn keeper's daughter - well he knew it was a highwayman, but the beautiful voice was unrecognized, he'd have to find out more about her, buy her CD or download it from the music service. "She's really good," he thought.

Speaking to himself, "Hope the lady DJ tells us who she is." As if the self-same lady DJ was in the car listening to Ivey, the song ended and the voice of the night DJ-mistress said in her smooth as warm honey voice, "Loreena McKennit, from the 'Book of Secrets' 1997 CD – Yep, a good voice like Loreena's will get you a record contract, but my 38-Ds got me a real good man."

The Deputy laughed out loud.

Okay- okay, focus, first item on the "list;" the status of the day. Looking East toward the mountain top, he noted the sun was locked and loaded for another day, typically hot, bright, and high-desert relentless, poised, still hiding over the top of the ancient mountain. Aurora, the Goddess of the Dawn, is waiting for her turn again. He liked Aurora, she was beautiful, better looking than RA with what, a crow's head? Much better looking than his local Native American Thunder God, yep, Aurora was his Sun deity of choice, and nope, this part of the checklist was normal.

The colors, even though he couldn't see them so far today, were most likely normal. He had checked them yesterday and yep, they always looked like plane 'ol dirt this time of year.

The monsoon season would give a brief respite from the yellow-brown to orange-red side of the color pallet, a spatter of green and a zillion desert flowers would appear like pop-corn going off when the storms rolled across the high desert.

Ahhh- those storms…like little gray circles of intense rain, at least little when viewed from up here. Inside the circle of falling water, it got real wet, real fast. The threads of lightening stitching the gray lower clouds, and in the daylight the tops of the storm clouds snow white and outlined against the blue sky like they were cut from white paper and glued there. He could watch them roam the desert floor down there for hours. Little patches of a pissed Mother Nature marching, drenching those in her path as she rumbled toward the east across the high desert. Flash floods for sure.

On the list, here and now in the fading starlight, the deep dried-blood-brown colored crags and steep rock faces of Sandia Mountain looked like dirty grey ice as they stabbed savagely upward into the nearly perfect inky blue-black sky. Waxing poetic on that checklist…but it was normal. Three peaks up a higher point had just become a brilliant green point of light swimming on darkness below. Beautiful, "And that view is why I'm here!" he thought for the millionth time in his young life.

The clear desert sky. There was the normal faint starlight struggling to compete, maybe to hold back against the creeping arrival of Aurora's blue and another day. Check that one off, the sky was progressing toward day - normal.

Fourth, another end of May New Mexico high desert day was working into its first third. Time marching on to what? Retirement, old age? Fishing! That's it! But not for a while, and not now…

and nothing wrong…yet the feeling. This pesky "something wrong" feeling he'd had all morning since leaving town to report for his routine, boring, patrol of the Sandia Mountain Native American Reservations at 01:00? Now, at about 15 minutes to 4 AM, it continued, this strange feeling of something wrong. Was it like that mouse or one of those nearly clear 100 legged things, bugs? Running along the wall you just see out of the corner of your eye, barely into your consciousness – there? Did I see something? Maybe? Maybe not. It was the end of one of those uncomfortable nights that everyone has, where the tape loops around and around saying "something out-of-whack here."

Actually, the something wrong was close, but still unknown to the Tribal Deputy Sheriff, and soon would take a turn…from a feeling of just "wrong" toward "real wrong."

Over the top of the mountain ridge line, and a few miles to the East. "Capacitors charged?"

"Check."

"AM Modulator section primed to 150%."

"Check."

"Receiving sensor-loop phantom power feedback current?"

"Check."

"Modulator section pre-heat?"

"Check, plate voltage at 85% and climbing, charge time to go in 90 seconds. The VLF frequency generators are stable."

"Okay then let's do it - excite and connect test modulation to the carrier frequency in T Minus 60 seconds –fifty-nine–fifty-eight...."

Like the young Sherriff's deputy, Doctor Joan Rand didn't know why, but she was sweating, okay, being an attractive woman, she was perspiring, or what do they say? Glowing...and nearly shaking – from...what...why? Well, pushing a button which connected nearly 5,000,000 amperes to a cable buried in the ground was a bit on the large side, but shaking? Yes, her brilliant and logical mind had worked out the uneasy feeling, finally isolating it to...fear. But fear of what? Maybe the inconsistent and unreadable data coming back from the miles of antenna radiators and connected sensing loops?

It was circling in her mind and was not able to be nudged out, even now with the big test - "Where was that 'extra' power coming from?"

Back on the west side of the ridge in the Deputy's Tahoe, he was looking into the fading inky darkness to a grey pre-morning valley. The next item on the mental checklist he mentally checked off as he peered into what sometimes seemed infinity.

Clear air and a perfect perch, he was the highest eagle in the desert, on the side of this narrow mountain road. The 11,800-foot mountain would keep the valley in semi-darkness, then shade for hours after the rest of the South-West came to daylight.

Most people on "graveyard" shift will tell you, at this early between morning day and ending night, the eye lids start to grow heavy. Circadian rhythms fighting for normal.

The radio cut off.

The deputy was in between awake and asleep, checklist fading to the background, and lots of delicate spider web connections between conscious and sleep un-conscious.

His mind strayed - things hid in those valley shadows. Was that it? A monster hiding, clinging to the rock, just over the edge of the cliff in the shadows, ready to grab a foot if he stepped away from his truck? The classic monster under the bed scenario everyone had as a kid, now edging into that plane between sleep and awake that he was drifting toward. He shook his head clearing the sleep-creeping-fog, and the bull-shit monster thoughts that had started.

Corporal Ivanov Longfeather looked from the postcard landscape framed by the windshield to his watch, then at least a part of the abnormal hit him.

Beads of sweat, then he noticed the total lack of wind. Bingo! Finally, something weird. Where was all this humidity coming from? It hit like a wave of invisible not-hot steam. Even in way hotter temps, the sweat normally evaporated as soon as it arrived on the surface of his golden skinned arm. This natural cooling let one be comfortable in all but the hottest New Mexico days. And the wind, at 11,800 feet on the side of this ancient rock, well, there was always wind…at least a breeze…there was a few minutes ago, wasn't there? Night up here was always cool and pleasant, but not now.

He put on his Sheriffs' cowboy hat with the Native American Regional Tribal – Sheriff Deputy five-pointed star, didn't need the hat – just a habit, and opened the door to the Chevy Tahoe/police cruiser. Ivanov, or Ivey, was one of a small number of Native American people with police experience who served as an interface between the Native American Tribal Police on the "Rez" and the civilian authorities. The plan was working well after a few hard spots in the first two years. Now both 'sides' saw the benefits. Cooperation between the Anglos and Native American law enforcement folks had never been better.

The truck's windows were open, so he did not expect any temperature difference, but as his boot hit the ground, the air seemed to get even heavier, thicker, hotter feeling if that were possible. No claw or slime-oozing tentacle came over the edge of the cliff toward his boot, "Well, at least that's a relief, but…damned!" he said out loud to no one, as he found himself leaning heavily on the side of the truck. It was as though he had put on thirty pounds since sliding into the truck just a few hours ago.

Then he thought of his first aid training… sweating, heavy feeling, "Ivey, you having a heart problem?" he whispered. No…no pain anywhere. He stooped a little to look in the side mirror, it reflected normal color, at least as far as he could see in the pre-dawn light. A quick shine of his flashlight showed that he looked 90% Navajo, but with light brown hair, and green eyes. This interesting combination made him interesting in an attractive way.

He didn't notice that the flashlight went out a split second before he switched it to 'off'.

At the base across the mountain, it was countdown 0 +2seconds.

Ivey shook his head, maybe the altitude? No, the air seemed even heavier than the thin mountain air normally did, anyway, he lived up here, so he was well used to the thinner air. The hair on his neck moved, like a wolf raising its hackles, suddenly becoming afraid, but of what? The cool rush from a minor shot of adrenalin washed over him.

Somewhere, miles away, now a little over 15 seconds prior, unknown to him one of the most powerful electrical-electronic devices ever assembled had begun its awakening with the hiss-clang-hiss of thirty-six 5,000-amp air powered-electrical line breakers closing on each of the three - 3 phase legs of 150,000 volt circuits. Twelve 14,000 horsepower GE turbine generators, started and warmed up 30 minutes earlier, rumbled and screamed like an airliner going full throttle for a takeoff- same engine, different use. These added to the 150,000-volt feeders from the commercial lines coming into the base, which now quivered and added their power to the load. The next in line devices, the oil filled and Freon cooled transformers, took the load with a shutter and groan...and then...an audible vibration, about a third the speed of a normal heart-beat seemed to permeate everything in the command center, a thump that was perceived...felt, but otherwise was not present. Joan watched things progressing as planned, then...what?

Back on the west side of the mountain movement in the moonlight gravel at the edge of the worn gravel road caught his eye. Then more movement to his left, near the high side of the road. Barely visible in the near darkness. The gravel seemed to be moving, he grabbed for his flashlight, it flickered and stayed dead. Using the universal flashlight repair procedure, he banged it on his hand, operated the switch and banged again. No help - what? The damned thing worked a minute ago? He then focused his sight into the slowly growing pre-dawn light/moonlight and saw the source of the movement, spiders, big and smaller, some brown scorpions, horned toads and lizards, then a side-winder rattler, all had escaped from their hiding places and were scurrying around in what looked like drunken circles, some ran off the side of the road into the thin air of the bluff, as did the snake.

Instinctively Ivey heaved his butt, with great heavy difficulty, even needing to hook his cowboy boot heal into the brush bumper, to up on the hood of the Tahoe, and watched the frenzy. Birds came from nowhere and screeched in the sky, furiously flapping wings as they struggled to stay aloft. The flurry of activity continued a few more seconds, then, all the creatures vanished, almost as quickly as they had appeared! Like the "America" song from the 60's said, "The desert is an ocean with its life underground." He knew it was so, but what had caused this section of "underground ocean" to go nuts?

He thought of the Navajo spoken stories of how animals, insects and rodents could foretell of an earthquake, by their behavior. An earthquake coming? Here? No friggin' way!

Then, a truly alarming thought popped into his mind- had there actually been bugs and stuff running around and disappearing in a few seconds? Where were the birds? Was he losing it? Yep, this definitely qualified as weird! Maybe that checklist had ended too soon.

He returned to the side mirror peering into it again. Ivey took a finger and pulled an eye-lid down, more open, looking into the mirror from a few inches away, still nearly dark, he strained to see exactly what? Okay, it occurred to him that he had absolutely no idea what. His face moved, like it was deforming, as though a wave of water was slowly moving just below the surface of the mirror, in that other place, where Alice explored the opium blasted mind of Lewis Carroll, then the shimmering mirror locked back normal. Bad light? Medical problem? Another shot of adrenalin at what he thought was his face melting. Or was it maybe he was teetering on the edge of passing out?

Suddenly, a very bright, white, 2-second-long flash of light in the sky sort of behind him away from town? But it seemed closer, reflected in the mirror, the source of which was blocked by his hat. A thought hit like a slap that the light seemed to be moving toward him. He released the eyelid and spun around, right hand instinctively on the butt of his Beretta 9mm pistol, half expecting someone with a very bright hand light or flash camera who had sneaked up close behind him. The light was gone. No one. No clouds, no thunder, nothing. Wait, not thunder, a single BOOM reached him far up the on the side of the mountain. A sub-conscious counter calculated light-to-noise. Maybe three – four miles as the crow flies. The boom, like a stick of dynamite, only much, much bigger and deeper. He remembered that it sounded more like the two-thousand-pound bombs he'd heard while in the Army. Imagination? With no wind, sound carried for miles and miles, then he heard a Burlington Northern Santa Fe freight blowing for the crossing at Avenida Bernalillo Street as the mile-long metal snake raced across the desert headlong toward a new unknown home, the crossing was a good fourteen miles away. Three miles was nothing. He began searching his mind-map of what in a three-mile circle could have exploded, but there was no smoke, no lingering plume of dust visible in the now dawn light.

Across the mountain in the command center, all hell had broken loose. Looking out the windows at the project's power sub-station, the staff saw every line breaker open in the same second, all with huge arcs of green lightning colored by the melting copper on the arc-balls. The instruments pegged to red, a few shattered and died in a puff of acrid insulation smoke. Technicians ducked for cover. What later would be discovered to be the disintegration of the turbine engines, the sound of incredible tearing metal, loud and scary...then silence – the turbines, which had stalled, twisting their out-put shafts into pretzels, flying apart in a shower of sparks, four of them bending their enclosures nearly in half, no "hummm," no more heartbeat thump. Glowing lumps of still half molten copper buss-bars and flash balls gave the silent equipment an even more ominous dying orange glow. Small fires were lit across the entire sub-station lot.

At Ivey's Tahoe, across the mountain ridge, that single boom. Not rolling thunder, nothing else. Not even an echo, well, no echo made sense, he was on the reflecting face that would kick back the echo a noise hitting from somewhere down there.

Looking into the valley ...nothing unusual ...or... something along the road back to town was wrong, something missing? But what?

He looked up at the fading stars, and saw ribbons of faint bluish green and blue light winding across the sky like the sidewinder rattler a little while ago. "Wow! What the hell is that?" he said out loud, searching his memory, it looks like those pictures of the aurorae-borealis ...what do they call them, Northern Lights? How come now and here?

And what was that? Something on the Pearson Bar-Nun ranch 4 miles down the hill as the crow flies, 15 miles by road to where the mountain began the 4 miles to mostly rolling hills and then flat desert. Smoke? No, maybe just dust...nope, nothing. Probably from a pick-up truck one of the ranch hands had as they went to check on their animals, or fences, or pot crops. He stared for what seemed a long time, arms folded across his chest, back against the truck, then gave up, nothing came across his radio... and no more wacked out wild-life.

The ranchers who owned the gently sloping land had leased the space for the E-R-Mag Labs ENet project. The 'antenna', once buried three meters underground and back filled, would become invisible, and the land could be returned to the skinny drifting cattle who eked out a meager living on scrub grass, and if really hungry or thirsty, a bite out of a juvenile prickly-pear cactus.

Life's tough for a free-range cow out here. Hell. Life is tough out here on the side of the Southern Serra-Madras - period.

Well, other than what seemed to be a hot shower without the water, bat-shit crazy wildlife, a big-assed boom, Northern Lights, there was nothing further here he could put his finger on, okay, he had to admit, all that was grounds for a weird feeling, which he noted, continued. And he had to admit, frankly these few events were actually more in one shift than he'd had in 6 months. And...wasn't all this enough? Well there was back then in the Fall, when a flash flood had him rescuing hikers from a tree 20 feet out in the in the rush of muddy water in a normally dry creek bed where they had been camping, since then na-da.

His police radio remained silent, no tankers flipping, no train derailments, no bored-shitless

Native American kids with dynamite stolen from the quarry on the other side, and up three peaks from his place on the mountain. Better get to town and see if he's just imagining something. But there was this heaviness thing, what was with that? He noticed a smell, he'd smelt it before in the Army – ozone?

Yes, Ivanov had feelings about things around him, had for years, since he was a kid. He trusted his intuition, his "feelings". Always had. It had served him well in Afghanistan as a Special Crime Investigator for the US Army MP's. It served him well as a cop, but, not too well as a single guy. Seems the intuition crashed when it came to women, damned that intuition. 'Sometimes it takes more than good looks' he thought.

Afghanistan.

"Hey Ivey, just like home huh?" How many times had he heard that during the twelve plus months he had been stationed there? He didn't even go into the reasons that the place God created and then, apparently got pissed at and forgot, sometime in the 8th century was not at all like home, yes, the mountainous portion of the Middle East, was nothing like his home in New Mexico. The seasons were harsher and seemed ass-backwards.

Then there were the people. They seemed to hate everything, America, Jews, Pakistani's, Jesus, George Bush, Obama, fun, women, especially their bodies, science, cartoons, music (unless it sounded like it was out of tune and playing backward) edible food, toilet paper, and, most perplexing, apparently even each other. The first civilian he had seen was an ancient man pushing a two-wheeled cart, inside the cart was a donkey, looking around like he wanted to jump out. A new twist on the horse before the cart? "Man, that's messed up," he thought as he shouldered his M.O.L.L.E. vest pack and moved to the Hum-V waiting to take him to his station. It turned out that 'backwards to conventional' personified this part of the world, at least what he would see.

Okay, that said, he had to admit 'His people' were admittedly a little slow on the uptake too, trusting the white guys who were displacing them a few hundred years ago, yeah, treaties that were not, and the alcohol problem was still there, and yes, aspects of their tribal plight were still troubling, but his people loved everything. The land, the mountains, food, oh-hell yes, women! Dress them in shapeless black cotton trash bags? I don't friggin' think so! Cover their face so ya couldn't see that day brightening smile nearly every man on earth loves? Okay, every man not gay should love. Stone them if they said howdy to a man not related? What kind of nonsense was that? Pass a law making rape legal? Kill gay folks? Really?

Even the Afghani mountains seemed different, when God left, he took his paintbrush, the colors were washed out, like nature never got around to painting them. Very light brown, almost bleached white. Rocco, the 'A company' comedian described it best, "This whole Goddamned place is made of sun bleached-constipated-dried-cat-shit piled nine thousand feet deep. Need a house? Just saw off cat shit bricks and pile 'em up." Why had that stuck with him the three years since Rocco said it?

Deep blue had faded to blue-grey, then a super bright flash of Sun shot across the mountain top, and popped Ivey back the here and now.

He re-opened the dusty Tahoe door, removed his hat, tossing it across to the passenger seat. It dropped onto the communications console just rear of the newly installed computer and rolled on the brim into the passenger side foot-well. Maybe the friggin' hat had gotten heavy too. He shook his head and laughed.

Twisting the key, the truck turned over slowly, but caught. What, even the truck feels heavy? The amp meter, added as part of the cop interceptor package, showed full charging, 160 amps! What had drained the battery that much? STOP IT! This heavy shit was getting out of hand! He flashed back to the bugs and amphibians scrambling…to…or away from…what?

The AM radio came back up as the engine started and didn't help at all, The Doors were 20 seconds into "Strange Days" on the ionosphere skipping oldies station. "That sounds right to me."

He looked at his watch, a military wind-up one he had just sort of kept when he left the Army, and shook his head. "Damned, I lost 35 minutes someplace? Was I dreaming all this 'weirdness?' A nightmare…a vision, sort of anyway?"

He would proceed uphill on the gravel road further to a wider spot around the next turn as he clicked the seat-belt, pulled the lever to drive, it was always tight, but ¼ mile further up the road in a passing area he could execute a 3-point-turn to head back down the road. He made the turn and headed back downhill. Daylight was just beginning its daily erasing of the shadow in front of him, he slowed as the rutted, wash-boarded gravel road began the drop into the valley bottom and town, sunlight just now hitting the desert floor miles away. Those washboard ripples in the gravel could bounce a car right off the road, and here off-road (like a 600-foot cliff) was pretty serious stuff.

The thermometer climbed as he descended, once on less steep ground as he passed the sleeping Bar-Nunn ranch it was already ninety degrees! Yet still just in the shade of the mountain. Damned, this was hot, usually 90 degrees came around noon, if at all this early in the year, and not this early in the day. He powered the windows closed and turned on the air-conditioner. Within a mile the sweat on his arm was gone and he felt cool and dry.

As he continued down the slope, he came out of a patch of scrub ironwood and mesquite bushes then into a road now in full sunlight. Suddenly he stopped on the deserted road and looked at the outline of the town now a quarter filling the windshield side to side, still sixteen miles away, and another 4,500 feet further below, down in the valley. His mind could not shake the 'something wrong.' Then, very slowly, like arriving at the conclusion that there really had been a mouse, he realized what it was. Well, maybe anyway. There was no wind here either and no heat ripples from the road, and the outline of the town was absolutely clear. Ninety plus degree asphalt in the quiet high desert and miles of blacktop with the Sun quickly climbing, bombarding it, and no heat ripples. There was not even that little line of blurry stuff right on the surface of the road, like a layer of water, where the road dropped away over a little rise.

Again, it reminded him of that pesky analogy of a mouse running along the wall while watching TV, on the very outside of one's vision. Something there? Or nothing? The radio skip was gone as the ionosphere had raised in the coming sunlight and was now tuned to an Albuquerque oldies station where The Doors ended the double play with "Riders on The Storm." The next song started with the voice of Arthur Brown, a one hit wonder, shouted his only first line of his only hit song "I am the God of hell fire – and I bring you FIRE!" That corked it, too much paranormal input; he chuckled, cleared his throat, and switched off the radio and clicked the fan speed down from HI to LOW, and made the left onto New Mexico State Route 165.

Damned! Was this really interesting enough of an event to cause him to stop the truck? Enough to ponder? So friggin' what? No heat ripples, surely there were circumstances where there were no heat ripples in the desert on the highway at damned near 06:00. "Get a fucking grip!" He said aloud, this time to the Deputy Sherriff looking back from his rear -view mirror, who even now looked edgy, and was frowning. He got the police radio microphone off the clip and pressed the transmit button, using the more powerful truck radio than the portable normally on his belt, which was now in the charger on the console.

A subconscious reach across time and space to see if the world was still there?

"Luna, you in yet?" Her normal starting time was 05:30, but as laid-back as the town was, she had some "flexibility" when she started.

A somewhat distorted but readable a voice came back, "I'm here, watcha need?" As usual, Ivanov could tell Luna had a mouthful of something, almost universally unhealthy, and always held in a square of unfolded, greasy aluminum foil. The woman should have weighed 900 pounds, instead had stabilized at around 260. Still, at four feet six inches, that was a lot of POLPF as the guys joked. Pounds of Luna per-foot.

"Nothing special, just checkin' in, I've been up on the hill between the tribes. Anything for me? Anything going on?"

'The tribes' was the nick-name of the three Native American reservations on Sandia Mountain separated by six miles of ranch land, and a gravel road.

"Well the lights went out for a minute a while ago, messed all th' clocks and stuff up, but nothin' else - Oh yeah, the guy from the TV place had a message on the non-emergency recorder, says your TV works fine for him, no waves across the screen like you brought it in for. You can pick it up anytime, but he's still got to charge you $30 for lookin' at it."

A pause, then, "The Sherriff wants everyone in by 13:30 and for you to stay over for a fizzyikal year budget meeting, you can take the time off tomorrow's shift."

"Tell Sam NFP," Ivanov put the microphone back on the clip, checked the rear view mirror and continued down the road toward town.

Now maybe an answer.

As he got to the "flatlands" he slowed for the only jog in the road, a kind of "S" turn where the ninety-nine percent of the time dry stream bed of Pin Oak Run crossed the highway, he continued to slow, looking to his left. Was it possible? Who? How? Why? Stopping, he turned on the light bar on top of the truck, drifted slowly until the vehicle could be seen by on-coming traffic in the unlikely event any came along, put the truck in park and, given how last time it was off didn't want to start, let it run. Unclipping the fob from the key, took the key fob and prepared to step out of the truck. He looked all around and checked the mirrors again, leaned over the console to the footwell, retrieved his Deputy Sheriff hat, semi-screwing it on his head, got the Motorola portable radio out of the console charger, attached the microphone and stepped down and into the heat, turned and poked the button to lock the Tahoe door.

Crossing the blacktop to a time-long, well-worn path he paused, and left the road. Just before entering a curve in the path, he looked back at his truck...there were heat ripples coming off the road.

Interesting. He continued along the path, dry weeds and barrel cactus sprinkled with trapped tumbleweed seed pods on the windward side. Ivey stepped over an outstretched point of red rock, subconsciously leaving extra room from the underside of the rock to his cowboy boot – snakes love those places, especially after a cool night, then climbed a gentle rise and walked another few meters into the rocky draw. As he stepped up to the top of the little rise, a warm breeze wafted over him. A sudden bounce in his step, "What the hell?" He seemed to lose the "extra" weight he'd been struggling to understand. Maybe the world was "back to normal."

Maybe not.

At the turn in the road to town, the "something wrong" became apparent in a space in the scenery that shouldn't be there.

He, and everyone he knew in "the tribes," had all made this little thirty second walk hundreds of times to the "Silver Tree." An out-of-place pin-oak that had somehow managed to sink roots deep enough to keep itself alive in a place where there were no other such trees for 1,500 miles or more. Just enough sun, and shade from the canyon walls. It was so strange and such a novelty that the kids had come to it for as many years as he could remember, making out under its proud branches, and partying in the shade. The tree had to be a hundred years old. Many had climbed the old tree and, sometime in the forgotten past, tied metal streamers to the branches, over time some had put Mylar, and tin pieces to reflect the light, even a few silver Christmas ornaments, causing the old tree to flash and sparkle in the sun. Someone in the past, long forgotten and so un-named, had given the tree it's rather obvious name, The Silver Tree.

Deputy Longfeather looked at the place he had spent so much time as a boy, young man and even as a soldier/cop returning from war. He had placed a silver Afghani good luck charm near the very top of this old, silent friend, this eternal tree a week after coming home. This majestic anchor to his childhood's past, and present home. The eighty-foot tree he'd seen out the right side of his Tahoe as he passed not 6 hours ago, and had sub-consciously waved at, remembering those good times.

The silver tree was gone.

CHAPTER 2

The Ride Begins

0 5:58 AM

Arriving at the clearing where the tree should have been, he saw the base of the tree was sort of there. As he approached, he saw a polished oak rounded and curved obelisk less than four feet tall, it looked burned. But as he touched it, there was no soot, no charcoal, just smooth darkened wood, the clearing and stump smelled of something electrical, ozone? He looked around for branches, leaves, acorns…anything, the surface was bare and smooth, not even marks like someone had raked it. So…this was the mouse his mind 'maybe' had seen. There was nothing there, no sign the tree had been cut down, no sign of anything being dragged away, just an irregular totally bare depression going out ten or twelve meters from the base of the remains of the tree, in all directions. At the remains of the tree, the polished "stump" were beginnings of the top of the tree's root system, exposed by the removal of a foot or so of sandy earth. The depression sloped gently to its irregular edges where it was only a few inches deep.

Something caught his eye across the depression. No…oh God no!… an arm was laying there apparently severed just above the elbow. Maybe a manikin, no blood? He bent to see if the arm was indeed a manikin, from a few feet away he saw a fuzzy movement at the end of the arm…ants! Must be real, ya can't fool ants. He stood, looked a few feet to the left, then from side to side…what the! A cowboy boot, jeans and a leg, again cut cleanly, this time directly across the knee joint.

With his 9mm Beretta in hand, he continued to look around the clearing, and leaned toward the portable radio microphone clipped to his epilate. He had noticed the radio was nearly dead up on the mountain and had kept it in the console charger for the ride off the Reservation road, the radio was now partially charged and was back on his utility belt, pressing the key - "Luna this is Ivey, get the Sherriff on the line."

"He's busy."

"Luna, get Sam right friggin' now."

"Roger, Ivey," Luna knew something was up, and it was serious.

The sheriff walked quickly to the radio base station console, having heard the conversation between Ivey and Luna, set his full coffee mug carefully down, reached for the microphone.

"Ivey this is Sam, go."

"Sheriff, 10-18 - my 20 is 165 - 12 miles North of town, stop at my unit and come in the path across the road. No more on the air. I don't see any immediate danger but respond 10-39."

10-39 being the code for an emergency response.

The Sherriff heard a wavering voice of a very nervous young deputy, "Copy Ivey, ETA…ASAP."

Sherriff Sam Bush wasted no time getting out of the office and into his Suburban, where he hit the lights and siren, and floored the truck as soon as he had made the turn toward the hills. His deputies did not ask him to come into the desert unless there was a damned good reason. He never questioned their judgment, and they had never been wrong. Within 16 minutes he was stopping in front of the Deputy's truck. As he reached to key his portable, he heard two rapid gunshots. Reaching back in the Suburban, he unlatched his Remington shotgun, and jacked a round in the chamber. Grabbing the microphone, he nearly yelled, "Ivey, talk to me."

Ivanov answered "I'm okay, just needed to scare a Coyote off, come on in."

Some 35 miles away in Albuquerque.

06:10 AM on the Southwest side, across the railroad tracks from the section - 8 housing near Trunbull Ave. This was not a good time for the cell phone in his pocket to vibrate, but vibrate it did. He was staring down at the last known, and reportedly highest-ranking leader of several Las Germen gang cells. They were in the dusty warehouse of a dusty side of Albuquerque, well, all sides of Albuquerque could be considered dusty, but the abandoned building supply warehouse, displaced by a new and better Home Depot a mile or so away really fit the bill for the gang's fencing, sex, and drug operations.

This large room had only a row of dusty (imagine that) clerestory windows of which 20% were broken allowing the hot day and smoke from all manner of inhaled and recycled stuff to escape across the top of the walls where they met the open zig-zags of the bar-beam ceiling. The remaining 80% unbroken glass letting in a tired yellow light into the otherwise dark cavern. Several sad, mis-matched dispirited couches were along the north wall, in a rough semi-circle facing a 75-inch projector type flat screen TV. It was attached to a Sony gaming system, and a Blu-ray player with an assortment of discs, some martial-art B movies mixed with mostly Spanish language porn, scattered like dropped playing cards around it. Cords went along the wall to 2 electrical outlets with 10 wires attached to a stack of plug multipliers. A pool table with shiny felt, had random balls collected along one side indicating some leveling issues. A pinball machine, missing a leg, perched on a crutch-like stack of milk crates. Lights were in rows along the ceiling, left-over from better warehouse days, some double rows of fluorescent fixtures, 95 percent either flickering or flat out, the remaining ones on were blackened on the ends, ready to join their dead bulb comrades, all were so dusty they appeared brown.

In the center of the pock marked floor where the rows of industrial shelving anchors had been pulled out when the shelving was sold for scrap and near the back wall supporting a mezzanine were three 55-gallon trashcans, resurrected from the graveyard of old oil drums, all over-flowing from missed thrown beer cans, soda cups and countless fast food bags and wrappers. A healthy crop of shiny green flies roamed the mostly empty food containers or were lazily circling in an airborne recon near the jackpot of fly-food recycling.

At the back of the room with the trash barrels, under the overhang of a mezzanine of empty offices now used for sleeping or screwing, and in front of a few defunct warehouse worker breakrooms, a Detective 2nd class was facing the 350-pound gang boss, "Tiny" Vas-Quez. Vas-Quez had a problem. He was nearly the only one of his gang not currently in jail but actually didn't know it, the rest of his crew had been swept up in a mid-night sting/raid at a local rave night-club where a rival gang was supposed to be elbowing in on their territory. Tiny was in fact nervous, someone should have checked in hours ago. The rival gang, well actually they were all cops recruited from several counties nearby and ready with badges, arrest powers, bullet resistant vests, oh, and tasers. This operation had carefully been planned and executed so far flawlessly. There had been over 2 months of leaked miss-information and drive-throughs from "strangers in out-of-town cars." Now the "last of the gansa crew" needed to be picked up and brought in. A cell signal blocking van had kept the whole thing out of communication while the arrests were made, and no one had been allowed their phone call yet, so why the vibrating phone?

Jaylee Washington was trying for nonchalant, and, he thought, pulling it off. Sticking to this part of the ops plan script, he had let Tiny's bodyguards, the only remaining gang guys not in the sweep, take his service pistol, a custom Glock 21, and his .25 Ruger clutch piece off his ankle. He continued the pre-planned dialogue. "Look Tiny, there is no reason to go out in a blaze of glory. I…we got you and you know it."

The ½ Mexican, ½ Creole grinned, "Look yo' self 'Big' cop. My crib is my last stant, 'n yo ass is done. Anyhow, how my peeps gonna see me if I juss walk in wit you? 'Na I gots yo guns."

Jaylee said, "Well, they might see a guy who's not scared of 'd Man and knows he's gonna walk when the lawyers with the shiny assed pants get you off."

Tiny considered this alternative. "What I gon' say 'Big cop', if I do like dat? You gon' say I help you? You gon' be my friend in court? Even so, they say you got me for cap-murder, like I gon' get the needle."

"I'll say that in court, but no blood on anybody will say it too, the needle isn't for sure and you know it." Jaylee saw a slight chance for this, maybe, to work out.

Maybe not.

"K Big man, - no prob, I come wit ya."

Tiny leaned over the mahogany door used as a desktop, a sheet of plywood screwed along the front hiding what was behind. Jaylee noted that he didn't have his hands on the back edge of the 'desk' like he should have had to help his fat ass stand up. Jaylee went to the balls of his feet, ready to move. When Tiny straightened up, he had a sawed-off double-barrel shotgun.

Tiny was left-handed, so Jaylee dove to his right. POP…POP-POP three shots hit Tiny, first round in the stomach, second in the sternum between the nipples, the .223 round bursting his heart like a dropped melon, third shattered his jaw, as the widening bullet went through the back of his throat, it severed his spine at C-1, the cerebral-cortex removing all vestiges of his spinal cord with the super-sonic bullet, all three shots thru-and-thru, all-be-it the second "thru" a ragged series of holes and gore. The shotgun dropped from dead hands, hitting the floor on the stock, both barrels went off, the full discharge taking Tiny's entire reproductive organs cleanly…well…as clean as the 40 pellets of two rounds of 12 gauge-#3 buckshot could manage, off his 350-pound carcass as he fell straight backwards. The blast-excised-and projected- remains hit the low mezzanine ceiling and somehow stayed glued up there. He hit the floor and a cloud of dust puffed out from under him, curling around his morbidly obese body. A few shaking leg spasms as muscles got random nerve signals. Another, but this one real, Jabba the Hutt died in a desert.

The flies were all in full panic mode, then condensed back into their pizza box and Burger-King wrapper heaven. A few appeared to re-conning the newly dead meat ambling aerially toward the settling dust cloud.

A SWAT team leader had been looking from behind a curtain draped doorway at the end of the building and had seen the move for the gun. His sniper also behind the curtain had taken his shots. He ran around the door/table used as a desk and kicked the shotgun away. It rattled across the dusty floor. He, helped Jaylee up from the floor - "You OK detective?"

Jaylee nodded, "Yeah, I'm good. Thanks Randy."

Because it was a clean shoot, all recorded by Jaylee's recorder, and the SWAT team leader's video camera's transmission to the van placed nearby, paperwork was going to be a snap. Warrants and interviews had been legally obtained and were carefully filed. No hanging legal strings left untied.

Bart rushed in and brushed the dirt off Jaylee's sport jacket arm where he had landed on the floor. "Two SWAT guys and I got the three 'bodyguards' in the wagon, I was on the way back when the shooting started, you OK bro?" Bart stepped around the "desk" and looked at the remains of "Tiny" Vas-Quez, "Damned, Jay - did you guys shoot his balls off?"

Several of the braver re-con flies had flipped up-side down and landed on the ceiling, cautiously approaching the fresh blood.

Jaylee said, "Naw, he must have done it himself. Oh jees, man, they're on the ceiling! Man...that ain't right." The mess looked a little like a hand was glued to the ceiling one grotesque finger hanging down giving them the bird. Shaking his head, "Let's get outta here!"

They checked out with the SWAT team leader, and Bart called in to their task-force office. Closing his soon to be out of style flip-phone he said "Captain says we're officially done with the 'gangs duty', Jay, but we got some money to spend on the grant. He wants the SWAT people to take the credit for this one. Now he wants' us to head for the desert, got a strange one out there."

They sat in the surveillance van and finished their ever-present paperwork, after-action report, but since neither had fired their weapon, it went fast. The SWAT team leader, Randy said a taped interview could wait a few days. Jaylee screwed the cap back on his ever-present water bottle, stretched like a Black Panther waking up and nodded.

Out to and into the unmarked but clear as day cop ride, Bart driving, Jaylee riding passenger in the dark blue Ford Crown Victoria, entering his final sections of the action report into his newly acquired laptop as they cleared the town and headed south for the desert, to Route 165 and the Sandia Mountains. Radio computer modems had been installed recently and were proving useful.

By noon the "Silver Tree" scene was taped off, and New Mexico State Police crime scene techs were sifting through the bizarre clearing, and out ten meters in all directions. Two folding canopies had been set up just off the road, one had folding tables and chairs placed on plywood sheets to keep them from sinking into the loose sand for detectives and techs, water bottles, sodas and canned lemonade in a cooler, a small box was open with Army style MRE's. Two empty dozen sized doughnut boxes sat under the table where the ever present ants were in a mini circus parade carrying away the crumbs and sugar leavings. The men and a few women were writing and talking. The other canopy being used for the forensic team to layout collected evidence. The arm and lower leg, and some other findings, were placed on a white plastic sheet. A man in a doctor's length lab coat was looking at the arm through a hand-held Sherlock Holmes type magnifying glass.

An old Jeep had been found in the wash, probably the way the people had arrived at the Silver tree.

Homicide Detectives 2nd class Jaylee Washington and 1st class Bart Williams of the New Mexico Gang Special Task Force arrived after drawing the call. Since the task force was running out of work, and rumor had it that there was no money in the new FY budget for them, they would be returning to their regular Albuquerque city homicide detective jobs, Captain Walker had given them this one to burn up the last hours still budgeted. The now ending ten-member task force was formed to help with Mexican gangs and drug activity cropping up in recent years. They had been good, maybe too good, and had worked themselves out of a job...at least until the supply lines and cannon fodder gang members could be recruited as replacements and put on the street again. Best guess, maybe 3 months.

Jaylee and Bart were the classic Mutt-and-Jeff cop team, Jaylee 6'6"-230 Lb. solid black man, dark complexion, a square face, mustache and short sideburns dropped from a one-inch-thick covering of black "mini-fro" hair, some salt starting early in the sideburns. He wore a lightweight cop cut sport jacket with space for the under-arm shoulder holster cross-draw rig, colored the shade of well creamed coffee, lighter brown almost white polo shirt, light tan cotton Docker's cargo pants, and tan suede just-over-the ankle desert shoes. A young Detective, prematurely turning grey, in his thirties, dressed in light brown head to toe.

Bart, 5'9", an older white guy, on the downside nearing retirement, thinning salt and pepper hair and a high forehead, a pot belly that he tried to hold back, with marginal success. He wore a "dress" pocket tee shirt with a conservative Hawaiian style shirt left unbuttoned. It had palm trees, hula girls and penguins, all in blues and grays, icebergs in the water, a sign stuck in the beach said 'let's hear it for global warming.' He carried a Ruger .380 tucked in the small of his back, the shirt draped over it. His black jeans had faded to dark gray, and his shoes were classic cop Doc Martin black lace-ups, he had one off, tapping it against the leg of the table, a small rock and line of sand bounced out.

The Sherriff and his Deputy, both in traditional uniform, sat across from the Detectives, Jaylee had a new bottle of water, Ivey noticed no sweat on it - normal, the rest had coffee. The Sheriff spoke, "Thanks for taking this seriously and getting down here so fast. I don't even know if we have a homicide, but my gut's leanin' that way. I've never seen such a clean cut, jees, a saw wouldn't cut so clean."

Bart nodded, then looked to Ivanov, slipping the shoe back on, "You grew up out here?" Ivey nodded, "And I think I'm safe in saying you've never seen anything like this either?" Bart's voice was a gravely one of a long-time-smokers, he had quit in a near-career-ending nicotine withdrawal episode that had threatened to implode some decades long friendships, now smoke free, except for the voice, for six months. Jaylee had laughed through the whole five-week ordeal as his partner raged around the detective bullpen and glowered at anyone making eye contact. Ivey gave another nod.

A technician in a blue lab coat entered the tent, bent to Bart's ear, and started to whisper. Bart turned to him, "Billy, these men are not suspects, Jees, bro, you can tell them too. I think we're gonna be a team for a while."

The Sherriff and deputy relaxed, a team was a good thing.

"Wellll, this one's a gonna make the books." Billy looked like a character actor hired for a homeless guy part, except for the glasses and the baby-blue CSI light weight polyester lab coat. He had a narrow face with a narrow hawk nose a little long for the head. A row of evenly spaced dots made a straight line across his forehead, a hair-plug job done by a rookie or someone who did not understand the randomness of human physiology. Long, rubber gloved fingers were animated as though he thought if they stayed still they would freeze. He had a carrot stick wedged between his right ear and head.

As he spoke, he drawled, "See, we got a young girls' arm, and a young boys' leg, we recon it's a boys' leg because it ain't shaved. Both severed like the best laser knife one could imagine. There's no blood 'cause the cut is cauterized but not burned, just enough heat to seal the capillaries and all. We cleaned out the ants, not much damage from them, shouldn't hurt the investigation. Oh, by the way there are four fingers over by the leg, same thing, no fingernail polish so my guess is they belong to the boy, the hand on the arm had nail polish. And by the way, the girls watch stopped at 04:01, I don't know but it's not damaged, just stopped. Cheap, but should be still working, the iPhone she had clasped in the hand was completely dead too.

"Then there's the remains of the tree. Deputy Longfeather here says the tree was there and appeared healthy when he went up the hill for his regular patrol." Ivanov nodded again. "Wellll, the stump has no water in it at all, looks nearly petrified, and it's smooth, like somebody sanded it into that shape. Then there's the rest of the tree. It's gone, and no sign of it being cut, dragged away, whatever. And finally, and this is just a guess, the first several inches of dirt in that clearing edge has been removed, and that tapers from a foot or so deep in the center of the cleared space, the tree stump or whatever, nearly the exact center of the space, top layer of the tree roots are gone to."

He looked at Deputy Longfeather, "No offense, but none of us can believe the tree could have vanished in such a fashion in just-a few hours. No leaves from the tree, no dead desert grass, bugs. Oh, look at this," he held out a plastic evidence bag, and carefully placed it on the table, in the bag was a medium sized brown scorpion, with 1/3 missing. The remains carefully taped to a piece of card stock, in exact position so as not to move in the bag. The line was clean and as straight as cutting a picture of the arachnid with a pair of scissors. The men looked at the bug, then to each other. "Even just the footprints of the deputy and the Sherriff, and damned few of those. The guys over at the Jeep said there's no sign of foul play, and the engine was stone cold, the battery of the jeep is dead too, like completely dead."

"We got a book bag from the Reservation Unified High School from the back, the sheriff's people are running the registration on the Jeep."

"There are plenty of footprints along the path from the highway, and back down the path to the wash and toward the Jeep, but, like I said, none in the clearing, we found the two 9mm shell casings the deputy said he left scaring the Coyote away from the girl's arm, they were where he said they would be."

Jaylee leaned back and stretched like the Black Panther again waking up. "Thanks Billy, no sign of a UFO? Four-foot-tall grey guys with big assed eyes? I think we're too damned far from Area 51, don't you Bart?"

Ivanov interjected, "But we're right over the mountain from E-R-Mag Labs Base, and they do weird shit over there."

The other four men looked at him. Jaylee continued, "Now look Billy, you and the rest of your crew need to get yo' asses back over there and find out what happened to those kids. Bart, the Sherriff's and my own self want to know what happened. I've been doing this more than a few years, and I can tell you that without a doubt something happened that's happened before, and if dats so, then…it damned well happened again, and if dats so Bart, the Sherriff's and I will find out who 'happened' it again."

Jaylee had a Masters in Criminal Justice from NYU, and had published two short pocket books on investigative technique. This semi-street Ebonics act was just one he used when he thought he needed to get someone off the dime. It worked, Billy shrugged, closed his note pad, got the taped scorpion, reached for the carrot stick, got a mechanical pencil - wrong ear - tried again and crunched the carrot, trudged back, ducking under the tape.

Bart, the senior member of the team, got out a yellow legal note pad from a small Dell computer laptop bag which he had with him, devoid of computer, and poised a clear plastic Bic ballpoint pen over the first blank page. "Okay, let's see if we can divide up the work here so, maybe, we can get some kind of a lead. You two," gesturing toward the Sherriff and Deputy, "why not take the background on these two kids, see if they have any friends who have high powered lasers and a construction company that could have come in here between 02:30 and 04:55 with a few bulldozers, a crane and a fleet of dump-trucks or a Sikorsky Sky hook helicopter and done this."

The Sherriff laughed out loud, "Bart, we'll do the background and get anything we can." His cell phone went off. "Sam here, yeah……. Ok….and anything on the girl?... okay." He finished scribbling a note in his pocket pad, ripped a sheet off and slid it over to Bart. "We have the address for the Jeep, it belongs to a Native American guy on the reservation, says he's 74 years old. Ivey, why don't you take this and check it out, maybe stolen?"

Bart copied the information onto his pad, then slid the note to Ivey. "Jaylee and I are available to coordinate with the Feds, since it's possible a Native American kid was involved – just let us know. The bulldozer thing was a joke, but has there been any construction around here lately? I'm still having a problem with a fairly large oak tree and a couple dozen cubic yards of dirt disappearing. I've never even seen a sand trap on a golf course so clean"

Jaylee opined, "And, partner, you know really well what they look like, you've spent considerable time in them."

Bart gave Jaylee the finger, everyone laughed.

Ivanov raised his head from the address he was studying, "To coin a phrase, the guys at E-R-Mag Labs on the Sandia Labs Base over the mountain do some weird shit. They just buried a boatload of cable in a grid up the hill from where we sit, said it was an antenna, but no other information, well E-R-Mag Labs was what was on the side of the trucks anyway. I never heard of a buried antenna, said it was part of ENet or something like that. It was finished last month." He described his inquiry a few months ago as he drove up to a ranch on the side of his mountain where a crew was inching along behind a ditching machine, a huge wheel with buckets carrying dirt out of a 1-foot-wide by 9-foot-deep trench. Following the wheel was a plow like device that fed a cable to the bottom. A set of scrapers brought the dirt back in the trench. He asked what they were involved in and was answered, well sort of answered, "It's a very large antenna for ENet. That's all they had said."

Didn't make a hell of a lot of sense to him, an antenna buried in the ground? And, it damned well was big though. Probably 1,200 meters from side to side and 2,000 from top to bottom, and that was just what he could see, as it wrapped around the mountain. Two huge triangles, the points of which faced each other made of horizontal wires spaced about 9 meters apart. They had been digging for best part of a year, burying a fat black cable of some kind, as big around as a t-ball bat, unwinding off twelve-foot high reels from the back of special low-boy tractor-trailers. "Lord knows how far it goes, probably back into Kirkland Air Force Base, which borders the second Native American reservation over the top of the mountain and into the valley just below."

Jaylee stood, walked out from under the canopy, and looked where Ivey was pointing up the side of the mountain. The ditches were now barely visible, but if one knew and looked for them, still showed the shadow of different coloring. "That would be an antenna that would have a very long wavelength, maybe ten hertz or less. The power to activate such an antenna would be enormous, unless it's a receiving antenna, but receiving of what? Nothing transmits on that low a frequency, and like you said, deputy, receiving a signal underground is very hard to figure. I can see the triangles, looks like a power Yagi, and the land there is on a 45-degree angle." As he stared at the side of the mountain it appeared that the place where the points of the Yagi connected were blurry, waving like a reflection of the mountain in a not-quite-still pond surface. He rubbed his eyes, and thought, 'That must be the heat.' A thought entered his mind, why he had no idea, "Deputy, has this ozone smell I picked up when we got here always been here?"

It was not.

Ivey, who had moved to beside Jaylee to point to where the antenna was buried, said, "Well, if you mean always around the tree, no, but it was and is still here since I came in the clearing this morning."

Bart looked at the Sheriff and Ivey, "Jaylee's got an EE in radio theory, a General Radiotelephone License with Radar endorsement, and a Master HAM operator's ticket."

Jaylee said under his breath, "Mans got to have a hobby."

This information juxtaposed with the statements to Billy a few minutes ago caused Ivey, like the Sheriff, to laugh out loud too. "You two have a few surprises, don't you? If you don't need me, I'll be going into the reservation, I think I know the old man at this address."

"Before you go," Bart said, smiling, "where the hell did Ivanov come from?"

Ivey looked at the ground, "Well, I don't normally talk about it, but my dad, a Native American, a Tewa-Navajo, worked over the mountain as a machinist for the R&D people at Sandia Labs after a 6-year hitch in the Navy, you know, over there where they do weird shit. He used to work with a lady Russian scientist who had defected from Cuba after the missile crises hit, a few years later, in the early 70's. The whole thing never made the papers, she flew a Russian/Cuban prop fighter 10 feet off the water and landed on the main runway at Cape Coral with five minutes of fuel left. Anyway, dad was assigned to keep an eye on her when she finally got to Sandia Labs, which he used to tell everyone was easy, she was beautiful."

"Well, keeping an eye turned to more direct contact, and they fell in love. I'm named for her first husband, who died in Russia, someplace in Siberia, keeping him there kept her in line and working for the Russians loading the island with missiles, then the Russian spy work after the crisis was over. When he died, that's when she split Cuba."

Bart said, "Cool story, how are they doing?"

"They died twelve years ago next month at a nearby base. Some explosives went off prematurely during a bunker test. A dozen people were injured." He turned, hitched up his belt, put on the hat and walked out from the canopy toward his Tahoe. Then over his shoulder, "It's okay Bart, they were good parents and I like to think raised a good kid. I'll call when I get anything. Should we meet at the office in the morning?"

Bart looked at the Sheriff. Sam said, "Let's make it a breakfast meeting at my office, may have some ideas by then." They all nodded.

As Ivey turned to go, they all saw him at the same time, an ancient Navajo festooned with beads, carrying a staff topped with beads, feathers and animal teeth. He walked up from where the jeep was parked in the wash, and approached the yellow tape around the cleared opening, stopping, he did not attempt to go under it into the clearing. Ivey said to the others, "I know him, his name is Paschelette, he's a hataalii." Puzzled looks from the detectives and sheriff. He said, "An Native American Shaman, let me handle this." Ivey walked to the old man who was looking into the clearing followed several paces back by the others, gave an almost imperceptible bow. "Singer… wise one, why have you come to this place? Can you help me understand what happened here?" The others came to where they could hear the conversation, but stayed a respectful distance.

The old man didn't seem to hear, Ivey gave him time, as he knew was the Navajo and Apache custom, the Shaman stared at the barren sand of the crater, then slowly looked from the center of the clearing to Ivey, deep set dark, watery eyes looked straight into Ivey's. Ivey saw a deep terror he had never…seen… no, not seen, this was felt like it was radiating from the old man, "Young Longfeather…I know a very powerful dark wolf has been set loose, and it has started here. What this Witch is, how…it is, even where this wolf now is…I do not know. I will get others from the council and we will pray for it to be sent back from where it came, we will ask that its spell be turned back on itself." He took a pinch of something from a small bag on a leather string around his waist, sprinkled it toward the clearing, pollen, Ivey guessed. "The young ones I saw in my vision are soon to be gone, they are close to the spirits now."

"What do you mean? They're dying! We know they are badly injured; do you know where they are? We know they are hurt…aren't they?"

"They are…gone…but here." He pointed to the sandy circle, "And yes, they are dying." With a feeble wave of his arm, toward the clearing, the old Shaman turned, and shuffled back to the draw, moving purposely back up the wash toward his reservation.

Bart said, "What did he mean? They are there? Should we get a search party? Jesus, in this heat and hurt like they have to be they won't last until nightfall!"

The sheriff was on his radio, and within an hour aircraft, locals, and soldiers from the base were collecting, and getting their search assignments, the crew already on site had begun searching the area, fanning out from the crater, all available deputies from the town, as well as several agents from the Border Patrol and State Police soon had joined the search. The Sheriff, the one most trained in desert search and rescue, was set up under the refreshment canopy, now the search command, and was giving assignments.

It was decided that Ivey should go back to his task of checking the Jeep's owner. The Sheriff said, "Ivey, we'll call if we find the kids or if there's any news to report."

CHAPTER 3

Wisdom of Age

Leaving the scene of the missing tree, Ivanov turned the radio on again, John Prine sang about old folks behind screen doors "Hello in there". This radio also was getting, well...okay, staying weird. He headed for the entrance to the Sandia Mountain Native American Reservation, entered and turned left on Saguaro Road, drove slowly looking for the address. A very old, but well-kept rounded-edge single-wide house trailer perched a few feet from the sharp edge of a dry gulch. The light green paint was all-but-gone, dull aluminum sand-blasted roof and sides now had that grey-not-quite silver look. By the gravel path-road, the wooden address board had, of all things, a faded Amish hex sign, maybe a rooster with some triangles around him? The path up to the porch was lined by several assorted types of flowers, out of place here, and obviously watered several times a day. They labored under desert dust and too-hot sun, still they tried to put their best face on and a smile for anyone crunching by on the gravel path they guarded.

Sitting on a rocker under the tin porch roof attached to the side of the trailer was an old man, faded red and dark blue plaid shirt with the sleeves rolled up, well-worn Levies. As he saw Ivey pull to a stop, he rose, the shirt and jeans looked like a brisk wind would blow them off the man's thin frame. His weathered face showed no emotion. Mostly black-grey hair was tied in a classic ponytail held with silver beaded string and hung down his back, hair and string the same length.

Ivey continued up the faded stone path the thirty feet to the porch, observed the flowers, bobbing gently in the hot breeze, some kind of Petunia? "Mister Foxlight? I'm Deputy Longfeather. Can we talk?" The old man gestured with a bony hand at the chair beside his. Ivey hopped up the one wooden plank step to the porch, noticed a tag on the old man's rocker that said, "Cracker Barrel" and sat in an identical one next to his. The underside of the tin roof was grey-galvanized, the wood holding the roof was pine with knots, some kind of clear varnish fading, but not peeling. The door to the trailer was brightly painted a glossy green, and showed no wear. Like the hex-sign and flowers, the green door, about half open, appeared rather out of place.

"Do you own a '68 jeep, faded red?" Foxlight nodded, "Do you know where it is?"

The old man looked up toward the mountain, pointed and said, "Grandson, Willy, uses it now. He wrecks it or something?"

"Did you see him...well let me re-phrase that, when was the last time you saw him?"

"He left here to get his girlfriend in town last night. He and she both works the evening shift at the Wal-Mart, he's off at 10, she's off at 11:30. Most nights they stay up and do what kids do, hang out with other night shift friends, sleep in the day, she's in some kind of high school-work thing, goes in to the schoolhouse after noon." He looked again at the mountain, then down at the dusty wooden porch floor. "He's dead...ain't' he."

Not a question, a statement.

This shook Ivey like a cold wind had gone down the back of his shirt. He looked directly at the old Native American. "I honestly don't know, but he may be hurt. We found some evidence of trouble over by the Silver Tree. Why do you think he may be dead?"

The old man, dark eyes now glassy, rung his hands. "I just know." He looked at the faded bare wood planks of the porch floor. "I had a vision, Willy and Macy was hurt...bad hurt...in the red desert, they were thirsty, scared, it was just dark and something, something was coming toward them... they were so awful scared, the vision ended, thank the Spirits."

"Look, Mister Foxlight, this is hard for both of us, believe me, but can you tell me if there's anyone, anyone at all who would want to hurt Willy, or his girlfriend?"

"No Deputy, Willy's a good kid, was a good kid, and Macy's a good kid too, she graduates," he stopped and rung his hands… "Was gonna graduate this Spring, in a, what-ya-call-it…a vocational program that let her work at the Wal-Mart for credits."

"Macy then is his girlfriend?" Mr. Foxfire nodded. "Do you have an address or phone number for her?"

"No, no I don't, but her dad's the manager of the Wal-Mart, works the day shift. You let me know when I can get him, I mean Willy, I'll tell the council, I'll want a traditional celebration. Deputy, it just ain't' right to outlive your kids, and now theirs." He looked at the floor again, a single tear ran down his face, he wiped at his nose with the sleeve of his faded shirt.

"I'm so sorry Mister Foxlight, but we haven't found Willy…or Macy yet. I…I…really can't go into details…see…we don't have anything much yet. I'll be sure to keep you informed. We're not sure… we have no evidence he's gone; I'll keep hoping for the best."

The short, level walk back to the Tahoe seemed to be very long and heavy, not unlike the heavy feeling on the side of the mountain this morning. But this was a different heavy, it was the heavy of hard emotion. The path seemed to be like walking uphill. The day's events were settling in, like a long, overdone, hot workout at the gym. The time since he got up to go to work some eighteen hours ago, now, seemed to hit him with a strange type of tiredness, half physical, half his mind's visions and then the medicine man - Paschelette's strange description at the Siver Tree site.

The drive to the local Wal-Mart was not easy, Ivey had practiced 'professional detachment' but it never worked for him. Foxlight was a tough one. Many times he had ended up hugging a mom or dad after they had nearly or actually collapsed on hearing the bad news no cop ever wants to be tasked with delivering, tears streaming down his cheeks as well. He kept swallowing a lump in his throat as he remembered the single tear on old man Foxlight's face.

Ivey parked in the spot reserved for "Police" and retrieved the hat now in its traditional place on the passenger seat. Funny, no police were ever needed here, but the thought of a parking space near the air-conditioned front doors was always welcome. He walked past an absolutely ancient hand extended with a smiley face sticker, took the sticker and slapped it onto the side of his hat to the right side of the 5-point star. He turned left and went to the customer service counter.

In a few minutes the page had Macy's dad walking behind the Service Counter, a single parent widower, things seemed to overwhelm the thoughts suggested by the smiley sticker. No, Art Plankerton did not know of anyone who might want to hurt "the kids", they were popular and well liked. Plankerton was upset, but different from Foxlight. "Deputy, you guys just keep working this thing, I know Macy's alive, I can feel it. She's in trouble, well, may be in trouble but alive." He turned to the lady processing the return of a box of Depends, wrong size, "Marilita, I'm going home, need to be there when Macy calls."

Marilita nodded, patted his arm, returned her concerned lined face back to the cash register keyboard.

Hope against hope? Willing the universe to conform to the wishes of a father who has just lost the last precious thing he had? Physic vision? Or just one of those "glass half full" people?

Ivey walked slowly out of the Service desk area, back toward the parking lot and the Tahoe. Wal-Mart radio began the Moody Blues "I know You're Out There Somewhere." He stopped, stood and listened. John Lodge sang "Somewhere… somewhere." What the hell, now a psychic Wal-Mart radio? Yes, he was emotionally and physically drained. Once in the truck, he plucked the microphone off the dash clip, "Sam, you on?"

"Go Ivey" the sheriff replied.

"Confirmed the ID on the kids, no help there. Details over the data link in a few minutes. I'm beat. Catch you in the AM."

"Thanks, Ivey, get some rest and I'll see you 0-7-hundred in the shop. I'm changing your shift until we make some headway, Okay? I'll update the guys on what you got. No luck on the search yet, I'll call you if anything comes in."

"Roger, Sam…till the AM – out."

As night fell, the coordinators from the various search parties were back at the canopy sipping nearly stale coffee, discussing the search, gnawing on a second wave of now stale doughnuts, the MRE's were long gone. The local Chick-fil-la, a business pad tenant in the Wal-Mart center, had delivered dozens of sandwiches free of charge, and they too were quickly gone. The sheriff had a 1/250 map, he had "X-ed" squares where the searchers had been. He looked at the search leaders. Shook his head. Several dozen exhausted men and women were along the road, leaning against a hodge-podge of vehicles, Army, Boarder Patrol, civilian, some ATV's, even a few horses tied to a trailer from a local rancher and his crew who had come to help. Wal-Mart spring-water bottles in most hands, 5 gallon pails for the horses being filled from an Army water trailer.

The total lack of tracks leaving the clearing, no scent picked up by any of the three teams of dogs sharing the water pails with the horses, who had been presented with the arm and leg to load their scent. Absolutely no trace of the victims had been found, leading the sheriff and all concerned to call off the search when the daylight began lowering the brightness on the desert's scene, soon fading into dark.

The inescapable conclusion, agreed to by all, was that the Native American Medicine Man was slap-assed crazy.

CHAPTER 4

The Detective and the Canary

The team of sheriffs and detectives decided that they were not needed in the search crowd, instead they decided to start investigation books on the missing victims, try to fill in some background. The sheriff, Sam, told them he'd keep them up to date on the rescue effort. Later the information Ivanov had found came into Jaylee's Blackberry PDA.

Jaylee and Bart had gotten into their plain dark blue Ford Crown Vic cop sedan, Bart opened all the windows to vent the 130-degree air inside of the car, then got his pad, and flipped notes. The air conditioner blasted hot, then cool, finally cold air, they closed the windows.

There were damned few notes to flip, he handed the pad to Jaylee, and put the car in drive.

Jaylee said, "Bart, why not take a trip over the hill to E-R-Mag Labs Base? I mean we've got nothing here, and maybe they have an idea, shit, maybe they have a new weapon or something and it fucked up." Bart, who had just turned toward town, swung a

U turn and headed back past the crime scene tape and down to I-40 then Southwest toward Kirkland AFB. It was toward the home of some of the best thinking in America, and, historically, some of the most dangerous.

Bart had come to his appreciation of Jaylee, well, actually black people in general honestly, but it was a growing experience. Jaylee was, as were many minorities, the beneficiary of Bart's personal growth. Bart was one of the last GI's to do a full tour in Vietnam. His lottery draft number had been #3! It was in early1975, and everyone was tired of war. The congress, pushed by the anti-war news media stories, was de-moralizing troops even worse than idiotic rules of engagement. Funding was fading, equipment was shot up and parts were hard to get. Nineteen-year old Bart Williams was a new Spec-4 in the 288th Combat Engineer battalion, two months out of AIT training in Fort Leonard Wood, a run down, under-funded, poorly maintained relic from World War II. Faded peeling lead paint barracks that should have been burned down 20 years earlier, with coal furnaces that were in such bad shape the windows had to be open to keep the burning coal's carbon monoxide from killing everyone inside. Combat practice bridges were built across the "Big Piney" river, so polluted with untreated sewage that it was used because it never froze. Those were Fort Leonard Wood's good points. Yes, Fort Leonard Wood, a festering zit on the ass of Missouri. The local town, Rolla, MO, population 1,213 with mostly sad, sagging strippers and sadder even more sagging whores. Rolla was so worn out that even the 3.2% beer was stale, it was, however the only GI's source of women for 40 miles.

The Army had brought Bart into a new paradigm, he was from the south and didn't like blacks. That was okay, they didn't like him either, except for the Platoon Sergeant he was assigned to when arriving in the jungle. A tall black man with the highest standards for uniform, training, leadership and a dedication to duty Bart had ever seen in his 7.5 months in the U.S. Army. Some seeds of doubt about his position on blacks were sown, and his feeling that lumping all of a color into a racist bucket was… well…stupid. Sergeant Leech was frankly a superior NCO and Leader, and lead by example.

This Master Sergeant overlooked the thin veil of Bart's racism. One by one he dispelled each and every racial stereo-type Bart had brought with him into the Army. All blacks were not stupid, all were not cowards, all did not hate 'whitey', most loved their wives and kids. To his amazement, many were at heart more conservative than he. All his preconceived notions of black people, born and bred of laziness of thought and outdated group-think, were proved by personal observation to be wrong. He found that being an asshole could as likely to be a black person as a white one. Stupidity was an equal opportunity employer, and anyone, even he, could be a coward.

Then, one cool rainy day, the final racist straw broke and was swept away…forever.

For the first hour and a half, the mission looked routine. Situational awareness was getting rusty as the assignment was now nearly a daily Combat Engineer task. Every day the Engineers would inspect the bridges across the canals feeding the cesspool rice paddies and remove normally simple booby traps installed every night by the Viet Cong. Leech had cautioned against complacency, "There is no such thing as a routine enemy explosive." He had speculated that the VC were really not interested in destroying the bridges, they needed them as much as the Americans. "I think it's sort of a dance, dangerous for both sides, and maybe if the poop hits the ventilator, they'll actually try to blow them up."

Today was different, a few shots from the jungle had turned quickly into a longer, more intense firefight than any he had been in. Bart Williams, the newly promoted Spec-4, and several others were now pinned down under a 50' mahogany log bridge over the muddy banks of a muddy un-named canal. They had been inspecting and de-fusing demolitions planted overnight by VC under the bridge over the stinking canal feeding another of the million rice paddy stinking pools in the area. A "milk run" until the bullets started flying. Bart, the acting Squad Leader and three black soldiers had been attacked. Two were wounded, one of those close to, or maybe dead. Bart was on the radio, and help was on the way, overland from the camp only three miles away. All choppers were off-line by the rain and intermittent fog blowing across the acres of water crisscrossed with walkway dividing levies.

Three VC had tried to get a firing angle by sneaking down the edge of the canal bank, 1 was shot for the effort, and 2 slipped and fell in the canal, where they were shot as they flopped trying to get back up the mud bank. A steady concert of bullets ripped the water not three feet from his legs. The VC knew they had the GI's trapped and were pressing their advantage. His radio man and he had dragged the two wounded men up high under the bridge, but to get a firing angle, they too had to drop back down to near the water's edge. Bean Saunders was to his right, now shot through the leg at the calf, but still fighting. Shorty Hayes was just above with the radio, and he had the right side. Bean yelled "Oh shit", pulled a grenade off his vest and literally dropped it in the canal, just six-feet from where they were.

Bart yelled, "What the ...are you crazy...you fucking ni..."

WHOMP! The blast threw stinking mud and water over all five men. None were hurt by any shrapnel which was stopped by the water, the sound was muffled. Three bodies surfaced in the canal, just twenty feet from the men. Bart stitched them with his M-16A1.

They sank.

"How?... why?... they would have come up right in our blind side, by the pilings!" Bart shouted.

Bean said, "I just saw a few reeds floating down the canal, one went under water, and when it came back up, water came out of it. I knew the light shrapnel from the M-26 wouldn't come out of the water, but that 2.5 oz of Comp-B sure knocked 'em out, just like the cat's fish in Savanna Creek."

They all survived, but were down to partial clips, M16's set on single shot, and no grenades when Platoon Sergeant Leech arrived with a hundred men who had had to fight their way hard the last two hundred yards to get to the canal. Sergeant Leech had been shot, but lead the platoon anyway, the second Lieutenant was killed, an OCS child only in-country three weeks. When it was over, forty-one VC were found dead, including the six Bart and his team had shot in the water and those on the canal bank. Bart became best friends with Bean and the others, two of them by letters and phone calls as those two new black friends had never returned to Viet-Nam, their injuries had sent them home. He had written a very well-done letter with Leech's help that resulted in Bean, who stayed in country with Bart getting the Silver Star. The other two men got Bronze Stars. He never used the 'N' word again. Leech had sent in another commendation, unknown by Bart, for his actions at the canal bridge, who also got a Silver Star presented a few days before he left the war for home.

The Tet offensive had begun.

And later in life, on the street as a Police Officer, Bart had never developed the usual 'us and them' attitude so many cops have toward minorities.

'Bart-man' was well liked by minorities, a tough, fair, by the book cop. Even when he made Detective, and even when he drew the call for the shooting of three black college football stars outside a club downtown.

'Lots of water under that canal bridge,' he thought as he looked at his friend and partner punching at his Blackberry in a ham sized hand with large thumbs poking the tiny keys. How do people do that and spell anything?

The sedan rounded the mountain and started down toward the National Museum of Nuclear Sciences and History, taking a right toward the entrance to the Sandia National Laboratories, then as directed to the contractor buildings of E-R-Mag Labs. Jaylee said, "I've been by there a few dozen times, and each time it reminds me of a friggin' county lock-up with all the high fences." Three 'duce-and-a-half's', 2 ½ ton Army trucks, with men from the nearby base passed them, heading for the search command point. It was now damned hot for May, and the bare area around the labs seemed to have large areas of water covering it. Light bent in the heat causing near mirage conditions, shimmering lakes of nothing disappeared and re-formed in the heat.

In the 50's and 60's Sandia Labs Base was the place where people were trained on the maintenance and repair of the American Nuclear Arsenal, with Picatinny Arsenal in New Jersey as the shipping and returning weapons point. Those Sandia Labs trained people did their jobs after "Nuke School" graduation, both places now had turned their specialized talents into research and testing of various government programs. Serious maintenance and replenishing of the plutonium pellets being done at Los Alamos. Bart, noticing that Jaylee was still on his PDA, and said after a mile or two had passed. "What you doing on that damned computer, got an idea? Jay, if they had something, do you think they'd say anything?"

Bart used computers, but they were never called a computer. They were "damned computers", even when writing a report. Jaylee had written a macro for Microsoft Word on Bart's desk computer that looked for "Damned Computer", and automatically removed the damned.

"Dunno, maybe I can fake 'em into admitting something…if they have anything to admit. I'm trying to get on the internet, maybe when we're closer to the base. What did Ivey say that antenna was? ENet? Nothing so far in here about that. All kinds of shit, like 12,000,000 hits around it but nothing directly related to E-R-Mag Labs like the gate guard said."

Jaylee had known Bart a long time. Since shortly after Jaylee graduated from high school in fact. In School, he was not a bully, even though he was the biggest kid in any of the grades in the several schools he had attended as his mother, a single mom, moved to find consistent work, even moving a few times in high school. People liked him, and when he went out for the football team, that likening extended to college level scouts lurking in the stands of high school games. Jaylee had graduated at the very top of his class, a solid 4.0 GPA. He had a scholastic scholarship on top of the football one, a fact that would be real helpful as it turned out.

Just out of high school in Phoenix Arizona, he found himself with a late model car 'loaned' to him, a nice apartment on a high floor of one of the condo buildings near the State University, Chandler campus. All part of the "fringe benefits" of an athletic scholarship, even the roommates, who were two seniors on the football team. Livin' large. Girls, cars, clubs, a credit card that always seemed to have money available. Little or no real schoolwork, and what there was, he had mostly done with tutors, even though he saw the work as easy assignments for him.

He was a star. His mother, a housekeeping supervisor for one of the Native American casinos a little way down I-10, started happy after the announcement of the scholarship, but lately was worried. "Hey, mom it's all gooood." He had said over her frown. His worthless dad had even come back into the picture, once the boy was a star, asking for tickets to the home games. The first season had gone well. By the near end of the football schedule he was a starter. But the end of the season had not continued quite so 'gooood.'

The center of the offensive line was comprised of 'The Three Muscatels' as they were known, a running back, Jaylee as lineman delivering opening blocks, and the quarterback left a downtown club, two men in dark suits came up, one on either side of them. One said something like, "How come you won last week?" to Chassy Pounder, the running back walking on Jaylee's left.

Pounder said, "Hey Dog! I ain't the only one on the fuckin' team!"

The guy said, "You could have tripped on the line on that last run. Lost by two!"

Pounder replied, "Well I fukin' didn't, so get over it."

The man then simply said, "A Hundred and Fifty large for one nigger not tripping on his size 13 goddamned foot on the line, like he took six G's for, is something I don't think we can just 'get over'."

As Pounder pushed the man, he yelled "Nigger? You fucking cracker, I'll show you a ni…" Jaylee heard a bang, then a bunch more. Something burned deep into his left shoulder, it was a bullet slowed as it had passed through his "friend" Pounder.

All three young men lay in the street. Jaylee Washington, the only one alive, shot in the shoulder. Pounder, hit over his left ear, two to the chest, 'Skeeter' Skidmore, the quarterback, shot through the neck, in the side, and knee. Two more holes in Jaylee's clothes showed near misses. As he fell, he hit his head on a newspaper vending box, slashing his scalp, knocking him out, probably saving his life as the shooter thought him dead as well, the other's blood all over him, and his pouring from a bullet notched brachial artery. Jaylee's injury resulted in enough damage so there would be no more football.

The eighth floor of the Phoenix MED-Star complex looked like any of the million hospitals across the world, attempts at cheery colors and shiny floors. The fifth floor was, at this time-of-day kind of special, the sun came directly into the hall windows at the end, giving one the optics of those near-death experiences all seem to talk about… "just walk toward the light." In Jaylee's room the normal assortment of special machines designed to use plastic throw-away stuff for which the hospital could and did charge Tiffany store prices sat beeping, flashing, and buzzing like large, trapped horseflies.

A young Phoenix Detective was talking to Jaylee as he lay there on the receiving end of several clear plastic tubes, one blood red…well that probably was because it was delivering blood. One machine was beeping slowly, just loud enough to keep full sleep from ever actually happening. Jaylee had two pints of blood added, the last one still a third to go, in a bag, the dark line going into his arm. He was woozy and like most who get a stranger's blood, had a headache, added to by the fourteen staples in his scalp, the shoulder hurt like hell and was in a cast.

The cop spoke. Not at all what Jaylee's mother, sitting in the roll-around "sleep" chair, which by any measure was designed the keep your ass sweating on the 'easy to clean' vinyl, while arms and feet were freezing in the "hospital cool." He was kind, and really tried to help the young man, not just with the crime, but it seemed with his life. He had gone over the expected questions, all in line with someone being shot. Then, "Jaylee, what happened to you is either the end…or the beginning. You can 'get even' by buying a gun and becoming one of them, or you can say never again. You can say 'I'm not a gangsta, I'm not a punk.' "

"The circus guy, P.T. Barnum said something like the only fear he had was believing his own rap. I guess Barnum was like one of the two guys you were with. We'll get the shooters, probably not for this, they were probably hired to deliver the consequences for not fulfilling a deal to throw the West Virginia game. Nothing points to you or Skeeter knowing anything at all about this deal. Pounder had deposits of three, four and in one case six large into his checking account for every game you guys lost."

Reaching into a grey polyester sports jacket, he retrieved a card. "If you think of anything that might help…call." He paused, looked straight into Jaylee's eyes. "If you just want to talk, just call, anytime." He wrote a personal number on the card. "Look, Jaylee, I think you have something special to give back to the people, to your mom. Take this for what it's worth. I looked at your high school grades. You're smart, maybe brilliant. Get off the jock wagon and really do the school thing. I was never smart enough to do what I know you can."

Jaylee never figured out just what about that short talk and the several other visits the detective had made to him both in the hospital, and as he recovered at his mother's home (the car, card and condo vanished when he was off the team) had burned into his consciousness, but something had.

The sincerity? The common sense? The bizarre circumstance of it's being delivered? All of those… and…something intangible. He felt comfortable with 'Bartman' and enjoyed his company…a father he never had? Maybe.

He did – the school thing. Finished that year at the University of Arizona, then went to New York University on a full academic ride, then got his MBA in Criminal Justice. The FBI and a dozen other law enforcement entities were lobbying him hard to join their organizations. But, five years after the bullet shattered his arm near the proximal brachial fosse, the top part of his arm bone, he applied to the Albuquerque police department using Detective Bart Williams as a reference, the name on the business card, and the mentor he had kept in contact with all through college, the man who had moved from Phoenix to Albuquerque as a Detective First Class.

Now partners for the best part of a decade, they were as close as any family members, closer than many brothers.

The police shields got them into the secure portion of the base, but not before signing in and a call back to their Captain. Jaylee asked the information officer where they could find information about the 'antenna' buried between the Native American Reservations on Sandia Mountain. A dozen calls later they were walked to a nearby building and shown through glass doors with E-R-Mag Labs logo on them, and into a reception area, then asked to wait across from a counter with a paid security guard who glared at them from time to time. A few minutes later, a portly, pilgarlic man looking to be in his 60's with a thin face that didn't go with the pot-belly and large, skin-fat tightened arms sticking out of a pale yellow short-sleeved shirt that had been bought for the neck size. The shirt's shoulders hanging over their edge, and sleeves which came mid-forearm. A stained paisley tie ended eight inches above the belt line. He had a mustache which was trimmed crooked, giving his mouth an un-natural sneer, fingers like sausages stained from years of chain smoking, and like Billy the crime tech's, kept moving, his flipping most of a yellow pencil. He looked tired and sweaty, and smelled like burnt electronics. "I'm Doctor Jefferies, what can I do for you." He did not extend a hand for shaking but plucked Bart and Jaylee's cards when proffered.

Bart and Jaylee gave each other a look that they had perfected over a hundred cases. It said, 'This guy will lie to us, he's a jerk off, ok, then, fuck him'. All unsaid, and no second thoughts. Jaylee charged into a bluff he had been turning over in his mind. "Doctor, did you record any anomalies on the ENet testing, real early this morning, say about 04:00? And if I might ask, why do you smell like a burned circuit board?"

Bart watched the good Doctor closely. "I… How…I don't know what you mean, what's an ENet? Yes, we had some stuff overload in testing a while ago." Jefferies eyes had looked down and away to his left, he was lying.

"Oh, you know, a big antenna buried in the high desert a few miles North of here, you know, the one tuned to a very low frequency that you've been testing." Jaylee smiled like Sylvester the cat with yellow bird feathers sticking out of his mouth.

"You gentlemen can leave now." Jefferies turned on his heel and took a step toward the locked security door he had entered from.

Bart said, "Doctor if you leave before we get a few simple answers, I'll have cops all over this place in fifteen minutes." 'Shit', Bart thought, 'why let Jaylee have all the fun bluffing?'

Jaylee looked at Bart with that 'you got brass balls' look, and added "Make that some here, Bart, remember, we want a crew over on the ranch digging up cable."

Jefferies wheeled back and pointed a stubby finger at Bart, "You touch that antenna and I'll...."

Jaylee swallowed the canary, "You'll do what to who about what Doctor? And If you don't get that finger out of my partner's face you'll have the unpleasant task of removing it from your ass. Look, we got a situation over on the west side of the mountain." He thought, 'looks like my hunch might have some touched a real nerve.' "You find out from someone with a pay-grade that will allow some info exchange and we'll keep the hounds tied up outside this place."

A guard at the door desk stood up, began to move toward the men. Jaylee looked at the guard, pointed a finger and said "You sit the fuck down or I'll arrest you for interfering in a murder investigation!" The guard sat down, picked up the phone on his desk, started poking in numbers, no longer glaring

"Murder! Keep your people from digging up that cable, it might be dangerous for them and for us here! There's a lot of power in there! I'll see if I can get clearance to give you more information… Okay…Okay…what kind of a 'situation' do you have?"

Jaylee described the scene by the remains of the tree, the body parts while watching Jefferies expression carefully. Jefferies looked like a rookie witnessing his first autopsy of a two-week dead victim. He was pale and sweat had popped out on his forehead, adding to the obvious sweat in parts of his shirt. Dabbing his forehead with a stained handkerchief he now smelled like a sweaty-burned capacitor. As Jaylee finished the summary, he waited. Nothing came, then he looked at Bart, thinking that nothing was going to happen here, now, "It's getting late now so, Doctor Jefferies will brief us tomorrow morning." Shooting a look at Jefferies, "Won't he?" Jefferies nodded. "'Till then, we'll leave things alone over on the mountain. We'll be here in the morning, say about 10:00, okay?" Another nod as Jaylee turned to go.

They left the doctor standing by the security desk, Bart said to the guard as he passed the guard desk, "Thanks for your corporation and understanding," once outside to Jay as the doors closed and the heat resumed with an afternoon vengeance. "Well, I got to tell ya Jay, there's nothing I like better than shaking a tree full of egg-heads and watching them splat on the sidewalk when they fall out. You think we were over the top?"

Jaylee said, "Well, I did until I got the distinct impression the good doctor was lying his ass off. I don't think he knows what happened, but I think he knows something did, the flicker of panic about touching the antenna leaves me wondering what he knows, and what happened this morning. Either the Doctor is a drunk and had a really bad hangover, or he had a long bad night from something else."

Bart laughed, "My bet is the latter. Let's go back by the Sherriff's place and set up a desk, start the casebooks and see if anything else has come in."

On the way back to the town and Sheriff's office, Jaylee went over the information Ivey had sent in that Luna had relayed it to the Detectives. Jaylee read the data on the likely victims from the Blackberry screen. "Shit Bart, let's just go back to Albuquerque, shoot some pool and soak up a few beers." He plucked his phone off his belt, punched a few buttons, when it was answered "Hey Luna, this is Detective Washington, when is everyone meeting in the morning?... 7 AM?... you'll have breakfast?... We'll be there, oh by the way, can you get us a desk and a phone?... Thanks, you're a sweetheart." He punched on the radio, Nanci Griffith was singing "Boots of Spanish Leather", Jaylee asked "Who wrote that song?"

Bart responded "Bob Dylan, released in 1964 on his album 'The Times They Are a-Changin' back when he was inking da hits, a few #1's a year back then. That music and lots like it got me through the Hell of Viet-Nam."

Jaylee said, "Bart you never cease to amaze me."

Bart replied, "Like I always say, I have the ability to remember countless facts and infinite details of shit that will do me no financial good what-so-ever."

They headed into town and to the favorite cop watering hole, on the south-side, but on the across the Burlington Northern Santa Fe yard from the now deserted Tiny Vas-Quez abode.

Leo Kotke followed Griffith "Morning is a long way off" with his impeccable slide guitar and lonesome voice.

How true.

PART 2

Credible Witnesses

CHAPTER 5

The Intersection of Time

Consequence is sometimes the mother of coincidence.

Traffic was heavy, but three particular vehicles approached the busy intersection of Camino del Pueblo and Avenide Bernalillo - Deputy Ivey from the West, Sheriff Sam from the North, Bart and Jaylee from the South, all were headed to the Sherriff's office a few blocks away, and none noticed the others. The unusual traffic in the town of Bernalillo was nothing compared to a real city, but here it was still called "the rush hour."

Ivey suddenly felt a wave of an oppressive heaviness in his chest, and the air seemed to get "thick" like the hot air before a cleansing thunderstorm. Where had he felt this? Why was this so strange and foreboding? He began pondering this, as his mind locked onto the memory of where he had felt the feeling, he began to sweat, not from the heat, not from the humidity which had suddenly appeared, but from an undefined dread. A dread of what? The feeling dropped another level toward hell and to a nebulous fear as traffic in the intersection ahead stopped. A glance at the traffic light showed it flickering, well, all twelve lights flickering, none full on. Movement to his left, insects and rodents! Running in, circles on the sidewalk beside his truck, people scrambling from the chaos! "What the…" A cat flat out running, pigeons flapping in the air, going in all directions, not flocking, just…flying tilted up like they had a string around their leg. Where in the hell did all these animals come from? And where the hell were they going?

Ivey looked back at the cars attempting to clear the intersection, a quick cop's practiced area survey still had him not noticing the other team members nearby. He keyed his radio…before he could speak his eyes widened and he froze…adrenalin flooded his system and he felt ice cold, then hot. His senses became hyper tuned, like Ray Walston on "My Favorite Martian" where antenna would sprout from the back of his head.

Out of the windshield, the scene shimmered, then became very light, as if he were looking at a photo that was way over-exposed. Everything in his line of sight suddenly looked like the Wicked Witch of the North had turned it to ice, white, sparkling ice. His mind was racing to find some anchor, something he could pin the scene he saw out of the windshield, his mind racing for some context. Was that real, or was he losing consciousness? Or worse?

As he watched the Honda Accord in front of him seem to turn from ice to glass, the edges of the car began to become ill defined, shimmering, like looking at a TV picture that is threatening to break into a roll, then it began to fade. The truck blocking the intersection could be seen through! Faint lettering on the side of the trailer appeared to be made of cellophane, the rows of boxes inside barely visible, also clear as glass. Suddenly there was a tremendous flash of bright, even whiter light, and a near deafening BOOM! A blast wave hit the Tahoe and seemed to lift the front into the air, then it bounced back to the road surface, rolled forward a few inches then kept dropping and seemed to crash into the surface of the road, on an angle toward a three-foot-deep hole where the intersection used to be.

The area roughly inside the confines of the intersection was gone. It had simply vanished! Some power line wires dropped into the chaos and flashed and jumped before their line-disconnect fuses blew, more "booms." To the side he saw a man dragging himself away, God, it was most of a man. The poor thing stopped moving a few feet later. Why he noticed he would never be able to say, but the insects and other animals were gone, back in their hiding places?

Jaylee was looking at a pretty Native American woman in the next car to Bart and his blue Crown-Vic. Her face suddenly flashed a look of absolute terror, he wheeled to the front to see a motorcyclist become translucent, like he was made of water, as was the Honda Shadow he rode, then he disappeared in a sharp, loud, very bright flash and bang.

Bart jammed the car in reverse and floored it. He got back maybe four feet and hit the car behind, then pushed both vehicles back another twenty where they crunched into a transit bus and stopped. Jaylee yelled over the smoking, screaming tires, "Bart stop! We're okay here! Stop!" He grabbed for the steering wheel and began to turn off the key, but the car died, he turned off the key anyway.

Bart looked at his partner, "I saw her cut in fucking half! Jesus, Jay, just like a big glass blade came down and just cut her in half! She didn't even have time to scream, move, nothing! God in heaven, what in the world do we have here?"

Tears were streaming down Bart's face. He was shaking, almost convulsions. He and Jaylee had seen some real bad stuff, but nothing anywhere like this…maybe no one on earth had ever seen anything like this.

Complete chaos ensued. A Native American woman was standing at the edge of the hole with her arms outstretched screaming for her daughter. A woman got out of the front half of a mini-van and looked at the sliced van. Half of her hair was missing in the back, right to her scalp. She suddenly realized her son was in the missing rear half of the van, she stepped out to the road and began slowly turning in circles, crying, wringing her hands, then began wailing. Several people on the sidewalk were trying to help the injured, but soon were overwhelmed by the scene, one man just sat down, his back to the drugstore wall shaking his head.

Many instinctively reached for and flipped open cell phones, then noticing they were dead, looked at the instruments in disbelief. It was a small snapshot of a society when all sensory and "routine" underpinnings are suddenly removed. Although relatively new, those little electronic anchors, those lifelines to help and rescue, cell phones, were suddenly useless. A primal fear of being in trouble and alone swept over some, but there were others, survivors, who just "kept on keeping on". It's what they did, just keep moving. Plodding through recessions, unemployment, sickness, divorce, deaths, and now the beginning of what? The end of the world? A death ray from aliens? Some government screw-up? Terrorists?

The Sheriff was a few cars back from the flash and events at the intersection, but he saw what seemed to be a stream of light going into the sky, like a white bolt of lightning, but with more straight edges, not as ragged like lightning, it seemed to bend to the South in an arc before it went out of sight above the site-line available from the windshield. He jumped from the Suburban, stumbled, it seemed to him that he had gained sixty pounds. He craned his neck and stared up where the stream seemed to have gone, nothing but clear, blue sky.

People were yelling, abandoning cars that were also cut in various places. The woman next to Ivey looked out of the hole through the missing front of her car, then noticed she had no legs below the knee, she screamed, a sound so anguished and painful it made his skin crawl, she fainted.

Sheriff Sam tried his radio, somehow feeling it wouldn't work. It didn't. He noticed the battery was dead. He quickly walked into a storefront and grabbed the phone by the cash register, it had a dial-tone, and he punched in the office number, "Luna, get the disaster book and call everyone in there. I have some kind of an explosion or something at the intersection of the Pueblo and Avenide. We need every ambulance and cop you can get here 10-39. No details now. Few to tell ya. I'll set up a command post, call it Avenide command, on Avenide Bernalillo - North side, until the disaster team arrives. Radios are dying."

Outside, he flopped, leaning against the Suburban, he scooted along the side, not sure he could walk, at the back window he got his crank-it-to-charge bull-horn. He moved back to the edge of the sharp edged crater, cranking the charger on the bull horn. Sweat drenching his shirt and uniform pants. At the edge of the hole he stopped. It was a rough circle, like the one at the tree yesterday, but bigger and deeper. It started at a sharp edge of a yard deep, and was cut in an irregular pattern, roughly circular. The sidewalks and all of the large intersection proper was gone. The cantilevered traffic light poles were cut directly over where the edge of the pavement was scored. It seemed a giant irregular sided cookie cutter had come from the heavens, punched a "cookie" and left with it. He thought of his mother rolling dough for biscuits and using a "Mickey Mouse" juice glass, bought as a promotion filled with Welch's grape jelly, once empty of the purple jelly used to punch out biscuits on the white porcelain drain board next to the kitchen sink. The memory came from a long, long time ago and from a place where 'normal' existed…certainly not here. Certainly not now.

With some effort, Sheriff Bush pulled up the bull-horn and spoke. "This is the sheriff, listen up. If you are not hurt, move away from the…" What the hell to call it. "The hole, please be available for law enforcement to interview later today. Folks, if you have any EMS training, come here to my vehicle, help is on the way." He could hear sirens as indeed; help was winding through traffic toward the scene. His radio went off. Suddenly the weight was gone, and a breeze came down the street, he felt lighter, like he had set down a hundred-pound bar-bell. Sweat began to evaporate, cooling him. That was a relief!

"Avenide command, this is Battalion Chief Lawson. Any update, any fire, what we got there? Over"

He keyed his mic, the radio seemed to have recharged somewhat, "Battalion, some kind of explosion, I don't know, no smell, no fire but several dozen injured here. I saw it happen, but I can't tell you just what the hell it was. Over." The radio died again.

Ivey, and the two detectives came to the Sheriffs truck, having heard the bull-horn. Bart was still a mess, but was improving. The sheriff turned to Ivey, "Ivey, let's try to get some security out there, better not step into the hole." Jaylee and Ivey fanned out moving people away from the edge of the incident scene - the mother of all pot-hole depression that had been a normal small city intersection a few minutes ago.

Bart leaned against the side of the truck, head in hands. Hurt, dismembered and shell-shocked folks that could be moved, were. Within three minutes EMS and Fire units began arriving, and soon were all over the scene, Town Police and Sheriff Deputies started to cordon off the twenty-meter perimeter of the hole, stringing yellow tape, tying it to the nearest available points or placed traffic cones close to the hole. New Mexico State Troopers began arriving.

New Mexico State Police Captain Randy Potet'e arrived in a little less than a half hour later in a Blue Bird RV bus built as an Incident Command Unit. All the cars not involved had been cleared, simply dragged back from the incident, all car and truck batteries were completely dead. The streets were blocked off by cones and Troopers back a few blocks from the scene. Deputies and State Troopers were busy interviewing people who had witnessed the 'event' none giving any details that were helpful. The most consistent comment was the intersections and everything in it turning to ice before the boom.

Soon the senior Fire, EMS, and various ranking police, as well as the Mayor, his chief administrative Assistant who also was the press liaison and the South West FEMA warden, who was in the area for an illegal immigration impact conference to be held in Albuquerque. All were seated at or pressed against the wall of the narrow Command Bus conference room table. The room was 18 feet long, 12 feet wide when the RV style slide-outs on both sides were extended as they were now, the room was well lit with indirect lights. A gentle rumble of the on-board generator was present, but not distracting. Wood and light colors added to a space where work could be done without the tiresome look of an over decorated space. The very light smell of diesel fuel and furniture polish was present.

Sheriff Bush had always liked the Mayor, for a relatively small time city politician, James "Jimmy" Jamus, or 2-J as he was called by friends, was a sharp and dedicated public servant. He looked around the room and spoke. "Gentlemen, does anyone here have any idea what happened to my main intersection, several cars, trucks, and God knows how many of my people?" Silence returned from the men and women in the bus. "Okay, let's see if we can rule out a few things." Pointing the two thirds remaining portion of a Slim-Jim spiced sausage stick at the fire chief, a replacement for a cigarette in an on-again-off-again battle with smokes, "Chief Lawson, was there an explosion?"

"No, Mister Mayor, the police bomb, and my arson people so far have detected no evidence or residue of explosives, or chemicals of any kind really. Some trace flammable gas was discovered, but it was found to be sewer gas from the several manholes left uncovered by whatever removed the… the intersection. Additionally, even though almost everyone heard a powerful boom, most describe it as a thunderclap, or a sonic boom, like we hear sometimes from the base over the hill and down the valley."

Sheriff Sam Bush spoke, "Jim, what I saw was not an explosion. There was no smoke, fire, or anything ejected from the scene. Everything in that intersection just vanished." He snapped his fingers. "Just like that," he pointed up.

"Okay," Jamus continued, "where do we begin? And what can we say to the press? Look, I know this will be everywhere by the noon news, and there are a lot of folks wanting, hell, needing, to know what happened." He bit off an inch of Slim-Jim.

Detective 1st class Lieutenant Bart Williams spoke up, "Mister Mayor, Detective Bart Williams here, I saw the event… I think we need to simply tell the truth. We don't know what happened here, and exactly how many people are involved. I'm normally not in favor of getting the press into an investigation, but something's started in this valley in the last thirty hours that we're gonna need some help figuring out."

Lawson's head snapped up, he said, "Detective, what do you mean in the last thirty hours?" Every head in the room shot to Bart as well.

Sheriff Bush answered, "Folks, we had begun an investigation of what looks to us here like an earlier incident of the same thing, out on Route 165. Most of two kids and a friggin' eighty-foot oak tree vanished, just like here." He pointed out the front windows of the bus at the crime scene-tape-draped void in the street.

That information hit the rest of the people in the conference area like a ice cold water balloon had been dropped from the ceiling bursting on the center of the table.

Luna, back in the Sherriff's office was busy relaying new information to the team member's Blackberrys, the Sherriff, Ivey and Jaylee had PDA's, Bart had one whose battery had expired some time ago when the Blackberry was stored in his locker in Albuquerque. His compromise was, however, a flip-phone. The Sheriff office phone rang. "Sheriff's office, how may I direct your call?"

"I'm trying to get in touch with a Detective Jaylee Washington, his cell number isn't working, he wrote this number on the back of his card. My name is Doctor Jefferies, I work at E-R-Mag Labs. Miss…. did anything out of the ordinary happen this morning?"

Luna nearly dropped the phone. "Doctor, please hold, it may take a minute or so." She frantically typed. "Got E-R-Mag Labs Dr. on phone. Call office ASAP. Wants to know if anything out of ordinary happened this morning." She sent the text to the Sheriff and Jaylee.

Jaylee got a chirp and the vibrating PDA, hanging from a charger cord plugged into the outlet on the bus being fed from the bus's diesel generator, unplugged it and read the message. He handed the PDA to Bart, who passed it to the mayor. Jaylee was leaning over the table to the speaker phone and was poking in the numbers for the Sherriff's private line. Instinctively, everyone around the table got quiet. When Luna patched him in he said, "Doctor Jefferies, this is detective Washington, I'm in an incident command bus and I'm putting you on a speaker phone."

Jefferies said, in an obviously trembling voice, "Co.. Command bus? I'm not sure I can be on a speaker phone. Who's there listening?"

Jaylee looked at the Mayor, and then to the FEMA officer, who spoke. "Doctor Jefferies is it? I'm Samuel Ogelsbee, FEMA Warden for the Southwest. If you have anything to add to our situation, I suggest you do so now. We have a lot of damage here and no real information."

"F..ff..fff.. FEMA! Oh Jesus! What is FEMA doing there? What happened?"

The Sheriff jumped out of his chair, nearly turning it over. "Another twenty meters of my jurisdiction disappeared, and God knows how many of my people with it. Mister...Doctor you better fucking start talking, NOW, speaker phone, tin can on a string, or whatever the fuck we need."

The Mayor put up his hand, Sam sat back down from where he had sprung from his chair. All people in his jurisdiction were indeed HIS people, and he took their welfare seriously… very seriously. Ivey looked at the sheriff, he had never seen Sam so emotional, normally Sam was a cool, composed lawman. 'Good to see a real person lives in that uniform', he thought.

Oh, Sheriff, those people's welfare, maybe their survival, was going to become more of a problem.

CHAPTER 6

A Skeptic Converted

Jefferies spoke, voice still shaking. "We...well we're testing a new communications antenna, completely harmless, I assure you. Nothing new, just a different frequency, and a new pattern of the radiators, a...an...and very powerful. I assure you, our preliminary tests indicated no problems, none at all."

Jaylee said, "Then why, Doctor, are you calling asking if anything happened here?"

"Well, the power registered as going into the antenna array came back into the transmitter at significantly higher levels than that sent out, it wiped out the finals in the transmitter, nearly burned down the trailer the cabinets are in. I was checking to see if a power line or something like it had fallen up on the mountain where the antenna is located. And then there is a problem we haven't quite figured out yet."

Jaylee held up his hand, not wanting an interruption... just yet anyway. "Doctor did you have something like this yesterday morning, say about

0-four-hundred, the problem Detective Williams and I spoke to you about yesterday about this same time of day?"

"Uh...well...yes, sort of, but Detective, I had security issues and just couldn't talk about them then, actually the incident I just described was yesterday morning."

The Mayor banged the table, introduced himself and said, "Doctor, you get a team of your people together, right damned now and get over here! I can assure you I'll have the Governor informed, and there better not be any more 'security issues'. Do I make myself clear?" Then before Jefferies could answer he added, "Oh, by the way, shut down the transmitter, and no more tests until we have a full understanding of the events last night, and this morning. Is that clear?"

The voice that came back was weak, still shaking, but clear, "Gentlemen, we did not turn on the transmitter after 03:45 yesterday morning, that's the problem I was talking about. We have disconnected all power to it, actually, the electronics and related systems required to activate the antenna are completely burned out, nothing working except the sensor leads, which are passive."

Bart looked white as a sheet, and said what everyone was thinking, "Detective Williams here, Jefferies, what the hell have you done? Jesus, man, what the hell have you done?"

Jefferies said, "The instruments showing power in the antenna are showing a slow non-linier curve upward, like the charge in a capacitor, a very big capacitor, then it falls, like it did this morning a few hours ago. I...I... I'll get a team over there within an hour, but I don't know what we can do."

The Mayor said, "Why not tear out the whole damned transmitter? What did you say, sensor wires? Shut it the hell down."

Jaylee said, "I'd be careful, Mister Mayor, right now we have some way of seeing what's going on outside the transmitter, if they aren't putting anything in, it may be the only way we can see what's going to happen out here...someplace." The gravity of that statement hit like another cold-water balloon. Then, turning toward the speaker-phone on the table he asked, "Jefferies, what's the level now, compared to when it peaked and fell?"

The men could hear tapping on a keyboard, Jefferies said, "Pretty low, maybe 1/10th of what it was."

Jaylee said, "In English, so we all can understand, what's 1/10th mean?"

Jefferies said in that same small voice, "9004×10 to the 24th Joules."

Jaylee said, "Doctor, you and the team, get the fuck over here! Leave someone at the transmitter who can relay the status of the charge...or whatever it is." And punched off the call. The others began to shout at him. He raised his hand slowly.

Sitting down from where he had reached for the phone, he said, in a calm full voice. "Gentlemen, the power of the biggest lightning bolt ever recorded was 1200×10 to the 3rd joules. There was nothing else he could tell us."

Leaning back in his chair, all eyes on him. "I do not know what they started, but it looks to me like it's going to happen again."

Ogelsbee spoke next, "Guys, this may well be way over my pay-grade. I'm going to call up the chain and see if Washington can give any assistance."

The Mayor raised his hands, and said, "Well I'm normally against an inside the beltway attempt at help, but I really don't know what we have here. Does anyone?" He looked around the room at the people assembled there. He got no response. "Mister Ogelsbee, make your call, but I will tell you right now, I will not secede governance of this town to anyone. This is my town, with my people, who elected me four times, as was Sheriff Bush, and the Sheriff and I will be involved in its welfare. Is that understood?" He looked at his assistant, a greying trim woman in a well-tailored business suit, maybe in her 50s. "Mary, inform the Governor's office of what you've heard here, be careful not to embellish in any way, and as usual, don't let them try to speculate on information we don't have yet. Advise them to keep the news people at bay if they can, as of now frankly we don't have any facts to give them."

She nodded, closed her note pad and left the room. Under his breath, the Mayor said, "She's an absolute jewel."

FEMA representative Ogelsbee, looking up from the cell phone in his hand said in an even tone, "I've not known you very long, Mister Mayor, but my gut tells me you got your shit together, so, in my opinion, keeping you in the loop and in front of it is the best course. You will have my full support. I'll work with you to de-rail any power grabs." He turned back to his cell phone, which he had been flipping end over end in his fingers, like a magician rolling a coin, stopped the flip, and started punching in numbers.

The Sheriff looked to Jaylee, who he, as did the others, seemed instinctively to know was the one who would act as their 'Bullshit' filter when dealing with the E-R-Mag Labs people. "Jay, shouldn't we, I mean us here in the real world outside E-R-Mag Labs have someone telling us how this thing is re-charging? I mean we won't know where it's gonna pop, but we might know when."

"Excellent observation," the mayor said.

Jaylee, slowly shaking his head, "Well, I agree, there's one assumption that we have to make, and that is we don't know if we can count on those PhD's on the base giving us real information. I mean Jefferies is a friggin' liar, Bart and I saw that first hand. And something's missing in the Doctors' information."

Bart said, "Yeah, like why call the Sherriff's office when their instruments showed problems? And what prompted them to shut off the test at what, four AM yesterday?"

The Fire Chief, who had been quiet spoke, "Guys, there is still one question I can't get my mind around." Everyone looked at him, Jaylee thought 'only one?' he continued, "I've been to some advanced bomb and explosive training, you may remember I was in charge of the bomb disposal unit in Albuquerque until this job was offered to me. What happened to, shit, I dunno, a hundred tons of material that was three hours ago in that intersection?" He too pointed out of the front of the bus. "My college physics says if it was turned from mass into energy, this valley would look like Nagasaki. So, if it wasn't converted to something else, like energy, then it must have gone someplace." He turned slowly around the table. Serious but blank faces looked back at him, he repeated, "Gone someplace." His voice died on the words.

Bart slowly placed his ever-present Bic pen onto his pad and said, "I can't get my mind passed the young woman I saw cut nearly in half, right down the middle. The right half of her went someplace, it didn't explode. And why that intersection? Pure chance, or was the energy that friggin' Jefferies found drawn to that place?" Bart had watery eyes as he remembered the girl's surprised expression as she fell. Jaylee patted him on the shoulder.

Ivey, who had been quiet said, "Well, we have to wonder why a tree in the middle of the desert? I mean where is that in relation to the antenna?"

Jaylee snapped his fingers, "Deputy, you might have something." Reading the labels, he pulled down one of the roll-up maps from several mounted on the bus the ceiling behind the mayor. Pointing to the mountain he said, "Here's the approximate location of the antenna." Then took a yard-stick and set it across the approximate location of the tree incident, then extended it into town, where it crossed the intersection in front of the bus. "Well, look there! It's damned near due North/South, not quite but close!"

Chief Lawson said, "Oh, it's magnetic North, not map north. Look, it's about seven degrees off." Lawson explained the difference of rotational North to the Magnetic North registered by normal compasses.

Mayor Jamus scowled from the map and rotated his chair at the head of the table back to the group, as he was closest to the map wall, then swiveled back to the map. He pointed the slim-jim. "The next discharge, if that's what we're calling it, will land someplace here, if the distances remain constant." He pointed to an area of the section of state route 85, then said, we had better not rule out North/South, then downside of the map with the ruler. He tapped a point within the bounds of the Native American Tribal Common Community College. He then looked further down the map. "Oh Jesus."

They all looked at a point in the center of downtown Albuquerque. The FEMA man spoke. "Guys, look, I know what we are thinking here, but we don't have anywhere enough data to do any mass evacuations. We have two incidents of something, which we can't even begin to explain. We have two data points of this unexplained phenomenon, and I don't think we can risk a panic based on that."

"Shit, still no one home in DC." He snapped his cell phone back on his belt after leaving a second voice message.

The Mayor looked back at the map. "Maybe we can evacuate the college, say a nut-case was spotted with a gun or something. That's manageable, and if the phenomenon happens again as our best guess has predicted, we should be able to save life and limb."

The New Mexico State Police Captain, who had been standing silent during the meeting moved off the wall, took a step to the table, leaning on his arms, looking around at the team members, "Gentlemen, I've listened patiently to what's been said, and it really sounds like a load of bullshit to me. What have we got here, a fucking death ray? Aliens, long hidden, broke free from someplace on the base?... It sounds to me like a gas main or some damned thing went off in the intersection. You show me something I can't explain, and I'll clear the campus, 'till then, I gotta tell ya, I'm out."

Bart walked slowly to the captain's arm, taking it gently said, "Follow me Randy, just follow me." The captain straightened, looked around the room, and nodded. The other men cleared a path through the tight quarters of the conference room, and the two men stepped down the front stairs of the Command Bus. The 'incident' scene was several meters away, there were still disabled cars and police vehicles between the bus and the hole. Events in setting up the command bus, distributing of resources and establishing communications had kept Potet'e from a firsthand look at the scene. Jaylee saw them duck under the crime scene tape and disappear out of view of the buss's windshield.

The impossible was going to become real.

CHAPTER 7

Book 'em Danno

Bart walked across the clearing, cones had been placed near open manholes and other hazards, loops of wire that had been buried in the road for the traffic light detectors, and some holes that went into the street with no obvious purpose. He walked Randy to where he and Jaylee had been before he had backed his car away.

He pointed to what looked like a pretty young woman, perhaps 18 or 19, laying on her side in very still water, with half of her body out of the fluid. The problem was she was laying on a cement sidewalk a few inches from the sharp edge of the hole. There was no blood, fluid, or any stains. Her clothing, an oxford style man's shirt, un-tucked and worn over a mid-thigh mini-skirt, was not burned or discolored. The mini-skirt was not even rumpled. Her left blue eye was open, a carefully shaped eyebrow held a slight arch of surprise that would stay imprinted on her face and in Bart's memory forever. Her mouth had no scream there, also just a slight look of surprise. A crime-scene technician was photographing her, one of a number of techs drifting around and through the scene, most with a shell-shocked look. The tech stepped back as the two men approached.

"Randy, I saw one-half of this beautiful child disappear, and the rest of her wheel and fall as you see her now. I don't know what happened to her, or the forty or fifty others in this place, but they did not die in an explosion."

Bart saw a look of complete shock turn to amazement as Randy bent, then stooped to look at the girl, then backed away some and took in the entire sight of the young woman, then, slowly turning, the rest of the scene. A third of a car, a bicycle with just the rear tire and pedal lying on its side. A hundred strange and weird sights. No smell, and no smoke, nothing charred, no fragments of flesh. The big Exacto-knife in the sky had cut the picture, and left a collage of scattered photo pieces around the scene.

The Police Captain straightened, waved for Bart to follow, and walked purposefully back to the Command Bus. As he ascended the stairs, the conversations stopped and heads turned. "Gentlemen, I'll do what-ever we need to do to clear the campus. I'll get a team on it now…how much time do we have?"

Jaylee said, "I knew you'd help, Randy, and I don't think any of us thought you were out of line with your skepticism. This is hard to get your mind around, isn't it?"

Jaylee continued, "As for time, I'd say we better have what we need in place at fifteen hours after this event, or about ten hours form now...That's unless the E-R-Mag Labs people have a different estimate."

FEMA Warden Ogelsbee said, with no attempt at controlling obvious anger, "Speaking of whom, where the fuck are they."

As if on cue in a high school play, a voice answered. "We're right the fuck here."

Bart rose and retrieved three more people from the State Police officer guarding the bus. As he re-entered the conference room, said, "Gentlemen, may I present Doctor Jefferies, and.." he waited for Jefferies to introduce the rest of his team, but Jefferies just stood there for a moment, surveying the people on the bus. He had changed and showered, no longer smelling like burned bong water. He now had a grey short sleeved shirt, same tight arms and the bottom 3 buttons doing overtime trying not to pop off and put someone's eye out.

He puffed out his chest, expanding like an anemic blow-fish, the buttons nearly screamed in pain, and said "Like the Detective noted, I'm Doctor Chris Jefferies. The ENet project was my idea, and I've been working it for thirteen years. I tested the antenna, and I feel it's safe. I'm here to prove Electronic-Resonant- Magnetics, or E-R-Mag Laboratories had nothing to do with the events you say happened over here. As the project director working for the defense department as a consultant, I'm sorry to inform you men, but I'm taking over this investigation, me and my team will be giving the orders, and we expect them to be followed, is that understood?"

Mayor Jamus looked at Jefferies, paused in the silence for a moment and said, "Really, very interesting, well, I do think you can help. Sheriff, arrest these men and the lady, take them directly to the place where we have calculated the next event to happen, and ask them to call us from where-ever the hell their harmless experiment sends them, I do hope their cell phone batteries are well charged." The Mayor turned to Chief Lawson, like nothing had happened, tapped a pencil on a clip-board he and Lawson had been examining.

Jaylee had cuffs on Jefferies in what had to be a world's record, Bart had his female assistant cuffed, and Ivey was clicking his on a small Asian man who had tried to sheepishly back out of the bus.

Jefferies had expected some negative reaction, but not this, "Wa...wait, you can't do this, I'm a contract government employee! I have my orders! Arrest, what's the charge?

Mayor Jamus looked up with an annoyed expression, "Well, I'm no prosecutor, not anymore, but let's try Manslaughter 1st degree, reckless endangerment, interfering with a police investigation, criminal negligence, those are off the top of my head. If I think a little while I might find someplace in the law books 'presenting oneself as a self-important pompous asshole'. "

The sheriff said, in a dead calm voice, "Jefferies, I'm a Government employee too, and unlike you, I actually have orders I not only can, but really want to follow." As Jaylee pushed Jefferies roughly toward the door.

Jaylee said, "You have the right to remain silent..." then smiling, "G. Gordon Liddy was a Government employee, and he got locked up."

Bart said, "Charles Manson caused people to be dismembered, and even though he had nut cases do it for him, he's still in jail." He thought, 'my prisoner sure looks good...and that perfume...'

FEMA Ogelsbee held up his hand, "Sheriff, before you take them away I have a question." Then to Jefferies, "Who gave you your orders, and were they higher than the Director of Homeland Security?"

Jefferies mumbled some unintelligible phrase. Ogelsbee nodded, the Sheriff and Ivey began walking them out again, returning to the Miranda speech.

The woman spoke, she had an angular but very attractive face, high models' cheekbones. Dark rimmed utilitarian scientist glasses perched across a straight, small nose, glasses which did not diminish pale blue eyes. Dark brown hair that looked black until she moved her head where highlights shimmered. She wore it gently curled, now banded into a pony-tail, a sweat band embroidered with 'nuke Greenpeace' started under the ponytail, came over her ears, crossed her forehead capturing any wandering strands of her hair, and returned. She wore a loose fitting white blouse, a fanny pack with water bottle, khaki pants that labored to conceal an attractive figure and failed, military desert camo boots completed the "ready for field work" outfit.

Yes, Doctor Rand looked ready for outside in the desert work, "Wait, please, wait a goddamned minute, Jefferies why the hell did you come in here with your usual E-R-Mag Labs big-shot- stuff? You know damned good and well we are supposed to help, and find out what happened here." Then without pausing for breath, "Gentlemen, I'm Doctor Joan Rand, assistant program manager, and Doctor Kough and I are here to help. As far as I'm concerned, you can stake out Jefferies at the next site if you want." Pausing, she crinkled her brow, looked at the Mayor, she added, "But I would like to know how and where you guys think it will be."

Jaylee laughed, unlocked her cuffs, Ivey followed with Doctor Kough's. Jefferies remained secured. He pointed to the map, and with Doctor Rand and Kough, went over the logic leading them to the Native American College Campus. She looked further and said, "Mister, I sure hope you're wrong, or Albuquerque is gonna have a really bad Sunday."

The Mayor said, "I hope so too. We've instituted a plan to evacuate the campus."

Doctor Rand continued, "Well, the rate of charge was moving toward another discontinuity at 22:30 tonight, we think we will be able to narrow that down as the actual charge is monitored and our calculations are sharpened."

She then moved to the door to the conference room and closed it. "Jefferies, I'm going to tell them the best guesses we have."

"Damned, Joan! You can't! It's classified! We'll all go to jail!" Jefferies wailed.

Jaylee reached over and tugged hard on the cuffs, Jefferies winced. "Technically, Doctor, yo' ass is in jail already, and I agree with the former ADA, yo' gonna do some serious time."

She continued, "Like the Project Leader said, this is classified 'Secret Crypto' and although I'm telling you this, it is still classified. Secret Crypto means it's secret information, the crypto means it's having to do with the transmission of classified data and information. Let me start by describing the concept of the ENet project. We simply wanted to build a transmitting antenna, full wavelength, tuned to the resonant frequency of the earth."

Jaylee whistled, "That's a frequency of between 7 and 8 hertz! You got to be kidding, the antenna, even at 1/4th resonant would be a kilometer or more long! And the power to excite it would be astronomical!"

"Very good, uh excuse me but I don't know what to call you."

Bart interjected, "He's Detective Second Class Jaylee Washington, the brains in the mismatched but extremely effective Albuquerque homicide team of Bart and Jaylee. I'm Bart".

"Homicide?" A very worried look came to her face, had people died here? She had not considered death. "Well, Detective Washington, the length of the actual antenna, and it's tuning elements are something over 12 kilometers, it's a power-element-Yagi design."

"Wait a minute." Chief Lawson said, "Why the hell would you want to do something like that?"

Jaylee said, "Doctor, with your permission?" She nodded, "What if, when you wanted to communicate with, oh say a submarine 10,000 miles away, and the entire earth was the antenna? Planes, boats, probably spacecraft could just put an ear toward, on, or in good ol' earth and, they hear the broadcast. Kind of like someone making noise when you're swimming underwater in a pool. The water is all around you and transmitting the sound."

Rand looked at the man she had tagged as a dumb-ass cop just a minute ago, smiled at Jaylee and said, "You are a detective, aren't you?" Then to the room, "Detective Washington is right on all points. If we were able to impress an AM signal onto the frequency transmitted with, and in sync to the earth's resonant frequency, any properly equipped receiver anywhere on earth could hear the message. Returning the message would be impossible, because of the length of the antenna and the power required to excite it, but consider the value in being able to get information to submarines on patrol, or unit's way out in the desert of, say, Afghanistan. Launch codes, stuff like that, any information deemed necessary. The Sandia mountain site was chosen because the geology, a mixture of metal ores and salts in the Sandia mountain range, presented the best conductivity toward the earth's core we could find."

Looking around, she saw still confused or empty faces, "Okay, indulge me a minute and I'll give a Cliff notes history of this project. Originally, some years ago, I think in the late 70's the project was scheduled to be tried in the Chesapeake bay at the very end of the Potomac river where it joins the bay, between the gun range in Dahlgren Virginia, and Indian Head logistics base in Maryland across the bay, to be run from part of the old Navy base there. Oystermen and other fishermen got wind of the project, and one, an electronics expert, argued that an antenna that powerful would kill any fish, eels or maybe even watermen that were across the wave form, literally electrocuting a fish because one end, say it's head would be a few dozen volts different than its tail. The wooden boats have lightening grounds along their keels, and that could catch enough energy to cause a spark, maybe explode a fuel tank or destroy electronic depth finders and radios on the boats. The Navy was forced to shut it down, but the concept continued. A a search for another area with electrical connectivity as close to the salt-water bay was attempted that could be found was started. Sandia mountain was chosen even though the power to activate the antenna would have to be over five times the energy that cables in the bay would have needed. Dr. Jefferies here was moved out here in 1993 to continue the work. As the project gained budget and engineering background, the staff was increased, Kough and I started in 2001, others since then to a staff of 55 now."

"And that's what and why we're in the high desert and based here on Sandia Base Lab property at E-R-Mag Labs rented space." Rand finished the concise presentation and looked around the room inviting questions.

Chief Lawson asked, "Doctor Rand, where is the energy coming from that Jefferies told us about on the phone before you came over here?"

Dr. Rand looked at Kough, who had as yet not spoken, he was an older Asian man, more Mongol influence than Japanese, probably Korean, typically slim, but slightly bent from too many hours bent over a lab table. His complexion had faded to an un-healthy yellow from hours in windowless rooms. He wore a light colored cotton shirt, but had chosen Levies that looked completely out of place being pressed and creased. He had an oversized NY Yankees baseball cap which wobbled on his head. He too, had a fanny pack and water bottle, and shiny ankle height lace up hiking boots which, as yet, had not seen any outdoor activity.

He said in good, but accented English "We honestly don't know. The power levels are astronomical. The energy at first look seems to be pure DC voltage and current, but we're not sure, and it builds, then simply disappears." He snapped his fingers, "Just like that, then starts building again."

Rand nodded an agreement, then followed Lawson's look to Jefferies, whose head was bowed.

Lawson said, "Jefferies, you got any ideas?"

Jefferies looked up from the floor where he had been staring, changing species from now deflated blowfish to canine, his expression was one of a wupped puppy, "Look, maybe I got off on the wrong foot. I had orders, but we really need to find out what's going on out here."

Mayor Jamus stood slowly and pointed a finger at him, "Doctor Jefferies, that is the wrong answer, but I think the truth. We have people killed here, some missing, and maybe more to come, and you fucking want to find out what happened? No mention of the victims, no mention of the dismembered people. I want to stop another event, what did you call it Doctor?" Looking at Rand, "A discontinuity? I'm so glad you admitted you're in charge of the ENet project. Like I said, you will stand trial for murder, or at least manslaughter. Now do you want to answer the question Chief Lawson asked, because if you don't, and I don't see a distinct change in your attitude, I'm going to have the Sheriff lock you in the jail until we get past this." He let the moment hang, complete silence for several beats, "Do you have any questions, sir?"

Jefferies now looked like a wupped, stomped on and kicked puppy, "I'm sorry, I...we...tested everything as good as we could. Chief Lawson, I do not know where the power is coming from. I do not know what happened here and up the hill toward the antenna last night. We did, however bring a truck-load of instruments and test equipment, and I have asked for re-positioning of a satellite with," he paused and looked at Rand and Kough, "some very special monitoring equipment which may be able to at least help define what and where the energy is coming from and going to."

Rand said, "Jees, Jefferies, stop being so close to the vest. Gentlemen, it's a spy satellite and can detect EMP's, or electro-magnetic-pulses, like a nuclear weapon produces. The data, with the other satellites in the constellation should be able to give us some actionable information, at least as to where the energy is coming from, and where it goes."

Kough spoke again, "It, the satellite that is, recorded the previous two events, but so far we have not been able to discern any useful information other than the exact time and place of the discontinuities. There is a team of electrical engineers pouring over the download the NASA people sent us, as we speak." He continued, "Look, the media has got to be told something, and since we have no idea what it is, they'll eat everyone alive here and, yes even everyone on E-R-Mag Labs if we don't decide on something until we have real data."

The Mayor said, "Well I hate to get into a media thing here, I mean we have people hurt and missing, but I see your point.

Potet'e said, "How about what I thought when I first arrived here, a gas line explosion."

That was the story and the mayor's assistant went back out to inform the news people gathered outside the cordoned off area of the intersection.

Ivey asked, "Okay, what's a discontinuity?"

Doctor Rand looked at him and said, "Sorry deputy, but I don't have any idea. We had to have a word to describe the discharges, I just called them that and it seems to have stuck." She moved to a white board positioned on the wall between two drape-closed windows. She drew a classic non-linier capacitor charge curve. "It appears there is a high flow of energy just after the event." She pointed to a vertical line dropping to a horizontal line she had made across the bottom of the board, tapping the line she said "time" and drew a sharp upward curved line which tapered and flattened out "energy" and at a point where it got nearly flat she spiked it down again. "Another event."

"So the issue is where is the energy coming from and where does it go? Guys, we are talking about an enormous amount of energy, high voltages and enormous current. We have to monitor it by remote sensors because it's diffuse, not focused, and our methods may be giving us exaggerated data, but we have to go with what they're sending us. We should see something like the mother of all lightning storms, but that's not what the instruments indicate. They show the energy simply vanishing."

Chief Lawson said, "Einstein must be rolling in his grave, we now have both mass and energy vanishing."

The Mayor rose from his chair, "This is interesting and truly, I'd like to continue, but we're not getting any new information in this bus. I suggest we get moving. Although the cycles seem to be in a pattern, that may not stand, two events do not a spreadsheet make. Potet'e is on the campus evacuation. Lawson, you have the staging of emergency equipment. I'll handle the press."

Sheriff Bush said, "Shouldn't we stick a bunch of camera equipment all over the place? I'd like to see if my mind and eyes were tricking me."

Jefferies said, "We have equipment to do that."

Jaylee wheeled to him, "I don't friggin' trust you. Why not you get the equipment, and Bart and I will assure the recordings don't vanish like the intersection?"

The FEMA man continued Jaylee's thought, "Yeah, and why don't we park this vehicle near where the event is likely to happen, then feed all the data your stuff collects back here?"

Jefferies put up his just un-cuffed hands in surrender, "Guys, I know I really messed up coming in here like I did. Fine, we'll route our sensor and camera inputs to the bus here. Any ideas where we can set this thing up, close but safe?" His tone and demeanor had completely changed, he was like the wupped puppy had rolled over and exposed his belly, all wind gone from his self-placed over-important sails.

"Mister Mayor, we finally have some good luck." His assistant had returned with her note book and was reading, "The college finals were completed last week, the campus is nearly deserted."

Potet'e said, "We can change the scenario from a nut with a gun to terrorist training, I'll get on that." He left the room, portable phone in hand.

Oh – if a nut with a gun were the biggest problem.

CHAPTER 8

Where's My Car?

Jaylee thought the day was going by like good sex, too fast and too tiring, drawing to an end too soon. Funny metaphor, but it seemed sex and what-ifs were on his mind a disproportionate amount of the time since Doctor Joan Rand stepped into the command bus conference room. Working with her, as she directed the wiring and tuning of the receivers and cables from several cameras and other data collection equipment, he found himself allowing some... interesting... fantasies regarding the good Doctor. In spite of this, he was a true gentleman. OK, she smelled really good too, something vanilla?

But for Jaylee, there was something scary about these events, and this insidious premonition kept a full blown, rip-roaring untimely hard-on Doctor lady fantasy from settling in. It was as if the wiring and work was preparing for an invasion of...what? Monsters? Aliens? A movie earthquake or global warming-where-everything-freezes bullshit disaster? He shook his head, Jaylee, get a grip man, you need context here - a tree in the desert, and an intersection in town are a problem, but really, how bad can it get? As he terminated an F-connector on a length of coaxial cable, Joan turned to him, "Detective, remarkable dexterity with hands and fingers so large, I have problems with those connections, but my problem is fingernails."

Jaylee looked up from the work, "Dr. Rand, please call me Jay or Jaylee." She nodded, he continued, "I actually do lots of delicate stuff, helps to calm the mind and limber the fingers." He twiddled them at her. They looked at each other, Jaylee flushed, Rand reddened. He coughed and snapped the new cable into the video controller. The sort of a cough to put a period on the mind sentence they seemed to be constructing; he said, "I have a HAM radio rig, and made most of the power supplies, computer interface stuff and the antenna myself from schematics. I like working with soldering pencils and blank breadboards, so yes, I'm good with the smaller electronic stuff…too." They laughed.

"You can call me Rand, or Joan…I get tired of the Dr. thing." Jay nodded.

It was 22:00, the bus had been positioned on the top level of the college campus parking garage. Getting the bus up there was no small feat, as the bus had to stay on the ramps connecting floors of the concrete structure, backing up every other one, air bag suspension deflated, even then it cleared three of the sprinkler heads in the garage by less than an inch. The main camera had been taken down from the back bumper of the bus for movement, and was now back in place, extended up to its max height of 30'.

Eight cameras had been set up, one on each corner of the garage, and four spread out to the limit of their transmission distances. The new, state of the art flat screen monitors connected to each were set on a slim, tall parson's-like table against the wall in the bus conference room, Velcro sticky tabs holding them in place against the wall. The main camera's screen, also a new technology flat screen monitor, built into the bus front wall of the conference room and connected to the camera on the thirty-foot mast, was extended from the back bumper. A joystick was on the main table and could command the camera to move, pan, attitude, and zoom. The trooper assigned to operate the bus was moving the camera in a panoramic arc to set context to the recording. He moved it back to center front, looking at the four-glass door entrance to the campus main activity building, containing a pub, pool, several exercise rooms and a gym. All were closed and the campus cleared of anyone not police or lab technicians.

A similar set of video recording equipment manned by E-R-Mag people was set up in the desert on the same line, but to the north of the mountain side ENet antenna, in case the discontinuity happened there.

Doctor Rand and Doctor Kough had several instruments feeding into Apple laptop computers on a similar table, short enough to fit under the monitors. Jefferies was actually helping, his attitude someplace else for now. He had an experimental wireless connection with a "desk-top sharing" program running, and could see the status of the energy building in the antenna as he monitored a sister computer an aid was working back on the base. Jaylee had stopped by Jefferies' computer screen several times and each time left shaking his head as the numbers on the re-charge line continued to grow.

The Jefferson Airplane were on the radio, "White Rabbit", and Grace Slick was imploring everyone to remember to "keep your head." Ivey came in the bus and in a loud voice said, "It's happening now." Everyone looked at a countdown timer Doctor Rand had on the table, 22:14:30, the counter still showed 54 minutes to go.

She said, "Deputy, how do you know?" She looked up to Ivey as she reached to turn off the radio, which had suddenly gone into static.

He said, "I'm sweating, and I'm heavy, like in one of those dreams where you're made of chewing gum."

The main screen on the wall of the conference room was full of movement – birds, pigeons, and what? Bats! Thousands of them all flying in circles. More movement, fuzzy stuff on the ground, insects and small animals.

Rand got up, pointing at the screen, stumbled and said "Woah! I see what you mean, hit the alarm!"

The team collected, moving into the room like drunks, staggering under a new weight that seemed attached to everything, even the people. Heads turned to the monitors. Lights in the bus flickered and strained to re-light. A strange noise was coming from under the bus, the on-board diesel generator had taken a full load, but what had loaded it? The south camera was showing some strange lights, ghost like shapes moving in the night, about fifty meters off the edge of the garage. The busses assigned State Trooper camera person turned the main camera on the mast in that direction.

The light was moving around like a cat prowling but faster, and shapeless. It was getting brighter, rays seemed to be collecting, dropping and moving from all directions into the amoebic mass especially up from the pavement. The objects near, and in, the light were rippling, like they were being seen under slightly moving water. Several officers positioned along the edge of the garage swung powerful spotlights onto the area where the light was undulating. One would have expected that the lights would negate the ethereal light, or pass a focused beam through it, but it became stronger, seeming to absorb the added spotlights.

The bronze statue of the college "mascot," in front of the entrance doors, a proud Native American Chief sitting astride his horse came into view, illuminated by the now circular ball of eerie light which had stopped moving, now 'parked' in front of the statue. Parts of it suddenly appeared to be made of glass. Bart shouted, "That's what happened to the people in the intersection!" Several people pointed at once, one of the men, leaning on the wall at the edge of the garage was becoming translucent, the man turned toward the camera, one hand held up as thought he was looking at it. His head snapped up, looking directly into the main camera, a bright flash of light and...BOOM!

He was gone.

The corner of the garage was gone.

Part of the Native American Mascot was gone, his arm, spear and hand.

The shell-shocked people in and around the bus stood there, in silence. A rough circle nearly eighty meters across was simply gone, as was the edge of the garage. Slowly, an ornamental tree, sliced nearly and neatly in half, fell away from the hole with an anguished CRACK and splintering of old wood. That was the only movement on the screen.

The people inside cautiously moved out of the bus to the place where the garage had been sliced off. The officer's thermos and lunch cooler sat less than three inches from the edge, and had not even moved.

The cut was four floors down and into the ground at the first level, even with the depression made in the ground and out the eighty meters to the front doors of the Administration building. Fire suppression sprinkler lines, also cut now shot water from all four level ceilings of the garage into the clearing. Lawson was on the radio to a fire engine and crew he had at the bottom of the structure, telling them to cut off the water. Another cookie cutter. The rough circular hole some eighty meters across was cut into the pavement. A square hole was exposed by the removed dirt, nearly dead center of the hole, and several meters in front of the remains of the Native American statue. It appeared black, and was about 25' square, a slowly rising column of white smoke was coming from the hole. No one spoke, it was completely silent. Deathly silent. Suddenly the bus generator which had been idling came back online, this the only noise at the scene.

Rand looked across the void, now re- lit by floodlights powered from the bus, not consumed by the event. She turned and looked back at the bus, eight feet from the edge. "That was too friggin' close." Then looking back into the void again. "Whatever's happening here seems to be getting more powerful. This hole is at least eighty meters across. The intersection was what? Maybe twenty?"

When no one answered, she looked over her shoulder again, this time noticing the other police, one was holding another, the other man's head on her shoulder. Potet'e was sitting on the bus step, his face in his hands. "Two tours in Iraqi, and he gets it like this." He got up and stumbled into the bus.

Rand said, "Oh my God, I'm so sorry, I'm so very sorry," to know one in particular.

Humanity had hit science right between the eyes.

Back in the bus, Kough and Jefferies had recovered from the weirdness of the vaporization of a large chunk of matter just twenty-four feet from their seats on the bus. They had started going through the playback loops. The batteries in the bus had drained, as did the laptops and radios, but the generator on the bus was diesel, and had continued to run, even though nearly all the circuit breakers had tripped. The trooper assigned to the bus had reset the breakers and equipment was re-booting. Jefferies came to the door of the bus. "Guys, people, come here!"

Potet'e had come back from the onboard restroom and was wiping his face with a wetted brown paper towel.

They gathered to watch. Jefferies spoke, "First, an overview." He clicked some keys and the main screen lit up. The picture was clear and well lit. It showed the roving lights stop, and collect, like someone shaping bits of glowing translucent clay into a larger ball with two hands. An eerie thought crossed Bart's imagination of an invisible monster like the one in the movie "Forbidden Planet" from the 60's. Where's Robbie the robot when ya need him? In that movie it was the subconscious force from the id of man, *the primitive and instinctive component of personality.* The id is a part of the unconscious that contains all the urges and impulses, the lizard brain. Hell, that made as much sense as everything else. Maybe it's a "real life ape-shit" id.

Parts of the statue became clear inside the ball, then the lighting of the scene brightened as the police re-directing floodlights downward from the garage. The ball of energy then began to quickly expand outward toward the open space in front of the statue and toward the parking garage, now bright rays of energy coming up from the pavement and adding to the energy ball. The ball covered the officer at the edge of the garage, directly in line with the camera angle, then all went white. A few seconds later, the scene came back, and was as it appeared in real time, empty, dark and silent.

"Jefferies, wasn't there a camera inside the perimeter of the event? On the corner near where the officer was positioned?" Jaylee said.

"Well, yes, but it can't possibly have anything on that loop, I mean really." He clicked some keys. The camera showed the statue, and the lights moving toward its location, then everything on the screen seemed to stretch, deforming into lines racing into the camera, then a bright white screen. Jefferies said, "see I told…" His voice disappeared. The picture faded back into a red brown desert, in plain, bright daylight. Something moved in the distance. They looked, mouths dropping open in unison. It looked like a miss-shaped elephant, then several of them, plodding slowly toward the camera, from some 100 meters away. A man's scream pierced the silence, recorded with the picture and blasted from the speakers. The animals seemed to turn to glass, and faded, then the entire picture faded out and turned to snow.

Potet'e dropped his head, tears freely running down his face. He twisted the paper towel. Shoulders heaving. The sheriff placed a hand on his back.

His son was the cop on the edge of the garage.

CHAPTER 9

A Human Face on Nameless Tragedy

Sheriff Bush leaned over to Captain Potet'e, "Randy, do you want me to call Betty?"

Potet'e looked up with puffy reddened eyes, took a deep breath, "No…Sam, I'll do it. Thanks, but… I'll do it. Just give me a few minutes. Sam, I don't even know what to say…what can I tell her? What can I say happened to him? Where the hell is he?" He slowly rose and walked to a small office space a little further back in the bus.

As the door closed to the tiny office, the FEMA warden looked at the animals Jefferies had frozen and expanded on the main large screen. He turned to Doctor Rand, "Let me see if I have this right. The thing re-charged faster, and apparently with more stored energy, maybe three times as much, if the size of the event is any prediction. Not only that but the events are on a north south line, but where the next hit is still a mystery, right?"

Rand looked from the screen, "Yes, I guess that's correct, based on the size of the crater we have out there." She pointed out the front of the bus.

Ogelsbee continued, "So, even with three events, we still don't know when exactly, where precisely, and how big an event we will have next time, correct?"

Rand and the others from E-R-Mag Labs Base nodded.

Jefferies said, "What I do not know is why we can't evaluate the data and make any definitive statements. There are forty people on the base combing the data from all directions. Still nothing, the evaluation programs are reporting programming errors. This means the data is outside the realm of any data fed into the programs before." He looked at the screen, "People, I'm scared."

Jaylee said, "Anyone not scared after this last 'discontinuity' is either a liar or a lunatic."

Ogelsbee stood, looking at the wall screen, then turned to the assembled people in the bus conference room, and said, "Doctor Jefferies, I want you to coordinate with whom-ever at the Sandia base airport, what? Kirkland? And order every bomb, missile, or any other ordinance available on Kirkland dropped on the antenna array and I want it done within two hours. I want targeting data on the best places to render the antenna dis-connected random pieces of copper. I will take full responsibility, and get whatever permissions needed, understood?"

Jefferies stood, "Wait! Wait! That antenna took 13 years of research and 2 years of construction at a cost of millions of dollars! You can't just..." The mayor just taking his seat, nearly shouted, "Jefferies, sit the hell down and don't say another goddamned word!" Jefferies sat.

Ogelsbee turned to Doctor Kough, "Send a copy of the entire video file to this address." He slid a card with the e-mail address across the table.

Kough solemnly nodded agreement, got out his cell phone and began punching in a speed dial number, the phone was dead, he had anticipated this, and had a charger plugged into the bus wall outlet, connecting the phone, he repeated the number calling sequence.

Doctor Rand got out a yellow legal pad and began diagramming the antenna, and where best to cut the conductors to render the wave amplification characteristics of a Yagi style antenna unusable.

The sheriff kept staring at the monitor. "It seems to me that the material and energy is not changed, but sent someplace. What are those things? They don't look much like elephants, and they don't seem to have fur coats like wooly mammoths. So, what are they? Why did they disappear before the picture ended?"

Kough said, "The assumption is they are on earth, maybe they're on another planet."

Rand shook her head, "They might be here either in the future, or past, hell, for all we know that scene is here, right here, right now, but in another dimension. If it's the future or past, if we have created a rip in time... The fire chief has made a damned good point, if something is converting mass to energy, the result is an atomic explosion, a rather ineffective one because we're talking dirt and concrete instead of refined uranium, but still probably a magnitude of 1,000 times more powerful than TNT. That, folks would be, in the case in front of this bus, about equal to the Trinity test, or about as powerful as Nagasaki."

Mayor Jamus said, "If we have opened a rip in the fabric of either time or space, we have made history here…but I don't think films of the event should be released just yet anyway, and that won't make the media very happy. Still, what does a rip in time mean?"

Kough said, "If we have done so we may well have begun the end of history. These events are getting bigger, and are being powered by God knows what. I'm not sure we can stop it." Punching numbers into a Texas Instruments-84 scientific calculator, he continued. "At this progression by the time the event gets to mid-America, or south a similar distance it will be three hundred eighty miles across, and that's just thirty-four days or repeats of the discharges." A few more punches, "In ninety-one days it will be consuming Canada or southern Mexico at a rate of 13,000 square miles a day, that is if it does not radically increase its charge-discharge cycle time. I'm worried that when the circles overlap, all bets will be off. All new parameters."

Bart said, "Thanks doc, you're a friggin' ray of sunshine."

Captain Potet'e returned to the room, pale and shaken. "I need to go home, Betty's a mess. But I have a request."

The FEMA man looked up from punching another message into a Blackberry, "Just name it Randy."

"I ...I need to know where my son went. I know we need to stop this thing, but we, the people who have lost folks, need to know where they went...what happened to them...and," his voice breaking, "did they suffer."

Doctor Rand went to his side, reached and gently took his arm, looked directly into his eyes and said, "I...we...will do everything in our power to find out what you and the others need to know, everything. You have my word on it." Then to the rest of the 'team', "I'm still thinking we don't actually have enough data points for any kind of an accurate plot of when and where the next event will happen, adding to what Ogelsbee said, three data points do not make predictable calculations possible."

The IT Trooper running the bus said, "I've got a squad coming up the ramps, he'll see to you getting home...Captain, I'm so sorry...I...," he shook his head, looked at the floor, and slowly turned away.

He nodded, thanked Rand, and with the female Corporal Bus Command Trooper, turned and slowly left the bus. It was a sincere but probably empty promise. The odds of a definitive answer were slim. Specifics unlikely. Results? Who could know, but

Rand's promise was heartfelt, and accepted for what it was.

Jefferies stood and cleared his throat. Everyone stopped their various activities and looked at him. "I think it's time we moved our operations back to the base. We don't have what we need out here to make any more progress. I know you don't trust us, and I don't know if I can get that trust…ever. But Doctor Kough is right. We might have started the beginning of the end, and I'm scared, and I can't do anything out here."

He began collecting his papers, and placing them into his laptop computer case, began shaking, then stuffed the papers in, slammed the case down. "All I did was design an antenna. I never thought…" He crumpled into a chair, placed his head in his hands, face turned to the Formica top, elbows resting on the edge of the table, his head slowly moving back and forth. He was a truly pitiful site.

Jaylee moved and sat in the next chair, his tone was soft, but direct. "Doctor, you need to do your best work, and you need to do it right now. There is a reason you were placed in charge of this project for all those years. You have institutional knowledge that few anywhere have. Now get out of the box you've been working in. Think in new directions and new possibilities. We humans, and maybe the Earth do not have time for a talent search, or a resume' committee to find if you or your team is the best. You are simply the best we have, right here…and right now." Jaylee poked a finger onto the table top several times with fingernail making a tap-tap-tap for emphasis.

Rand was looking at him, thinking, 'This guy is something else, a leader, and smart…handsome too…damned Joan, get a grip! Grinning, as her star tingled,' she must have felt her face redden as she looked away and started disconnecting cables – but the thoughts of the muscular, smart, and at times funny 'new guy' in her sphere kept creeping in.

Jefferies nodded, and stood again, his cell rang, answering it, he grunted an okay, then looking at the to the room as he punched off. "The soonest we can expect an air strike on the mountain is two o'clock this morning. The base commander is checking on the order, and there were no armors on duty on the base, no pilots or planes on hot reserve. I'll be sure everyone in kept in the loop." He turned and left the bus, followed by Doctor Rand and Doctor Kough. Their equipment was left on the bus, Rand said that if the world existed in a few days, they would come back and pick it up. If that statement was designed as a joke, no one laughed.

Time to blow up a mountain.

CHAPTER 10

Armageddon replay – a rewind in time

Ivey and three other deputies were tasked with assuring all the eight scattered ranchers were clear of people, and had finished racing among them, clearing people off the side of the mountain. Two families could not be found, and were presumed to be away from their ranches, yellow tape was across the few roads, and roadblocks were set up and manned by New Mexico State Troopers. Three camping sites were cleared of their people, and a squatter in an old truck-camper was rousted and removed from the scrub brush. Now, some three hours later the deputies had gathered high on the bluff near where Ivey had been when the first event had taken place, up to the wider area turn-around spot. He remembered the sweat, heavy feeling moments, and the feeling of…what, dread? Thinking back, it was just a feeling that something was not right with the world. How right that was, he chuckled to himself, oh, how right that was. He glanced at the others, two orange dots drifting around like anemic fireflies where the smokers stood, and a faint shadow next to him, Danny Deitle, two years ago the guy most skeptical of the joint Native American - Civilian Police project, now his best friend. All four now leaning against their trucks looking into the starlit night.

Waiting for Armageddon.

The Deputies were sharing the vantage point with two Army forward spotters with laser targeting guns, maps spread open with Rand's Xs placed where the antenna could be neutralized, the red glow from their night vision flashlights barely visible to the deputies just a few yards away.

At 01:48 a C130 flew over the mountain and began sewing a row of flares. The plane made a ten-degree right turn and appeared to be heading due North. The spotters flipped up their night vision equipment. The airplane was halfway across the antenna array when there appeared, to the men watching, a giant point of light that came upward from the ground, not at the speed of light, but rising easily at a speed that one could follow, glowing, expanding, swirling, soda being pulled up an equally expanding tapered glass straw. Another was coming down from, what? A swirling cloud where there were no clouds? A whirlpool of blackness, the visible stars turned to streaks near the apparent center of it.

The points of energy met at the airplane.

There was a terrific flash of light, and a ring of light spread out from the point of 'impact' as a shock wave would. A BOOM rumbled across the valley. No more flares continued the line. The light from the flares already hanging below their parachutes showed a white cloud of smoke, then suddenly, nothing where the plane had been. Ivey was on his radio, "You guys in the valley see that!"

Several radios' keyed at once, stepping on one another so no communication could take place. Sheriff Bush kept his keyed, "Radio silence unless there's something to report! Ivey, you guys up on the mountain okay."

Ivey said, "Yes, no damage here. I didn't see any wreckage falling from the place where the plane was hit!"

A female voice came upon the tactical channel, "Rand here, the base air traffic control has the point where the plane disappeared from radar at the exact center of the antenna. There must be some energy there we can't detect, over."

A flare drifted slowly under where the cloud and aircraft had been. Suddenly, as before, a light beam seemed to rise from the ground, and another drop from the heavens. The flare vanished with another blast ring, and another Boom.

A voice, which was obviously Jefferies came up, "I'm with strike command here, I've coordinated with the combat controllers, the fighters will not cross directly over the center of the antenna. They said the bomb attack will be from skip releases, and rockets, they will be JDAM guided munitions. The strike will commence in four minutes, over."

The men on the bluff moved behind their trucks. Ivey waved the others to come near him so he could be heard over the wind that had suddenly begun to blow down the side of the mountain. "Skip releases will throw the bombs up as the planes pull into a near vertical climb. They aren't as accurate, so they hardly ever practice them. If one is off by enough so the bomb's guidance can't adjust, it could land on us."

One of the others said, "Shit, Ivey let's get the hell out of here!"

Ivey replied, "To late, here they come."

The twin turbine screams of McDonnell Douglas F-15B Strike Eagles came up the valley from the South.

The first fighters let loose a volley of rockets. Ivey noticed a dozen or more Apache gunship helicopters taking up positions just outside of the lines the fighters were taking, right on the edge of the flare light. The rockets thudded into the ground, exploded in a yellow-orange flash and a dull grey cloud of smoke and dirt. The explosions leaped upward, seemed to freeze in the air, then, like they were being sucked into a giant vacuum hose, were pulled back into the ground. Several dozen rockets repeated the scene, a few that went over the middle of the array were incinerated by the pincers of light. It clearly seemed that more and more of the rockets simply were curving, flying in an arc, going into the same spot on the mountainside, their detonations now just orange flashes which disappeared instantly.

The Apaches didn't wait for position and cut loose with several hundred four-inch rockets from their pods. Again, the explosions happened, but were rewound like pushing a button on a VCR, and again several rockets crossed the plane where the light shot from the ground and from the sky. Three rockets, milliseconds apart, crossed the barrier and were hit in separate, distinct, and exactly the same manner. The booms were so close together they sounded like a short burst from a heavy machine gun. Now nearly all rockets were impacting the same place, and the explosions receding or "rewinding" into the spot where they went off, no dust or debris flying out from the six plus pounds of composition B in their warheads.

One of the blast rings radiating out from a rockets' destruction went through a F-15 as it was pulling vertical for a skip release, two 1000-pound bombs had just been let go from the underside of the fighter, and the pilot had gone full throttle with afterburners, turning away from the still ascending bombs. The ring cut both vertical stabilizers cleanly off the fighter without even a flash or spark. The Tomcat continued upward, the pilot maintaining control with the wing control surfaces.

He closed the throttle, and as the plane stalled, the weapons officer and he ejected.

Ivey and the others hunkered down near their vehicles on the mountain, and had lost sight of the bombs for a time. Then, almost simultaneously, two enormous blasts lit the early morning pre-dawn sky. The explosions, unlike the rocket's plumes, continued to grow, eight more bombs quickly hit on top of the first two, the targeting of Rand's points on the antenna were useless, every bomb went to exactly the same spot. The remaining fighters, unseen in the excitement, had released their weapons as well, now just twin blue tails of afterburner light, thundering away from the mountain. Nearly at the same time, and almost on top of the bombs hitting, the stricken F-15 landed, nose first at terminal velocity. Fangs of energy, like slow motion fluid tubes of lightening exploded from the hillside. Hundreds, then thousands of them, arcing out in all directions, but like the explosives, soon froze in space. Time standing still.

Slowly, very slowly the smoke, dust, rocks ejected from the crater where the bombs had hit, everything, spun to a stop, hanging in mid-air and illuminated by the Tom Cat's fuel fireball. A snapshot frozen in time and space. The sound faded away, echoes dying. No sound, no wind, no movement. Barely heard was the scream of the leaving jets and rapid thump-thump of the Apaches who were also leaving, then this sound too stopped.

The men on the hill stood cautiously. Ivey was almost afraid to look at his companions, fearing they would be frozen as well. A fear, a childhood dream of the entire world frozen in time…except him? Had time stopped? Was he frozen forever here, stuck in a postcard picture of the end of time? Indescribable all-be-it a subconscious relief washed over him as he saw they were moving. Two of the deputies were filming the events with hand held digital cameras. One removed it from the filming position and looked at the screen, then looked at the other filmier, the batteries were dead.

Barely noticeable, the ground under the incredible scene began to move inward, looking like it had become liquid and was going toward a drain. Ivey pointed and shouted "Look, Jees guys look!" the deputies and Army foreword spotters all peered into the valley below, the light from the flares whispering through the dust and smoke casting incredible shadows, like monsters moving behind a translucent screen. The smoky air and items near the earth began to be pulled in first, then the sphere of the "pull" expanded outward. Soon all the hanging chaos suspended in the air was moving inward. The material near the center was rushing at a fantastic rate, rocks, scrub trees and smoke, a blur as it spiraled into the mountain side. A giant whirlpool of solid material moving into…what? Ivey thought and then said, "a backwards volcano!" There was still no sound from the mountain, complete, cold, dead silence. Jaylee turned to Bart, at their vantage point further down the mountain toward the valley floor and said, "A force so powerful even sound waves can't escape?" Bart looked at his partner, and shook his head, Bart was un-characteristically silent.

Ivey yelled to the other men, "Where's it going? If it continues…we better run over the mountain or we'll be sucked it there too!"

When the air was cleared of all the smoke, debris and fire, the vacuum cleaner like phenomenon seemed to slow. It did not completely stop, but slowed to what looked like the sides of a hole in the beach sand collapsing on the kid frantically shoveling it out, the kid who would work for three hours shoveling sand against the tide, but who could not find the energy to put his socks in the dirty clothes hamper. Clearly, the energy of the explosions and their shock waves had become part of the energy, being collected in the mountain.

Rand thought as she looked at the screens and TV monitors, 'What kind of force, energy or physical entity can convert explosives, electrical, even light and sound, into usable energy. Is this phenomenon actually rewinding time in the space around it? A rewinding we are able to see from outside the event horizon?'

She stopped, a cold chill going down her spine, goose bumps on her arms, why had she used the words 'event horizon'? What part of her mind had connected the mountain hole and antenna with a Black Hole and its outer influence point – the event horizon?

What indeed.

The soldiers spotting with the laser targeting devices were yelling into their radios, something about the loss of targeting data and the munitions hitting as though they had been guided into exactly the same place. Then Ivey noticed they gave up. The spotters radio batteries seemed to be dying. The heaviness suddenly came to Ivey's mind as the extra energy of the adrenalin rush faded. "Hey, you guys feel like you're wearing lead underwear?"

Deputy Deitle said, "Dude, what the hell are... Jesus, I see what you mean, I can't get up, help me!"

Ivey, already standing, lumbered over and helped Dietle to stand, then the others. Deitle continued, "Man, I'm so friggin' tired, I could just crash here and sleep a week."

Ivey nearly shouted, "No – God no we have to get out of here, what if whatever is sucking the energy out of the explosions and even our radio batteries is sucking energy out of us! We got to get away from here!" He reached into the Tahoe whose battery was completely dead, and from a Faraday bag retrieved a fresh battery. Rand had suggested the radio wave proof bag it may work to keep the antenna from sucking the battery empty. He clipped it onto his radio and it came up. He then reported that he and the others were walking over the top of the mountain. Sheriff Bush said a NM Trooper would pick them up and to start moving.

It suddenly occurred to Ivey that there was light enough to see the valley, dawn still hours away. In the last several minutes, the flares had been pulled into the earth with the debris. The sky was faintly luminescent in a kilometer circle around the antenna location. A curved sided, cone shaped darkness was pointed directly at the middle of the hole, not a shadow, the scenery on the other side was visible, but distorted like looking through an old-time coke bottle. The hole was still slowly increasing in size, now ten meters across. The hole's growth had continued, but clearly continued to slow.

From the North, a helicopter came down the Sandia mountain range toward the scene. Oblivious to everything that had happened, the Channel 3 News crew, in the air for aerial shots of a Rock Concert in Albuquerque, had seen the flashes of light and was investigating the thunderous explosions seen on the side of Sandia Mountain. The Blue and White Bell-Jet Ranger slowed, started a circle. The tail of the craft snapped toward the hole, the pilot dipped the front of the plane toward what he thought was a sudden gust of wind. Ivey heard on his radio's tactical channel, "News Chopper, Kirkland Traffic, emergency, emergency, clear the area, this is a military exercise and you are in a danger zone, over."

The pilot responded, unheard by the men on the mountain, as his craft hung in the air, "Chopper three, three niner tango, acknowledged, we're fighting a strong headwind. Will leave area ASAP, over."

"Kirkland traffic, emergency, get as low as possible, if you cannot get ground speed, expedite landing with emergency procedures, do you copy, over?"

"3-3-9er Tango, we copy, but…shit…we're not able to get ground speed, air speed 180 knots, I'm taking her down."

The men watched through their binoculars as the craft, full throttle and leaning heavily away from the center of the incident, the unseen hole, nosed hard downward still canted hard into what seemed to the pilot was an invisible wind. The craft dropped toward the bare earth. The pilot tried to flare at the last moment, but the craft continued down, hitting hard, the main rotor bent and sliced the ground, one blade flew off, then the other which cart-wheeled up, over, bending like wet spaghetti, and then into the hole. The doors of the craft sprung opened as the men jumped out.

They ran, leaning into what looked like a wall of wind. They fought their way out from the Bell-Jet, and within just a few yards were able to stand, then a few more yards away, run, but were running like the participants in an "Iron-man" race carrying refrigerators on their backs. At fifty yards the three men, one with a camera now back on his shoulder, stopped, turned and watched the helicopter being pulled backward, toward the hole, up-hill from where it had unceremoniously been set down. The skids dug parallel trenches in the earth. As it got closer to the hole in the mountain side, the craft appeared to grow longer, stretched, transformed into silly putty.

The clear perception was that the tail rotor and rear fuselage was traveling toward the hole faster than the front of the craft. That was clear. But it was not being torn apart. The men witnessing this all found the scene so out of context, so strange, so out of phase with everything in their personal knowledge base, so out of sync with every physical thing they had ever seen, that they stood frozen. The men on the mountain top stared, a cigarette dropped from a loosened jaw, the only movement there. The two deputies videoing the scene kept the cameras up and pointed, even though the batteries in the cameras had died minutes earlier.

As it grew closer still, the phenomenon continued, until the Bell-Jet Ranger was a blur racing toward the blackness of the hole. Suddenly, it was gone.

The news crew turned again and ran, they had witnessed something they had no context in which to store the data presented them. Primal flight response was the action their three minds simultaneously selected. As had happened millions of times since a Neanderthal man ran from a predator jaguar dropping from a tree branch in history unknown, it saved their lives.

The soldiers found their truck batteries were also nearly dead, as their radios struggled, but also soon died. The soldiers elected to stay until help arrived, not wanting to leave their equipment and vehicles, even with the warning about energy vacuums from the mountain at work, the postulation they had overheard from Ivey.

The deputies finished collecting a few bottles of water, got their weapons from Ivey's SUV and began the long walk up the dirt road toward the mountain top, a lazy circular path that never got closer to the strange phenomenon still glowing and visible on the side of the craggily Sandia mountain. They walked in silence, a hundred yards down the road the weight lifted, a wave of dizziness hit the men as their bodies adjusted to the sudden change in blood pressure from the weight change, Ivey saw spots in front of his eyes, "Like driving off this mountain to the Silver tree, he thought." Still, they were silent, processing the scenes they had witnessed, but not able to fit cogent words or thoughts around the events. Of the three deputies, only Ivey had seen large munitions explode, and none of them had seen anything like the rest of the scene. Finally, Deitle said, "I normally would brag to everyone I know about some shit like this, but don't think I'll be tell'in this story, don't friggin' think anyone would believe it."

Maybe not now, but they will.

PART 3

And the answer is ... your best guess

CHAPTER 11

New Visions

Three hours later, still just before sun-up. Doctor Rand sat with others on the team in an actual conference room in the E-R-Mag building, light blue carpeted walls up to chair-rail height, low dropped ceiling and indirect but plentiful light. The room smelled like glade air freshener, some kind of new mown grass…or something, and mixed with furniture polish and carpet shampoo. One end of the room was an opaque screen wall where a recording of the air attack was playing. Centered in the room was a large dark, polished wood table with hinged ports for connecting plugs and phone chargers, undefined other connectors, and sixteen chairs, with another twenty in separate rows paralleling the table chairs, along the outside opposing walls. At a table by the back door sat a doughnut box that looked like Fort Sumpter after day one of the civil war. One-half a plain cake doughnut holding down the inevitable box-to-trash-can trip. Rand said, "I've been wracking my brain to figure why we are not getting one single piece of useful information out of the mountain of data we have collected. Our analytical programs are crashing, the data keeps coming up as corrupted. Where are we losing it here?"

Jefferies was standing near the screen, a laser pointer in hand, he motioned to a media technician seated at a small workspace within reach of the main table on the right backside of the room. "I can't get my mind around the way the energy from the explosives was captured, and seemed to be re-cycled into the center of the antenna."

Jaylee and Bart sat in the row of chairs along the side, across from Rand. Jaylee had been listening to fifteen minutes of conversation, each speaker telling the others that they didn't know what they had there on the screen, or more importantly on the other side of Sandia Mountain. He rose, did one of his 'panther waking up stretches' which never could be ignored by anyone not familiar with the 6'6" fireplug coming to life. "Let me presume to give some direction to y'all, based on my ten years with Bart here, of thinking about problems in which I have been presented with all the data, crime scene evidence in my profession, but stuck where I couldn't get my mind around the crime, to coin a phrase."

"I purpose your data collection and processing programs are failing because they have to narrow a definition of what they are looking for. Open them up from electrical or electromagnetic energy to just energy."

"I submit we are seeing something no one has seen before, at least in recorded history and by humans, especially ones with a PhD. Look, what did Ezekiel see in the desert 4,000 years ago? A spaceship, a helicopter? What did he write down? A wheel in the sky. He did the best he could in the context of his experience. Now 4,000 years later, we don't know what the hell he saw. If he had put down just what he saw, a silver object with rotating slats over it that made a whop-whop-whop sound, we'd have it."

"Do any of you here actually believe we have documented all the types of energy in the universe? Christ people, isn't 9/10 of the mass in the known universe just called 'dark matter' because we ain't seen it, can't feel it and don't know how to put it in a box to weigh it?"

"What do we need here? Gene Roddenberry to come up with anti-matter? Look, I'm not bustin' your nuts here." Shooting a quick look to Rand, and another woman, "Just an expression of inflicting incredible, all-be-it motivational pain Doctor."

"Let me propose that what we have out there is not something beyond our understanding. It is, however, something new. Climb outside the box your college and training has constructed around you, and find out what is out there," swinging an arm metaphorically at the mountain.

An older man, tan work clothes, grey hair over deep set eyes presided over by a bulbous pockmarked nose and face rose to speak. He had the requisite pocket protector, sleeves rolled up on thin arms, standing at his chair. Pointing a boney finger at Jaylee, spoke up, his voice nasal and whining, "Easy for you to say Detective, our math needs values for the computer to grind on. If we can't define it, we can't work with it. I'm used to facts, not changing the analysis to fit the problem, and I've been doing this for a long time." A dinosaur just waiting for the comet. He looked around the table for support.

He got none.

Jefferies had had it. The frayed end of his emotional rope arrived, snapped through the top pulley and let the weight on the other end of his rope and his 'Acme anger anvil' drop, landing directly on the doubting While-E-Coyote who had challenged Jaylee. Jefferies wheeled on the man, "Doctor Hassert, you are relieved of this project. Please get you stuff and get out of the way! NOW!"

Hassert looked at Jefferies, mouth open but unable to speak.

A period of silence followed in which one could have heard a grasshopper fart at twenty paces. Jefferies continued, glaring, "The detective is correct, he does a lot of that. Being correct. Anyone who will not embrace the far-out propositions required to stop this thing, get the fuck out!" He banged the table hard with his fist. The scientists jumped, some looked worried. Violence? The F-bomb? Not in their program.

Indignantly, Hassert stacked his papers and retreated from the room. Jefferies said in a loud voice after him "And everything connected to this phenomenon is Top Secret Crypto, and if you or anyone here leaks a god-damned syllable about it, they WILL go to Leavenworth for a real long time!" He sat down, shaking his head, then picked up a sheet of paper and began reading. The paper visibly shaking in his fingers. He was not doing well here, and he knew it.

After another silence, Doctor Kough cracked the cement silence, "Well, we may have slowed or at least changed the dimension of what we have on the antenna. The rate of re-charge has slowed, unless more changes are forthcoming, we have thirty-one hours until the event discharges again, still, most likely in downtown Albuquerque, probably around midnight tomorrow". Everyone looked like they had seen a ghost, pale washed out faces from which the blood had drained, jaws dropped. Albuquerque. Hundreds dead or…what?

By noon on Saturday the 'Discontinuity Project' had 100% of the E-R-Mag Labs and the nearby Sandia base resources focused on evaluation of the available data. Except the dinosaur, who was taking paid leave. Words like 'singularity' and 'worm-hole' floated amongst the encrypted instant messaging network. Jefferies had continued the 180-degree flip started in the police command bus, and was feeding data to anyone and any place that his people suggested. A paleoanthropologist, or doctor of ancient animals from Phoenix was online with the project and was examining a computer enhanced version of the animals in the garage recording.

Several hours later, the 10 AM update conference was just getting underway. The news director from

Channel 3 was ushered into the conference room/project center. She was quickly introduced by the Air Police Sergeant door guard, after Jefferies had briefed the Base commander of the "problems" the military was now taking charge of security, given the weight and possible national damage implications. The AP guard had been told to expect her.

To the scientists and others, she appeared like a transplanted Hippy Chick from Max Yasgur's pasture in Woodstock, NY. She wore a sailcloth billowy cream-colored dress, sandals, over-sized bust swinging as she moved, without constraint of a bra, round metal framed glasses with slightly tinted lenses which did not diminish light green eyes, and a drop dead gorgeous oval face framed with fluffy, curly blond hair. As she entered, the backlighting from the door behind her produced a perfect X-ray of a well-proportioned woman projected through the light clothing. She walked with a self-assurance and grace that grabbed all in the room. Approaching the end of the table, she leaned over, defying cloth and gravity to keep a breast from escaping, and said, extending a hand, "Doctor Jefferies, great to see you again!" Her other hand opened her canvas bag/purse and set a thumb drive and a compact disc case on the table.

Jefferies took the hand, and said, trying to keep his eyes from gluing themselves to the 44D's an arm's length away, "Ms. Peg Hanny, good to see you again too. Haven't had the pleasure since the open house last fall. You have some video for us?"

Jefferies snapped a finger and sent the CD case, and a second finger pop for the thumb-drive across the polished table to Rand's extended hand. She turned and handed them to the media technician, who plugged the drive into the computer tower, then the CD into the side of his multi deck DVD player, the tray closed as Jefferies continued the obligatory introductions around the table. The screen on the end of the room changed, the first clip was obviously the cameraman shooting the ending seconds of the Bell-Jet Ranger. From the angle off the port- front of the craft, the stretching was even more pronounced.

Peg said, "Well, that has me screwed up, I have more questions that I can even begin to get through, and the NTSB is yelling bullshit over the loss of the aircraft and wants to know where the wreckage is so they can investigate, as does the insurance company but folks that ain't why I'm here." She signaled the media tech to start the next clip. "This was from the camera mounted on the front of the 'copter, just over the searchlight. It was transmitting on another channel to a receiver on the mobile camcorder data-pack the cameraman was holding and recorded this on its drives before the batteries in everything died."

A shaky picture from the helicopter camera showed the three men receding and the marks dug into the dirt from the skids clearly visible. The scene seemed to move away faster. Items were stretched, like the rear end of the craft. The frame could have been taken from the rear platform of a passenger train going into a perfectly round tunnel. As the dot receded, the lighting got brighter, and with a spin and crash, the scene was daylight and in an obvious desert. A pure red sky with deeper red, what? Were they clouds, or dust from the crash hanging over red-grey sand, rocks and what may have been scrubby plants, she froze the frame, the shapes were not plants, maybe more like lichen? A number of people huddled some 50 yards away, apparently hearing the noise of the helicopter arriving, turned sharply to look at the camera, some stood. As one pointed, the picture faded and turned to snow.

Everyone in the room was absolutely still.

Peg said, "You folks are having the same reaction we did. What the hell do we have here?"

A very tall young man in a lab coat characterized by a pocket protector stuffed with eight identical .07 Pilot Black Ink roller ball pens, entered the room, walked over to Jefferies and whispered into his ear. Jefferies turned to Peg, "Your timing is incredible, Andrew here has some information that we have been looking for…Andrew?"

Andrew, the very, very tall, very tanned, very thin very young man in a geek outfit, stood, one half covered by the lab coat, which was even slimmer, as though it was given to him when he was twelve and was not replaced as he grew. In one step he popped another disc across the table to Rand who again turned to the tech, a gave Andrew's disc to him. He still looked to be a teenager, taller than Jaylee by three or four inches, straight nose that ended in a round button, brown eyes so dark the centers looked black, a dusting of zits drizzled across his forehead ended at a short black hair cut which had been made with a square and ruler, one expected to see a magic-marker line drawn so the barber wouldn't go outside the lines. He was not as skilled as Jefferies at avoiding tits, his eyes drawn like filings to the 44D magnets.

Peg nearly laughed, completely amused. She said completely deadpan, "Please, continue Andrew."

The young man, noticing that every one of the thirteen people in the room were looking at him looking at Peg's tits, turned a bright shade of red faster than a Lobster dropped into a boiling water pot. He coughed, cleared his throat and, with a voice that required three words to stabilize from squeaky to intelligible said," I... We've been working on the video from the camera on the garage that was zapped by the...the...uh, whatever it was that zapped it. See, everyone was looking at the scene sent back like the camera was pointing North, like it was pre-zap. I thought, what if it had turned or spun when it went away? Well, I started overlaying the landscape skylines from other directions, my assumption was the camera didn't go anywhere physically. No good, it went someplace."

The technician had the film on the screen. He gestured to the scene of the animals, desert and sky, but yes there were mountains barely visible in the far distance, Jefferies thought 'I never noticed a skyline'. In the next frame, a line had been traced on the mountains. "I used the terrain matching software developed for cruise missile flight-to-target navigation. I ran my mountains there," he dotted the craggily line on the frame with the laser pointer, "with the entire database. Here's the closest match, and it's a 94%-er for the entire mapped earth."

The next frame was a map of the Southwestern 1/3 of the United States, with an 'X' between Miami and Globe Arizona, two small towns several miles apart. Another click and the blow-up was a mountain and hills leading up to it labeled 'Pinal Peak', an overlaid arrow was pointing south.

Another click and the two lines were overlaid; the match was nearly identical.

"The problem is that the crags' in the video are clearly rougher, and Pinal Peak has had trees on it for at least 8,000 years. Using the 8,000-year date as a data point, the Phoenix Museum of Natural History anthropologist identified the animals as indeed mammoths, but the southern version, less hair, very rare indeed. So, we have a time machine."

CHAPTER 12

What Time is it Anyway?

Andrew had said it with the same intensity as one who had deduced the thief who had eaten his slice of left-over chocolate birthday cake stolen from the break room refrigerator, or solved a Clue game – Colonel Mustard in the library with the candlestick.

Peg stood, then sat back down. She said, "Andrew, why in the world is Globe Arizona in the Cruise Missile flight to target data base? Is Globe an Al Qaeda training camp or something?"

Andrew looked from the screen, directly at her tits, then up to her eyes, "No, I don't think so, Miami is a copper mine or something, and Globe is nothing, see the targeting program takes the top and side mapping photos of the earth loaded by NOAH satellites, and converts them to the outline we used in the comparison, same thing Google earth does if you ask it to give a 'street' view' where the camera hasn't actually been on that street. The cruise missiles can't rely on GPS because in a war those satellites would be the first to go, so they navigate by skylines."

Jefferies held up his hands, "If we have a time machine" …he stopped there, "Andrew, see if there are any landscape markers in the video from the helicopter." Then to the second woman scientist, a mousey young woman halfway down the table. "Maurine, I want one of the test robots, the one fitted for the testing we are ready to do for disarming IED's. I want it fitted with a cable lanyard, and sent out to the antenna, let's feed an EMP battle hardened and powerful camera into the hole and see if it can transmit any better information. Let's include full spectrum recording, not just video. I want as much useable data as we can possibly collect."

He turned to Peg, "Look, Peg, I know you have a hell of a story here, and I'm not asking you to sit on it, well not all of it anyway. We figure the next event, like the one Andrew is telling us about, will happen in the center of Albuquerque, if it goes south on the line if these events I briefed you on over the phone are the beginning of a pattern. A story of a time machine eating chunks of New Mexico could cause panic and loss of life."

"There's an understatement for you." Bart whispered to Jaylee.

Peg looked surprised and alarmed, "Albuquerque! Jesus, Chris, we have to do something! Albuquerque… damned. Any better location, I mean where in Albuquerque? That's a big place!"

"FEMA is working on clearing out the portion of the city that we think might…shit Peg, it's an uneducated guess. We don't have time to evacuate the entire city. That's the best we can do. The scenario is a chemical spill from a freight car. Folks can get their arms around that and can move without panic. The story is set to go out in…" looking at his watch, "45 minutes.

"Peg, we could really use your help here. That's why you were allowed in, and why you have all the information we do." Jefferies looked at the woman, pleading in his eyes.

She said, "Give me the scenario information. We'll have it out in an hour…but Chris, keep me in the loop. When this is over, I'm gonna get a Pulitzer, and a breast reduction."

Jefferies nodded, and whispered out of earshot, "If it's ever over."

Bart whispered to Jaylee, "If she reduces those boobs, I'll arrest her for destroying a national treasure!"

Jaylee laughed, "I'll sell what they take off on e-bay and retire. Coffee?"

Watching a paper cup drop onto a stainless-steel platform, then coffee sloshing into it, Jaylee wondered aloud to Bart what the beginning of a black-hole would look like. Bart said, "You mean one of those things that sucks in everything around it? A colossal inner-planetary vacuum? Don't they call it a black hole because even light can't get away from it?" He handed Jaylee the cup and dropped coins into a slot. Pushing a button, he got no response, wracking the coin return, still nothing. "They ought to call these things black holes" He banged the machine, coffee came down, sugar, cream powder, and lastly a cup bounced onto the steaming platform. He went to the change machine.

"That's what I mean." Jaylee continued, "I'm disturbed by not being able to see through the thing on the videotape near the center of the hole in the mountain. Stuff traveling through a field that strong, where even light is bent as it passes through the vortex."

Bart took the $2.00 cup of freeze-dried dish water from the machine. Second time a charm. "Okay, let me tell you what I think, as a guy who doesn't know shit about antennas or 'dark energy' or much of anything. I figure it's no accident that the thing is moving north/south. I remember from science in grade school that the earth is a big assed magnet. Some kind of lines come out of the South pole and go into the North pole. The teacher said it was because the center of the earth is made of iron and that's what magnets are made of. So, what if the antenna, when they kick started it, began to collect energy from the earth. Now it's powerful enough to be sucking energy from everywhere, even a 1,000-pound bomb. God knows what the energy is from the sky coming down and meeting the other coming up is about."

Doctor Rand had moved up silently behind them, coins for the random coffee generator in hand. "Detectives…" then to Bart, "That's as good a theory as any I've heard. I'm going to get a team on the proposition you have outlined." She dropped the coins in, the machine purred, and got off a cup of coffee, one sugar, two creams. A woman's touch?

Bart said, "I was also thinking, was there any source of energy crossing the North/South line from the antenna near where the events took place? A power line or something? I still can't figure why the tree, why an intersection in downtown, and why not where we had figured on the campus."

She had produced a note pad from her lab coat, and was writing, "That's also good, I'll add that to my team's direction."

Bart looked slightly angry, forehead crinkled, "Doc, you ain't jerking me off here are you?"

She looked up, with a no bullshit, serious look "No detective I'm not. Your thoughts are different, plain simple logic unpolluted by the information we, here, have about the antenna…our tests, the bias we've accumulated after working on this project for years, and what the models theorized would happen.

I will get a team on these ideas. I will either validate the propositions or discard them, but there will be a reason for doing so, and you will know that reason." She wheeled and started away. Then, over her shoulder, "Make no mistake, when I jerk someone off, they do not need to be a detective to know it." She winked and turned back to the hallway.

Jaylee said, "Damned, I like that Doctor."

Bart, slightly red, but grinning said, "Hey, what's not to like."

CHAPTER 13

I'm from the Government and I'm here...

Government, on any level and in any capacity operates much like an aircraft carrier moving at two knots. It takes time to increase speed and to turn. Things were beginning to happen in Washington concerning the mysterious events in the Southwestern desert.

Bart and Jaylee had returned to their station and had given Captain Walker an update. He had made the usual noises about not being sure they were supposed to be involved in a 'scientific fuck up that even the papers can't describe'. The simple playback of Kough's statement from Bart's recorder, that essentially, the beginning of the end of time may have started, concluded, and short-circuited all further discussion. "You guys go, if it's really hit the fan, justifying your time is like re-arranging the deck chairs on the Titanic. Please do me a favor – let me know if it's time to kiss my ass goodbye! I'm gonna get hammered tonight just in case…I would be thoroughly pissed if the world ended and I had a dime left in the bank." The two detectives went home, ate, showered, shaved. Jaylee picked up Bart and they arrived back at E-R-Mag Labs base. The project update meeting called for Saturday at 22:00 saw exhausted, in some cases sweaty team members shuffle in and take seats.

Jefferies stood at the end of the table, "Several NSA special satellites are moving into position to scan the area around and location of the anomaly, Doctor Rand, anything to report as yet?"

Rand spoke, but did not stand, she held a sheet of paper and placed it back on the table, "The data from the Spectra-scan sensors on the Mag-pop III satellite have been forwarded from Houston. Frankly there's not much useable information yet deciphered, but I can say that there is a tremendous amount of pure magnetic flux diverging from the normal patterns of the poles. It's like another 'middle pole' has been created, this one very, very concentrated. For the purpose of the programmers and number crunchers I have called the place here," playing a red dot laser pointer on the hole displayed on the conference room's end projection display. "in Sandia Mountain the 'X-pole' because it's the crossing of the flux from the North and South poles."

"Next, there is a strong presence of all frequencies, that is, all bands and all spectrum of electromagnetic transmission we can measure present at the time of the events, which quickly dissipates, replaced by the purer, magnetic energy I mentioned. It's all present, and it seems to be collected and focused as it nears the surface. Analysis of the light coming upward from

X-pole and down from God knows where shows it to be magnetic plasma, so much energy that it glows, and contained by something we have not yet begun to figure out, unlike a lightning bolt that wiggles through plasma paths burned in the atmosphere. Speculation now is that the objects, the C-130, flares and rockets crossing this focused flux acted like Franklin's key, flown up into the thunderstorm by the luckiest man alive in the 1700's. Lightning was reported to have come up from the ground and down from the sky, connecting at the key, and forming a bolt that ignored the idiot on the land end of the string.

"Finally, data from the crawler robot has not yet been analyzed, the energy team is on that now. Let's see," she thumbed through a few more papers. "That's it for me."

Jefferies looked over his glasses, "Maurine, anything yet from the video on the robot?"

The small, thin to the point of anorexia, light skinned black woman, short cut relaxed hair, close set eyes held closed nearly to a line, and glasses held with a plain black lanyard, shot the laser pointer handed to her from Rand at the screen on the end of the room, nodded to the media tech, and punched the button lighting the red dot with a claw-finger nail. "We sent the robot in at 20:14, it was proceeding at its controlled speed of two MPH until it reached a point 31.41 meters from the hole…uh the X-pole. At that time the speed recorder in the vehicle began to show it moving faster, quickly reaching 999 MPH, the highest reading the instruments on the driving control console could display, but look at this."

A split screen showed the camera aboard the robot with a time stamp on the left, a camera recording the robot from some control point a hundred yards away on the right. The on-board camera seemed to show the little tracked robot picking up speed, and soon racing toward the X-pole, objects, rocks mostly, blurred as though they were racing by, the telephoto camera from a hundred yards away saw the robot continue at the slow speed. The time stamps remained in sync. As before with the TV news copter, the robot seemed to be made of rubber and was pulled, until it finally snapped into the hole.

Maurine continued, "Note the cable trailing the robot was not stretched, pulled into the hole or destroyed, in fact, we re-wound it." She produced a length of cable, one end of the wire was obviously cut with a tool of some kind, the other had a strain relief, and the bolts that had held it to the back of the robot, the bolts simply sheared at where they would have gone into the threaded bolt holes in the robots' frame.

"We did get video back, not through the cable once it had been pulled off the robot, but from the transmitter, we also recorded a lot of full spectrum data, as Doctor Rand mentioned, although the analysis of anything but the visual is incomplete." Again she nodded to the tech, and pointed at the screen again, another claw jab. The now familiar desert appeared again, and there were several human looking people nearby. "These people seem to be clothed in somewhat modern dress. A number of them seem... well... incomplete."

Bart literally sprung from his chair, which toppled over, pointing at the screen. "Jesus, those are the people who vanished from the intersection! Hell yes they are incomplete! The rest of them is scattered around the Avenide incident scene!"

Everyone in the room looked shocked. Somehow the connection between the people from the helicopter video, now this one from the robot had not been made with the people from the intersection. Bart continued, "We need to get them a Doctor, food, water, first aid stuff. Shit, people we need to get them weapons, God knows what they have to defend against, dinosaurs? Cave men? Who the hell knows!"

Rand stood as well, "Hold on detective, just hold on. There were no dinosaurs 8,000 years ago, and for all we know no humans either, at least not where we think those people are. If they are in the past, even 8,000 years, we just can't send a couple dozen M-16's. We could change history. We could...Okay...Okay water, food and first aid. But no weapons."

Heads nodded around the table.

Andrew the geek said, "Like, what's a Doctor supposed to do? A swan dive into the X-pole? That is if we can find an MD whacked enough to need to begin building a practice 8,000 years ago."

Bart looked around the room for some help, everyone was avoiding his eyes except Rand, Jaylee, and Jefferies.

Both Bart and Jaylee had noticed a new face in the room, positioned along the wall to the right of the table near the screen wall. A stocky man in a dark blue $2,000 suit, cream colored silk shirt and a tie with B-52's inside circles in a parody of the peace sign. He had an angular face, clean shaven but a perpetual beard shadow, intense brown eyes, a nearly black-brown unibrow across a permanently crinkled forehead. A mouth comprised of thin colorless lips held in a semi-permanent dyspeptic smirk.

He positioned his papers on the empty seat beside him and rose. "Excuse me, but we will not be sending anything anywhere."

"And just who the fuck are you?" Bart said, still standing and with no attempt at playing nice.

"I'm John Milton, I'm from Homeland Security, and I out-rank everyone here. As Doctor Jefferies will attest, I have all the levels of authorization needed to shut down this whole incredible, even for the U.S. government, fuck-up. Ogelsbee from FEMA is out, his stunt with $3 or 4 million in Airforce ordnance and worse yet dropping it on a rancher's land got him nearly canned, and if I have anything to do with it, he will be fired. Anyway, I'm in, I'm number 3 at Homeland, and I make the rules."

"We in Washington don't know what the hell is going on here, and we are not convinced there is a 'time machine' or anything else. We also are not convinced that it is not some group of terrorists who have stumbled onto something and were bringing it into the Swiss Cheese Southern border, and it went off here, a weapon of some kind. In fact, we don't believe much about...what do you call it? This 'X-pole' thing at all."

Jefferies turned in his chair, a pleading incredulous look stamped on his face, "What do you people call the phenomenon in the video? The readings from our instruments?"

"Look, Doctor, I saw the Millennium Falcon jump to hyper-space, an alien space ship level the White House, even Sylvester Stallone hold his own against a real boxer, for God's sake most unbelievable of all, I saw Michael Moore say he was a patriot, all sorts of shit on a TV screen, and, most of us in D.C. don't believe that either."

Jaylee stood pointed at Milton, "John, did you just call me and all these good people here liars?"

Milton looked up at Jaylee then leveled his gaze back at Jefferies, "Well, detective, two things, first, I don't give a rat's ass what you think I did, and second, sit down or I'll call Walker and you will be removed from this base before the phone disconnects, understood?" Jaylee, with Bart gently pulling his non-pointing arm sleeve backed off and sat down. Milton swung an arm with a pointed finger at those in the room, "In fact, what I just said to Detective Washington here goes for every damned one of you." He raked the room with the stiffly pointed finger, looking way too much like a stubby Uzi machine gun barrel. He sat back down.

Doctor Rand stood, looking calm and as professional as she could. "Mister Milton, we are all but convinced that there will be an event of some kind, and I must agree, like you, we don't know what it is here we are dealing with either, but whatever it is will most likely happen in the middle of Albuquerque if south, and maybe if we're luck in the desert if to the north. I, along with the others here have looked under all the rocks we can find and see no terrorists hiding."

"Unlike the Millennium Falcon, real people will be affected, not actors in plastic Storm Trooper armor or a six-foot balsa wood Independence Day model of the White House. It will be about one hundred and fifty meters in diameter, and if it's in the wrong place, several hundred people will vanish." She paused for effect, then tapping the table with a finger. "And thanks to your superior deductive abilities and professional demeanor, sir, the thirteen people in this room will swear they tried to stop it, and you, John Milton, and Homeland Security, stopped us."

"Your move." She sat down, not making eye contact with anyone in the room.

Milton stared at her with a look that would have drilled holes in titanium bricks, "Very well Doctor Rand, you freaks and whack-jobs here can continue, but if the event happens, and I really doubt anything will that we can't tie to some nutcases, but if we can't figure it out, it will be spun as your fault, probably not that much of a spin. The whole expensive problem will come home to E-R-Mag Labs. On the other hand, if you are able to stop it, or more likely you're just delusional, and nothing happens, don't try some 'we saved the world horse-shit', because we in Washington will not put up with it. We see this whole damned thing as another 'we need more money' bullshit power grab."

Milton had done his homework, seeming to know all the players in the room. Scary. Still looking at Rand he collected his papers and closed his attaché case, stood shaking his head. Moving past the table, slid his hand on the dark green Formica top as if moving something on a game board, "Check."

He turned on his heel and stormed from the room. Then at the door, "Just because I'm leaving you here to make up the next improbable line of pseudo-science bullshit doesn't mean I'm gone. I'll be around every corner waiting for the consummate fuck-up that I'm sure will present itself. And when it does, you can play with time machines from Leavenworth. Have a nice day."

Rand looked at Jefferies, "Chris, I do NOT want this numb-nuts to call a Check-Mate." Turning to the countdown clock near the ceiling over the screen wall, then to the rest of the team leaders, "We have 21 hours 14 minutes to get control of this antenna. Slow it, stop it or control it. Can we do it!?" She banged a small, determined fist on the table looking around at the rest of the team. "Well…are you with us?"

Completely out of character, the assembled room full of exhausted scientists and mathematicians jumped to their feet, and actually cheered.

Jaylee stood by the door as they left, serious looks but determination etched on every brow, and in every step. As Rand came by, he gently guided her aside. "Doctor you are the most amazing person I've ever seen in action. Uh, and I've seen a few." He dropped his eyes from hers to the floor, "I…uh… If we get out of this thing would you consider…I mean like a dinner or something, maybe a movie with balsa wood buildings getting blown up?" She nearly laughed at the roughest man she had ever met kicking his shoe like a sixth-grade schoolboy asking a girl out for the first time.

She crinkled a little smile onto an obviously tired and stressed face, "Sure, frankly, I like your style as well." Then as her eyes looked back to the clock, "If we get out of this thing, and Jay, the more this thing goes apeshit, that's a real if." Then, with a pat on his arm, she brushed close and moved passed him and into the hall, gluing a cell phone to her ear.

In spite of the warning from Milton, the decision was taken to send food, water, a written explanation of what seemed to have happened, all in or packaged with bio-degradable materials. Several cotton tents, candles, matches, cotton and wool blankets, and a large pad with black markers. Instructions were given to write in big letters what they needed, who they were by name, and if they were in danger from animals or natives. Another camera would be following the supplies in a half hour from their being sent into the X-pole and hopefully would send back what they had written.

A live feed was set up from the camera to the conference room.

PART 4

Life in the old West

CHAPTER 14

Some Vacation

Firefighter/Paramedic Arthur Cheete looked at the stack of supplies, which had appeared with a crack! And had dropped from four feet in the air onto the reddish sandy hillside. He waved for the others to come over, well, those who could that is. Fourteen people had been on their way to work, or school, a few like Cheete were getting off the night shift, sleepily driving home...then...what?

A macabre assortment of parts of another six people had come along with them as well to this place. Yes...this hot, dry, nearly lifeless place. The place more than one had said was hell, or at least purgatory trying to be hell. Maybe it was the lack of life, or the color, mostly reds and grey-red browns. Even the sky was a reddish hue from sun-up to dusk, fading into violet and then black. They had not seen a normal white cloud since arriving.

People were not the only things to come along, two entire cars, three partial autos, part of a minivan, a nearly complete short trailer truck carrying

464 cases of disposable diapers, and a motorcycle, complete with the rider. None of the vehicles would start, even the interior lights would not light. Completely dead batteries. Even the batteries in several wristwatches, cell phones and two PDAs were dead.

Like an Amish farm, there apparently is no electricity in purgatory.

Several of the people had parts of, or entire limbs missing. Infection, bleeding or other consequences of a severe amputation did not seem present. They were not in shock, and most had little pain, although some now had the irritating "phantom" pains and itching of a limb that was not there.

The few items of food, and the few sodas and coffee that some had in their cars were long gone. The miraculous arrival of the supplies a minute ago, a little more than two and a half days since arriving in the sand pit was literally a lifesaver.

On the first night a corner portion of a concrete building of some sort had appeared, toppling over as it collapsed, a man who was on the top of the disintegrating structure was thrown across the sand. He had apparently been on top of the structure when the corner had been sliced off. As people ran to his aid they stopped short, one man yelling an alien had appeared. Closer inspection showed the young man was dressed in what several had thought was SWAT gear, the black riot helmet sending frayed nerves into a twilight-zone conclusion. Okay, weren't they in the twilight zone?

Cheete, the Albuquerque firefighter and Paramedic just off duty, had set the man's two broken legs as best he could with the meager supplies at hand, rolling a tube of newspaper around each leg and securing it with some clear wrapping film salvaged from a pallet of diapers. A block of the concrete wall had apparently bounced over his legs as he, and it, rolled away from the other falling concrete. Unlike the amputees, the young man was in considerable pain. His only relief coming from a bottle of Midol one of the women had in her purse.

Four of the healthiest men had gone on an 'exploration hike' to what looked to be a mile or so to the North, if the Sun was any marker of direction in this strange place, and if distance could be estimated in the desert. They were checking out where apparently some kind of aircraft that had exploded in the night sky, then six more explosions, a jet fighter of some kind had crashed, and finally a helicopter with no rotors had appeared, all this on their second night in this seemingly endless desert. Strangely, the helicopter did not arrive a mile away, it had arrived nearly on top of the cars and truck… and survivors.

The explorers had not returned. They had disappeared over the dune between the vehicles and the 'crash site' at dusk and were not seen again. Had someone heard a scream?

The remains of the several dead people, including the right half of a young woman, several limbs and the lower torso of a man were buried in the sand a dozen or so meters from the 'camp'. On the second night something had dug them up and removed all traces of the remains. The sand showed what appeared to be large bird-like tracks, a little over an 18" from end to end, but there were no details in the footprint due to the softness of the sand. The fresh, but bare skeletons of 2 people were literally under where the contents of the intersection had arrived. Cheete had looked them over, and determined that they had been stripped of their flesh by knives, one had a leg missing, the other a hand and part of the arm. Bloody clothing was strewn around.

Some thought they could see shadowy shapes moving around on the very edge of their vision, like they were staying just out of site, especially at dusk or pre-dawn. Some thought dark shapes would poke up from the horizon looking over a dune, then disappear again.

The sky, desert, and distant mountains were nearly the same red-brown, sometimes where land ended and sky started, was lost. The sky, the bright but muddy red, seemed to have dust or smoke suspended, the dawn and sunset were bright red as the sun sank into the expanse of sand, a giant glowing red bubble shrinking into an expanse of unmoving lava.

Cheete had taken the SWAT man's pistol, tried to test fire it, no luck, he had jacked three separate rounds into the Glock, none fired, even though the primers were properly dented. Removal of a bullet revealed the powder had turned to a clear jelly like substance. A discussion with the SWAT man added nothing to a solution. The pistol was worthless.

The diaper truck's trailer had provided some shelter, but the sun made it un-bearable in the afternoon. A wall of cases of diapers like big bricks placed along the sides of the trailer provided shelter from all but the most direct noon day sun. The nights were passed with diesel soaked diapers finally lighting, and providing protection from something moving around the outskirts of the camp, unseen but clearly perceived. They had all taken to sleeping in the truck after sundown and the heat of the day cooled, bathroom breaks were done with no less than three people at a time, and a torch of the diapers, not lit, but ready.

A mechanical rubber tracked robot had come through a few hours earlier, no help at all.

Now an hour after the robot, this arrival of manna from heaven. He passed around the letter that had come with the supplies. Heads shook, some cried, and no one smiled. The past? 8,000 years? How the hell was this possible? How could they get back? Lots of questions, but no answers. Maybe some soon…'maybe never,' Cheete thought.

But now there was a task with a deadline. On the pad, he wrote each remaining person's name. Next, he requested splints, first aid supplies including antibiotics, and some kind of weapon. He drew a pistol and an X through it. He then wrote '4 men exploring – 2 days gone' and ended the note with – 'Please…help'.

A FLASH IN TIME

Twenty-four minutes later, another flash of light, more supplies and the remains of a video camera appeared. In another thirty minutes and another flash, he had a large combat aid box, with the U.S. Army Field Medical Manual. Along with this were three bayonet like knives but made of iron, three simple wooden bows with several dozen wooden shaft arrows, the tips were iron as well, and a case of flares.

Cheete gave a flare to the young boy, just 11 years old, Christian Halloway, who had arrived in the back 1/3 of the mini-van. His mother's ponytail, but none of the rest of her had not come with him. "Chris, see if you can light this thing." The boy, despondent, but willing to try to help, walked a few feet away and read the instructions on the side of the flare, then, scraping the cap on the end gave a spark, a little puff of smoke, but no flame, finally it struggled and lit. He shrugged and returned to where Arthur was getting out two air-splints, Cheete put out the flare by stabbing it into the sand – no sense in wasting what may be needed as a weapon.

Cheete stood and called to the others "Folks, we need to set up these tents, and get the water and food into the truck. There may be animals who can smell the water and food, if so they will be snooping around when the sun goes down." He purposely did not mention the grave robbers, whatever they were.

Six females, one of whom was another child, a Mexican girl Chris's age, and two men shuffled over. "Art, I've done some work with the Scouts, I think I can do the tents." Gus Hammond said as he struggled and picked up a tent bundle, his left hand was missing at the wrist. He had his arm out of the window of his car waving at a storeowner when he watched, as he "turned to glass", and landed here, in his car, with no left hand. "Where do you think we ought to set it up?"

Art said, "Close to the truck I guess, I don't know, do you think we should try to make use of all the shade we can?" Art was doing well at not making all the decisions, and spreading responsibility throughout the group as he identified strengths and skills of the various people.

Gus nodded and headed to the truck, two women followed. Obviously the water and food worked quickly as everyone's strength was returning from what they had consumed.

A second man not going with the exploration team, an older slightly stooped man, white hair, white mustache and white eyebrows over a reddish round face, which suggested the South-West as a poor choice of place to live, came over to Art, one of the strange knives in hand, "They're afraid we will change history, that's why they gave us stuff that will disappear in a few years, even out here, simple iron, wood, little plastic. They also will give us food, but no real way to carry it, like a back-pack. They want us to die right here, not go hunting something that will be some race-horses' great times 200 grandfather or something like that."

He looked at the sand, then continued, "What do you think will happen to the time-line if we die 8,000 years before we were born? Will we fade from our people's memory? Will we pop out of their existence and lives in an instant. Will our stuff, houses, cars, shit, even kids vanish? Will those guys in the pill box in Grenada I killed 8,000 years from now succeed on wiping out the rest of my platoon on the jungle hill?" He shook his head.

He looked at Art, still inflating and testing the splints, who looked up, "Mister…Doctor Pocker, I'm an optimist. I'm also planning on taking my retirement shortly and for a good long time. I'm gonna go back to the reservation and drop a line in the river, maybe never pull it out, just watch it stay there as the water goes by. So, whoever runs the timeline better know, if we suddenly disappear because we were never born, I'll be truly and completely pissed. Please help me with this, the young man with the broken legs needs us now," then looking nowhere in particular… "Whenever 'now' is."

Mort Pocker shrugged, took a few rolls of cling, and two chemical ice packs, then followed young Chris and Art to the place near the rear wheels of the short trailer, on the dirt on the underside of the truck where Randy Potet'e Junior was laying, still in obvious distress. Mort had a few minutes earlier unpacked a blanket and positioned it on the sand under the injured man. A water bottle and two ½ eaten packages of food, granola energy mix, and a package of beef jerky, beside it.

"Randy, we have some splints which will help when we have to move you, like into the truck at night. Mort has a cold pack, and Chris has a few APC's, they're aspirin, military style. If you need it, there's morphine, but I think it would be bad for you, might sink you into shock."

Mort squeezed the ice pack and exploded the chambers, mixing the chemicals, then handed it to Randy, who tucked it behind his neck. Randy then scooped up the water bottle and downed the three white pills. Through clinched teeth he said, "Thanks, guys really. Any idea yet where we are?"

Cheete filled him in on the somewhat cryptic message that had appeared with the supplies. "You need any more water, food, anything?"

Randy shook his head, "You did get my name on the sheet didn't you? I know dad and mom are worried sick, he saw me...well, he saw me leave."

"You were the first name on the list."

An hour later Pocker walked up to Art doing busy work organizing the supplies and first aid stuff. Mort had been over examining the motorcycle. "You up for trying to start the Shadow?"

"Mort, we tried that, the batteries dead, the motorcycle is too new to have a magneto." Art replied.

"Yeah, I know, whatever electrical bullshit got us here sucked everything dry. But, my friend, lead acid batteries, even dead ones will self-re-charge a little in a day or two. If the battery in the bike has enough charge to excite the alternator on it, then we can start its engine, then use the bike to charge one of the small cars, then the truck. It's worth a try, but I don't know anything about riding a motorcycle."

Art studied the man, "Well, I rode years ago, I guess if riding a bicycle stays with you, so would a motorcycle. Jees, I wish the owner hadn't gone on the exploring trip. I suggest we push it to the hill, and I jump it while going down." He called to Chris, his 'adopted son', "Hey, boy, common over here and give us a hand." Gus looked over from where he was keeping Randy company, offered help, but was told they had it for now.

They walked to the bike, pushed it ten yards to the gentle hard packed mud slope. Art tested the brakes, found neutral, pulled in the clutch and stepped the transmission to first gear. Mort turned on the gasoline petcock.

Art clicked the key, a faint glow appeared on the light just above the switch. He wasted no time, and signaled Mort and Chris to give him a shove. The bike crunched through the gravely dried mud and picked up speed, at about 10 MPH, he popped the clutch, the rear wheel slid, then began turning. A few feet later the engine coughed, wheezed, misfired, and caught again, this time it continued to run. With no small difficulty, Art stopped the bike on the hill, and let it run. Mort and Chris ran down to him, "Good man! Can you turn this thing around without flipping down the hill?"

They moved the motorcycle slowly sideways on the slope, then Art pulled the clutch, stepped back into 1st gear. He rode deliberately and with great care along the side of the hill until it flattened out, then made his way back to the camp.

On arrival, the women, children, Gus and even Randy from his place near the truck were clapping, Gus slapping the side of his leg. Mort gave him a hi-five. They decided the Honda civic should get the first charge, a set of cheap battery cables from an 'emergency auto survival kit' in the trunk hooked the motorcycle to the car and started the process. The amp-meter on the bike showed the Civic was getting juice. Chris was assigned to keep the throttle up and could sit astride the bike. He was shown how the gearshift worked and warned not to touch it.

Mort got Art, pulled him by the arm over to where Gus and Randy were. Away from the Honda Shadow where they could hear each other. "I got some worries here, and please don't think I'm losing it." He looked at Art, then Gus, "See, about one day after we got here the corner of a building appeared, nearly on top of us, hell guys, if it hadn't fallen the direction it did, some or all of us would have been crushed, then the helicopter damned near took us out." He shook his head, "Now the little bomb robot and supplies are coming in right in the middle of us."

Gus said, "So what's your concern? As it stands, we don't have to go anywhere to get the supplies, or have very far to carry them."

"That's true, but what if another intersection comes through, or another building or part of one? I think we need to move the camp away from this ground zero and do it fast. Another day is ending in 8 hours, and something has happened about every 24 hours."

Art nodded, "Mort, you're a smart guy, we're lucky to have you here."

Mort looked at the pitiful surroundings, dirty, wounded, amputated survivors, dusty red, hot desert, wrecked cars, and laughed, really laughed, "Yeah, I'm just a lucky guy."

In spite of themselves they all laughed. Randy moaned as the laughter rocked his legs. Art would have bet he would never laugh again before the motorcycle had started, and now this irony placed before them.

In four hours they had the Honda Civic started, then the truck. They had loaded everything into it and had carefully driven a hundred yards away from the old camp, the new location was on top of a hill, good view all around. Art had driven the motorcycle and truck, Mort the Civic. The other car, a Ford of some kind was too damaged to consider starting. Maybe get any gasoline out later? The truck was placed where it would provide the most shade for most of the time. Discussions were underway for someone to take the motorcycle and see if the other men could be found, maybe tomorrow.

Evening dropped with the sun leaving a cloudless sky and sinking into a lifeless red sea of sand. They continued to work on the new camp.

Unknown to anyone, a very long time in the future a mistake had been made. The logic used to conclude that the Pinal Mountains got forested 8,000 years before the 21st century was good as far as it went. Those mountains had been there unforested much, much longer than that.

101,310,416 years from the cooling red skied evening, in a place where a dense magnetic portion of the iron core of the earth would eventually migrate toward, while the desert arrivals worked on the new camp site, a geek scientist named Andrew's clock went to 0 hours 0 minutes.

As the 10 men and women staked the tents in their new position, an incredible flash of white light arrived with…what?

CHAPTER 15

A Pain from DC

Jefferies ordered the staff to sleep for 4 hours, most had, none well.

Jaylee and Bart began working a plan to neutralize the loser Milton, so far nothing short of a 148 grains of copper jacketed lead between the eyes had come to mind. "All we gotta do is get his smart ass on the South side near 21st Street for twenty minutes, soon as he runs his mouth, he gets capped." Bart said as he and Jaylee turned into the conference room.

In the short meeting before the ordered R&R, Milton had interjected wise cracks until Rand had lost it. "SIR! If you cannot appreciate the gravity of the possible end of the fucking world, at least have the common decency to shut up and let us try to do our work! While you do not believe any of this, we do!" She had sat back into her chair, hands covering her face.

Jaylee had expected tears and was ready for a career ending whup-ass on the feckless Milton. When she dropped her hands, however, she found

Jaylee's eyes and winked. Then went back to her laptop in front of her. Jaylee pondered how lucky Milton was, and saw in his mind's eye a scene from the movie 'The Matrix' where a bullet was passing Nemo, here the idiot Milton's head, a little squiggle line tracing its path. Yes, John Milton had dodged a bullet in the form of a ham sized fist operated by a real big, strong, pissed guy.

Milton had shrugged, and sauntered back to the corner chair, sat, and contemplated his fingernails in an overstated theater 'don't give a rat's ass' body language pose. He had stayed there until Jefferies had sent them away for the rest period.

Now, with the countdown clock at 19 hours 41 minutes, they were back in the room. Milton had not been informed of this meeting, and unknown to the E-R-Mag Labs team was in an Albuquerque strip club stuffing dollar bills into garter belts. Just in case Jefferies had the hallway door locked. The team had come in from an outside door down the hall, one and two at a time.

Jefferies had sprawled on a couch in his outer office, closed his porcine eyes, but did not sleep. Visions of the young man's pleading eyes looking at the command bus camera from under the helmet as he turned translucent and fell from sight with the corner of the garage, and had vanished, was stuck in an endless tape loop, playing over and over on the insides of his eye lids. It was the moment Jefferies had changed his outlook on the 'problem', the instant the theoretical had become the actual. The moment his life had changed from detached project manager to responsible human, aware of the consequences of his actions apart from a favorable review at his next yearly evaluation. Finally, sleep nowhere to be found, he had lay there, looking at the ceiling, hoping for an answer to the problem he could not even define, not enough information even to ask the question. 'I'll take weird assed magnetic time travel for $200.' ZAAAAPP! "The first of the daily doubles!"

Andrew the geek, who could have been in a mini-time machine himself, not a hair requiring placement, clothing change or molecule different than the first meeting, stepped to the clock, consulted a slice of paper and with ease reached the ceiling level clock and poked the set buttons. When he left the clock it read 4 hours 01 minute. "The X-pole is charging faster than we had expected, it seems to be moving discharges into the night. Even though it had started at a slower rate than before, it seems somehow to be keeping to a roughly 24-hour cycle. The bombs and all re-set it to close to midnight, now looks like around ten PM." A dead pan voice, the possibility of hundreds of people losing over twelve hours of normalcy as they became lost in space somewhere was lost to him. He sat back in his chair, folded like a sixth grader in a second-grade desk.

Kough said, "I wonder if the ionosphere's changing layers at sunset makes discharges easier to project?"

Jefferies stood, then sat back down looking at the ceiling, then spun his chair in a complete circle, "Dr.

Kough, do you really think this is a projection? That is something being directed? If that's so who or what is controlling the hits?"

The notion that some intelligence was directing all this had actually crossed everyone's mind, maybe being prompted by the loser dumbass Milton? Most had chalked up the idea of some alien directing the strikes as not possible, but there was that nagging back of the mind fear.

Kough placed a few papers on the table, looked at them some more, leaned back in his chair and then said, "I really don't know, but I'm sometimes wishing it were. If some unknown alien or even earthbound enemy were directing this thing it's something we could martial our forces against, a common enemy to focus on. Maybe force an error, maybe find a way to stop the charging of the antenna. If it is being directed it might be someone in the middle of a learning curve, I mean really, a friggin tree? An aging Native American statue? That's actually the best argument, the seeming randomness of the events, for it being some kind of phenomenon."

On the projection screen was a blow up map of Albuquerque, a cone shaped shaded area like the weather channel forecast maps for hurricanes was crossing the city, north to south, another cone going into the desert south to north. Jefferies stopped his circling and rocked forward out of his creaking surplus government chair, stepped to the map, and pointed, "Anyone want to suggest a place where this thing might hit?"

Rand said, "The supposition that the events were happening in a due North/South course actually are proved incorrect, or at least over-stated. They are close to magnetic North/South lines, but the last event on the campus was a hundred eighty-four meters or some 12 degrees off from North. In addition, the spacing we thought might be in place is also off. There is no precise correlation between the three events we can find. Our best guess where the event at the college would be was on the sports field to the South of the Native American statue and courtyard. Couple that with the X-pole appearing where there was previously nothing, and we're stumped. The center focusing Yagi radiators of the antenna are close, but several meters up the side of the mountain from where the hole actually appeared. The antenna cable radiators are, however in a direct line East-West to the hole."

Jefferies moved back to the table, but did not sit, leaning on his arms and over his chair, he shook his head, "The damned Feds have not allowed us to evacuate anyone. They want specifics that we just don't have a location, and more to their point I guess is we can't say what the hell it is we're dealing with. They are saying they 'don't want a panic.' And I suspect Milton's reports have them thinking there might not be anything real of any dangerous consequence happening here. I was able to get the train car derailment story stopped at Channel 3 just in time. Peg is waiting…I don't have anything to tell her."

An arm went up near the end of the table, the owner, a middle aged man who seemed to be something like the tire mascot constructed of nearly white spheres stacked only with clothing, stood as Jefferies nodded his direction. The round head sat on round shoulders, rounded arms stuck from a close fitting, short sleeved white lab coat. Black eyeglasses seemed painted on the fat little round face which had not expanded proportionally with the head. A band of light grey hair stood on end from the ear-line, providing a scarce contrast to the head. Eyebrows above the glasses were thin grey lines ruler straight over little slits of eyes. As though to prove the man was not actually a black and white TV picture from the 50's, some color was presented in the form of a nose, bright red, which balanced above a prematurely grey mustache completely concealing what must have been a small mouth. The man, Doctor Thomas Peters, withdrew the arm, which had remained extended like an old railroad semaphore which had been forgotten in space as the other hand shuffled papers.

Bart leaned to Jay's ear – "That, my friend, is one very strange looking man." As the man started speaking in a voice requiring Bart and Jaylee to do a classic comic double-take. He sounded like the guy who did the voice over of Slasher movie trailers.

"Doctor Jefferies, you asked for some best guesses on what we have here, so I have a few."

Jefferies nodded; Peters continued. "Well, I examined the phenomenon of the aircraft, flare and rockets crossing the center of the X-pole and being destroyed. He waved to the media technician who tapped some keys, the dark telephoto picture and roar of the C-130 came up on the screen. A flare dropped from the cargo door, then another. The plane banked and started up the valley. The video slowed to where it could easily be seen in a frame-to-frame motion. Those in the room watched sadly as the inevitable unfolded. A point of light started up from the ground, and out of the frame, but well known to them, its mate came downward from the sky. The video slowed to a frame by frame click-click-click. The point of light filled out, and the other one from above came into view as the camera person saw it and made the camera adjustment.

"Please notice this one from the ground has a purple hue, the one from above reddish. That got me thinking of the opposites attract theory of magnetism, and electricity. The purple hue turned out to be shifting the light it produced to ultra-violet, the top one shifting its light output to infra-red." He paused, like the movie trailer guy letting a point sink in. "Analysis of the magnetic energy from the ground shows multi frequency but otherwise ordinary magnetic flux, positive here" he laser pointed to the low end of the spike, "and the negative up here." The dot circled the upper reddish point of light.

Another pause, "Folks there was no detectable energy from above. Now I will go into pure guesses with little or no hard science to back it up. Let me say here I don't mind at all being wrong." He looked at the airplane on the screen, now frozen three seconds from disaster, "In fact, I hope to God I am."

"We know there is something there, some powerful energy." The red dot buzzed again around the upper point of light, "and since our instruments cannot detect it, I propose it's dark energy." The room mumbled; heads snapped up to the screen even though no new information was displayed there. "Look, Hawkins said in his paper a few years ago that dark mass will follow known mass, effectively cancelling it out, so, a re-statement of the anti-matter postulations Einstein played with to fill in the voids in his relativity theory. I think this dark energy will follow known energy. The connection is some actual solid mass crossing where these forces are poised, in balance, ready to try to cancel each other out."

Another pause, "If the energy available to the real energy side, or the earth, if you will, gets strong enough to actually connect with the dark energy, then all the mass and energy on earth will go to all the dark mass and dark energy available in this part of the universe. And it will happen." BAM, he slapped the table, "just like that, and at the speed of light."

"Now," he looked down at the table, "please prove me wrong."

Silence so thick it could be physically felt hung in the room, several scientists had begun in-putting into their computers. Rand raised her head, "Thank you Doctor Peters. The dark matter and energy postulation has some intriguing aspects, and I too hope you're wrong. Like Dr. Kough says, makes ya want it to be an unnaturally directed event, one that we could fight. There's still a problem though. Doctor Peters do you, or does anyone for that matter, have a theory as to how this thing, the X-pole, has been able to create connection to a past time? Any conjecture on how energy, ours or the universes', can open this rift? Any idea why these objects leave E-R-Mag Labs Mountain, and appear several hundred miles away in the Pinals?"

Andrew, the follower, copying Peters, raised his hand, Jefferies nodded to him. "Well, suppose the actual place they arrived was actually right where the X-pole is now, I mean, say, the continents, you know, the shelves or plates, whatever, moved that far. I've been thinking that maybe all time exists at one place. Like if I moved back in time a few days, this place would be here. If I moved a hundred years, the dirt, stuff and all that was moved in the Manhattan project to make this base wouldn't, so maybe I'd appear where the physical stuff came from."

Jefferies looked up from a paper, "For that to be true, our 8,000-year thesis is trash, what's the best guess for the iron core shifting the several hundred miles from Globe AZ to here?"

Andrew was poking his MAC Book, "My best guess, as calculated from other points I've worked on, is uh, 101.3 million years. I suppose the Pinal's didn't have trees then either."

Maurine shook her head, returning to Andrews first point, "Okay, then if you went someplace in time where the physical stuff was from many places, like from the top floor of a shopping mall, then parts of you would be in China, India, hell everywhere but the U.S., or by that logic wherever the stuff in the mall came from."

Jefferies stopped finger flipping his pencil and tapped it on the side of his coffee cup, the rooms occupants re-focused their attention to the end of the table, "Andrew, don't get me wrong, that's as good a theory as any, but I'm with Doctor Rand. How does all this connect to a time-space continuum? Folks the answer is here in the data, but it's like reading a Chinese Horoscope written in ancient mandarin. We need the key to translate the data into answers." Jefferies continued, "Manny you had something?"

Doctor Manual Sanchez looked like the rest of the scientists in that he appeared very tired, he stood, shuffled some papers on the Formica table-top, and cleared his throat, taking a deep breath, he addressed the room in his clear, slight Mexican accent. "I have some troubling data and, I have to say, like the others here who have opined on this thing in the mountain, has no real solid basis for a conclusion. But there's enough here to move what we on my part of the team have deduced. We've been processing data from some of the NASA satellites tasked with looking at the sun, and their collecting of data on the magnetic activity as it relates to coronal storms and magnetic fields surrounding those events. NASA notified us of some strange readings coming from this array of solar observers, so we thought a look might be worth our scarce time. It might turn out to be that it was a very good use of that time, or at least seems so.

He continued, "First a little background. Tesla, the inventor, Nikola, not the car guy, had experiments surrounding the transmission of power through the ground and air. His work on the towers explored electrical transmission using a radio frequency resonance to create electrical energy through two coils to generate high voltage, high frequency currents. For those here with an electronic background, his experiments used near-field inductive and capacitive couplings – basically tuned to a specific frequency air-gaps. His experiments discovered that the near-field inductive waves actually are a short-range wireless physical layer that transmits a low power, non-propagating magnetic field between devices. Capacitive couplings transmit power between two networks by displacing currents produced by the inductive electrical fields, at least that's what old Nick was thinking. The tower he created was thought to be the ground, or one wire of the circuit, and the air was the other, or at least as he postulated it to be. He had some experiments that are not well documented, and the strange tower in some of his photos are not well explained. One question never answered is did Tesla have other towers that he was trying to transmit to, and how effective was his transmission scheme?

Westinghouse and Edison went nuts and spread fear about death rays and exploding birds who crossed the invisible paths of this energy ray in an effort to stop his experiments, and apparently they were successful. For them it was an effort to stop competition as they were stringing wires everywhere they could. They could and did attach a meter to the used end of each wire and started charging for their electricity…anyway."

"In the 60's the Russians had a series of these towers erected to see what they could find out, but their towers were suddenly and quickly dismantled, and any data was lost in the KGB catacombs. In the 80's some information came out that the towers were somewhat successful, but that they projected much farther than the intended range of the power transmission, in fact they caused 'ionospheric cascade storms', and even seemed to attract magnetic energy from the coronal storms on the sun! The Russians abandoned the whole project fearing that a massive coronal pulse could follow those lines back to their towers, maybe even destroy the entire electrical system on earth."

"So, as we have been filtering the data from all the sources we can get, we actually have detected, as with what the Russians did that I mentioned earlier, magnetic energy following some kind of lines of energy back to earth, and yes, more specifically to here, and into the X-pole. If my information is correct, and if the Russian fears were justified, which I pray isn't the case but may well be what's beginning here. People we have to stop this thing before the X-pole attracts a sun flare that could kill all living things on earth, and if not at least fry all electronic- even electrical stuff, and do so everywhere on Earth."

"Imagine if a coronal flare a million miles across focused itself into the X-pole. The explosion of that much energy going into a funnel…well I'm talking the total destruction of everything with a wire in or on it, everywhere including all the spacecraft, aircraft, ships, anywhere on earth, even toy RC cars and food trucks."

Bart whispered to Jaylee, "If this X-pole fucks up the Bueno Taco truck on 4th and River Street, I'm really gonna be pissed."

Jaylee looked at his friend, "Bart, if Sanchez is correct, the X-pole will be making Taco's out of all of us."

Jefferies was shaking his head, finally speaking, "Manny, we have to keep up on that energy flow from space. If this thing can connect to Sol, then we're thoroughly and completely screwed…anyone have anything to add to Dr. Sanchez's teams' findings?"

No one responded.

Rand, who had taken up sitting beside Jaylee said, "This shit-storm just keeps getting weirder and weirder."

Jefferies looked at Andrew and then to Rand. "Any better guesses than this cone here" tapping the projection screen which had been returned to the cone map with his pencil, "as to where the event will happen?"

How and where indeed.

CHAPTER 16

Turn off the Lights When You Leave

Nothing in the world of commercial electric power distribution is as boring as a Spring evening in the desert. In a power sub-station switch yard. In a tin shed building.

AmeriSouth Power Consortium Power Allocation Switching Sub-station manager Jim George, the 'man with two first names' sat playing Suk-udo from a pulp-puzzle magazine. The Manager title was interesting; he was the only power company employee on the evening shift. Feet on the desk, to both sides of the room a row of the newest flat screen monitors with colored lines running horizontally and vertically on them, starting 3' from the floor and going to the ceiling. The displays were side-by-side to form a continuous wall of screen, angled to appear to be bending around the corners of the room so the lines could easily be followed. Yet those simple lines gave the status of ¾ of the electric power generated in or passing through the Southwest. The Western Interconnection is a wide area synchronous grid and one of the two major alternating current

(AC) power grids in the continental U.S. power transmission system. The other major wide area synchronous grid is the Eastern Interconnection. The three minor interconnections are the Québec Interconnection, the Texas Interconnection, and the Alaska Interconnection.

All of the electric utilities in the Western Interconnection are electrically tied together during normal system conditions and operate at a synchronized frequency of 60 Hz or cycles per second. The Western Interconnection stretches from Western Canada south to Baja California then continues into Mexico. East -West it reaches eastward over the Rockies to the Great Plains.

In early 2006, new DC lines were connected. Interconnections can be tied to each other via high-voltage direct current power transmission lines (DC ties) such as the north-south Pacific DC Intertie, or with variable-frequency transformers (VFTs), which permit a controlled flow of energy while also functionally isolating the independent AC frequencies of each side. In the next few years there would be six DC ties to the Eastern Interconnect in the US and one in Canada, and there are proposals to add four additional ties, sometime in the future when it was figured out who was going to pay for it, and when the money would be recouped. Two of the current ones came through the AmeriSouth station.

George stood, stretched, went to the bathroom, returning he went to the window and surveyed his 'kingdom,' a wide expanse of metal, wiring, large grey blocks with snake guards on the bottom, insulators and more wiring on the tops and sides. Snakes cause more power failures than any natural event in the southwest, squirrels in the northeast. The domain under his personal control, square-mile wise, was approximately a quarter of the western United States, and, from his location on the outskirts of Albuquerque where, purely by accident, one of the dozen largest junctions of the U.S. Power Grid resided and was controlled.

As it happens, this place and its potential impact was created 90% by accident because the United States power grid wasn't designed, it sort of simply happened. It was the product of various power companies becoming interconnected in the early fifties, sixties and seventies. Schematically, the grid was a series of loops overlapping and connecting. Close examination of the power companies will show little or no altruistic motive in this scheme, it was about not building one additional watt of generating capacity if not forced to, and never being in a position to see an electric meter slow and stop turning, even if the electrons doing so were excited and placed into the grid from 3,000 miles away. The United States Power grid is an old, shambling out-of-date contraption that is just waiting to collapse into so much copper and melted aluminum. Adding to the threadbare electrically conductive rope holding it all together is a new problem. Renewable energy. WHAT? A problem? Well not if the sun is shining or the wind is blowing, but just when most electricity is needed, around 6PM to midnight, the wind lays down and so does the sun. Solar panels in 2006 were expensive and turning their DC power to useable AC was expensive and unreliable. Couple this to the aging generation plants that can't be turned on as easily as the little buttons on countless microwaves preparing hot-pockets for dinner. A steam plant needs at least 4 hours' warm-up before they can add to the grid's needs. That said they need to be ready at nearly the speed of light when solar, or wind can't supply the load.

He wondered, how many other underpaid single, as in alone, people across the world could screw up such a large portion of normal life in America or England, or Russia or France, no, wait, weren't the French already screwed up? Radar control points for FAA? Water supplies, like for New York city or Boston? The hubs and server farms of the new and ever-expanding internet? What about sewer treatment plants just south of Washington D.C.? What about nuclear weapons people? Someone was guarding them, somewhere, just one whack job, or one terrorist with clarity of thought, reasonable IQ and a desire cause trouble, not loss of life…at least not at the start of their terrorist action. George supposed the loss of life was equivalent to power over the victim, yes, dead people for lunatic Muslims, that's it. No dead people or pictures of people hurling themselves out of 100 story windows on the towers, no terrorist power.

If one were to look at the schematic of the grid, it gives the impression that if a section of one of the loops failed, it could be cut off, and power could be fed around the section in trouble.

Reality is quite different.

First, not all loops are equal, some carry much more power than others. Second, no two loops are the same size, some in the northeast are a hundred miles around, some out West are several thousand. Third, most are 'protected' by cutouts and breakers designed and installed in the fifties, slow to act and difficult to re-close. Ain't no power guy gonna spend a dime on something that ain't broke, (old and ineffective, maybe, but not broke). Fourth, there is no one in charge of the operation of the loop, it's a free form energy movement system, complicated formulas for adding power to the grid (selling electricity) or removing power (buying electricity) depending on a power company's resources to generate or use it.

Jim George's job is to look at the load and call for more generation to be "ready hot" which is generators turning, but not excited to produce power. Then when the line voltages start to drop they can bring their output online almost instantly. Ever more frequently, and with the EPA taking a few thousand coal plants off-line, there just isn't enough reserve capacity for the several dozen Georges across the U.S.A.'s grid to connect to. Worse, the utilities hate to go ready hot, because sometimes they don't get the call, and the gas, oil or coal used to get ready is wasted money down the drain. Actually, it takes nearly the same amount of energy to keep the system ready hot as it does to produce money-making electricity, so idling is not a good option.

Unknown to George was the damage to the E-R-Mag Labs base after he and others had worked to have every generator under his command at ready hot a few days ago when a new device was to be tested. Whatever it was had taken the load, then faulted off-line a few seconds later. The Federal Government at E-R-Mag Labs Base was still going to get the bill for all the preparation, nearly $100 K.

Now he was watching over a normal evening where the full air conditioning load of Summer was still a month or so away. The grid was humming along well within the needs of those 36+ million little electric meters stuck on everyone's wall.

So, here at Jim Georges' switching yard in the desert Northwest of Albuquerque, 42 miles into the desert, a number of tasks were routinely and mostly automatically handled. Power arriving or passing through the station was 'conditioned' that is the phase angles were corrected from the lead and lag introduced by the lines length which added inductance. The loads, or the users of the electricity, caused "reflected power" which needed to be cancelled. Large capacitors and selectable inductors countered this and returned each phase of a three-line circuit to its proper 120-degree relationship with the other two phases. Voltage was corrected by passing the power through a device called an auto-former, a transformer able to change its internal ratio of input to output to manipulate voltage.

Of course, there were rows and rows of switchgear, circuit breakers, and on top, lightening arrestors. Large copper bars called buss bars sitting on porcelain insulators connected the entire matrix together on a massive framework of galvanized angle iron, 100 feet tall in places. Lastly, a network of sensors and control wiring that collected the actual state of the power coming to, being manipulated in, and going out of the High Mesa AmeriSouth Power Complex. This matrix of sensors fed the collected information to George's flat panel touch screens, and up a tower to a just installed micro-wave link to the other far-flung members of the grid.

Forty-four separate rows of steel towers marched across the southwest, converging on the 110-acre complex. All the high voltage lines and the current they carried required a great deal of physical spacing between the various components. Once they terminated from copper or aluminum wires the individual circuits and entered the world of buss-bars, and the hundreds of devices in the power switching station, where on the evening shift, 7 days a week, 5 of which were Georges. In the yard the 60 cycle hum was ever present, and the faint scent of ozone was always detectable if the air was still.

These forty-four rows of towers came into or went from this location, most with three - 250,000-volt three phase circuits, or if one looked at the tower, nine wires (some 2 or 3 wires on each insulator) and a few top wires to collect and dissipate static electricity and try to keep lightening from hitting the actual electric carrying wires. A third of the towers were the 150,000-volt feeders going to local (if 150 miles' radius is considered local) destinations. He could, at the request of the suppliers of, or customers needing power, switch and route the intangible, invisible yet in many ways the actual real life's blood of modern society... electric power. Two of the tower soldier columns brought 950,000 Volt DC lines from the new solar and wind farms as far away as the Columbia river Gorge in Oregon, a new addition in 2005. Some construction equipment and crews were beginning work on another DC connector, rows of tower foundations being drilled into the desert sand and rock stretched into the distance to the East. The DC to AC inverter cabinets had just been upgraded to still experimental IGBT -insulated gate bi-polar transistor components, which decreased their size by 2/3, while increasing efficiency to 93%.

George's world was safe, double fences topped with razor wire, paid security in between with a 'guard dog' named Fang, who could knock a man down and kill without mercy, well, actually it might take a while, twenty minutes by licking him until he laughed himself to death. The guard staff drifted around the 1-mile perimeter approximately every hour, most of the time in a battery powered golf cart, a few preferring to walk if the weather was nice.

The guards, armed with Tazer guns, which so far only had only seen action in rendering Towanda Wilson down on the floor, screaming insults at her shift relief who had accidentally discharged the weapon directly into the left cheek of her ample ass as she was bending over to retrieve a candy bar from the guard shack vending machine. The amplitude of her ass exceeding the limits of the amplitude of the Tazer, as she bounded up, pulled out the darts and nearly choked the offending relief guard with the wires.

9-11 terrorists had not thought of these stations, but Homeland Security had, and mandated these top notch, if double digit IQ, rent-a-cops.

George had spent too long, years in fact, in the chair watching his monitors, and some settling was apparent in his pear shape. Balding and graying, he still had a sparkle in blue eyes set wide apart on a pear-shaped head circled with a ring of dark to light grey hair, the bald spot, routinely concealed under a variety of hats which had the distinction of being a baseball cap advertising football franchises.

A failed attempt to look younger by growing a goatee colored brown with beard dye instead gave Mr. George a silly neither young beast or old fowl appearance. His small triangle of nose presided over a non-descript face, thin lips nearly devoid of color. He wore a crisp but worn yellowing white shirt and red tie, darkened at the knot from countless loosening when the sun and co-workers left and tightening when the sun came up, getting ready for leaving work. Different white-wash-yellowing shirt, same tie, every day. It was loose now, top button of the shirt open, a sprig of grey hair over the top of the faded white tee shirt, moving toward matching yellow of the outer shirt. Worn blue Dockers held with a worn tooled western belt, now on the end hole and missing the loop, allowing the end of the belt to stand straight out, like Dilbert's tie, only lower. White socks concealed in tan Wellington work boots completed the man.

A bag of ravaged Cool Ranch Doritos sat beside the chair like an old cat, waiting for a hand to drop and provide attention. A diet root-beer teetered on the edge of the desk.

Ninety-nine miles away Andrew's clock went to 0 hours – 0 minutes.

George heard a rattle overhead, he'd heard this noise before, the wind moving the guy wires in their restrained towers and insulators. He dropped his feet to the floor from the desktop with a cowboy Wellington boot 'thump', stood shuffled back to where he'd just left and looked out the window, expecting dust and papers to be moving by in the expected wind. Damned, he was tired, and felt heavy, too.

No wind. A beep drew his eyes from the window, a monitor on the three circuit Hoover Dam feed. The sensors were reporting and showing on the flat panel display a current drain that was at a rate of increase outside of normal. Another beep, the 150K outgoing feed to Albuquerque South was dropping in voltage, now down to an astounding 89K volts, and still dropping. As he reached for the auto-former controls to manually boost the voltage, two more lines went into low voltage conditions, and the current from the incoming feeds was rising fast to compensate. Ohms law, in a Dollar Store flash-light or the United States power grid works the same. The DC super line's voltages also were dropping like a lead balloon. He knew automatic breakers would begin their opening sequence in seconds.

Fifty meters in front of the control house the first set of motorized breakers opened, then the ones on the next lines started their disconnect sequence. The bright blue-green arcs of the open-air disconnects lit the night, but, unlike their designed operation, which was to stretch and extinguish the arc, the man-made lightning bolt just continued, growing longer and wider. The excessive current, a hundred times what was expected kept the plasma of the arc from breaking, and something seemed to be pulling at the plasma arc upward, so they looked like a classic upward spike in a graph paper line.

Impossible! The disconnects had to successfully open and stop the current flow...! And fast! More tried to disconnect, more streams of lightening that did not stop. Flash balls on top of the breakers, the spheres where the arc should have concentrated and stopped, began to melt, sprays of luminescent molten copper flew in all directions, surrounded by the lightening, now bright almost white/green from vaporizing copper.

A shape, Fang the dog was racing flat out across the gravel path toward George.

The wall of the control house in front of George was shimmering, vibrating, or was it the chaos outside? Then it became as clear as the glass window he was looking through, he turned, the rest of the room was 'normal'. He stumbled, heavy, like he was made of lead. As he turned back to the window from the control panels, everything from a distance of six inches from his toes disappeared, including the little erection like end of his tooled leather cowboy belt. The BOOM and concussion that followed knocked him flat on his ass as he skidded across the floor. The Doritos, whacked by his arm as he passed the chair, erupted in a snowstorm of never to melt triangle chip snowflakes.

George scrambled to his feet, then looked out at the now open front of his control room.

In the moonlight he could see a flat rough circle at least 150 meters across, completely empty. Well over two-thirds of the sub-station/switching yard was simply gone. A few wires gave tired sparks where they had landed, then stopped even that. As he stood there, he noticed the complete and total silence. He then noticed how dark it was, not just because the moonlight was the only light, but the complete horizon including over toward Albuquerque to the South, as well.

He stepped out and looked in all directions. There was no artificial light anywhere, and he could see a very long distance.

John Milton was looking out the window from seat 2A, of an American 737-300 First Class seat. He had just taken off from Albuquerque Sunport, on the way back to DC. No time for bullshit geeks playing with lights in the desert, time to schmooze with the big guys back inside the Beltway. Ahh yes the life of a top bureaucrat inside the DC Beltway, his booze, coke and hookers were waiting.

As he took in the lights that made any city beautiful from the air at night, they vanished.

A cloud? No, he could see a drizzle of auto headlights. What the hell? He waved for the Flight Attendant, who answered a 'bing' from the cockpit and was on the intercom phone with the pilot. She ignored him. He unbuckled his belt, and began to stand, she looked at him and said in a strong voice devoid of any airline cheer. "Sit down and buckle your belt sir, now!"

He did so.

CHAPTER 17

Got Power?

The people in the E-R-Mag Labs conference room instinctively looked up at the ceiling lights as they blinked, shuttered and came back to full power. All knew that the countdown clock had told the truth, but what and where had the next hit happened? Trying to get back to their work, Jeffries's cell phone went off. It was Jaylee calling from a police chopper 3,000 feet over Albuquerque. He, Rand and Bart were assigned to try to determine where, and how big the next event was, and video the whole thing from the air. Peg had a camera woman on board, but no reporter was allowed because of the weight restrictions on the aircraft. They had been well to the West of the city, and the helicopter was pointed back into town. They had seen a flash of light to the Northeast, then…nothing.

Jeffries poked a small cable into the side of the phone, then speaking toward the triangle speaker on the table, "Go ahead Jay, you're on the speaker phone."

Jaylee said, "Well, Doc, I sure hope Albuquerque is down there someplace, all I can see is a few auto headlights. I've asked the pilot to climb higher, but he said air traffic is holding everything at their present location and/or heading, we're hovering over the middle of what I think is downtown. It's completely dark as far as we can see in all directions, the spotlight won't reach the ground from this high, and the co-pilot says his night vision goggles are just mass of bright green dots. The batteries in this thing all but died, but thank God came back."

"The lights blinked here on base, I guess we're on generator power."

"Wait a second…Okay, ATC says they lost their mid-range radar, and are trying to tie into Kirkland, ATC, wait… Okay we can climb to 5,000 but have to stay where we are."

The pilot began a slow hundred-meter circle to climb the 2,000 feet for the 5K ceiling.

"Jay, can you see any lights at all other than the vehicles? Ask the pilot how far away you should be able to see."

A few moments later Jaylee responded, "We just got to 5,000 feet, so he says we can see at least 100 miles North, South and West, the mountains are to the East, I still can only see vehicles, a few lights from Kirkland, and the jackrabbit runway lights from Sunport. There's a building with a few lights on it, the pilot says it's the hospital."

"Jay, as soon as you can, get permission to go down to searchlight height and see if you can find the place where it happened." Everyone knew what 'it' was.

"Roger, will advise, out."

Jefferies disconnected the phone, and placed it back on his belt.

Maurine spoke to the media technician, who nodded, then tapped in some keys, soon they heard the voice of an air Traffic Controller come over the ceiling speakers. The woman, in cool practiced precision was questioning pilots in her slice of the sky for visuals of the various towns and cities her radar showed they were flying over. Maurine was at the pull-down map circling the towns reported as dark as the various aircraft reported in. The technician switched to the frequency of other controllers looking out in the other directions. All the ATC people were trying to get an idea of how big an area the blackout had affected. The young man on the E-R-Mag Labs media console computer, chewing and popping gum furiously, poking glasses back up his nose into position every 3 seconds was quite good, no one had suggested he canvas the other ATC frequencies.

Within a half-hour the extent of the blackout was identified, it was the largest in terms of land area in U.S. history, eleven States and a quarter of the country in terms of land area effected.

High-definition cameras and the support crew at the X-pole location reported a blinding stream of energy that had arched from the Northeast across the sky and into the hole in the mountain. The video recorded information was a complete whiteout.

Over the night the Police helicopter crew did not find the place where the flash had happened, the further out into the desert they went, the more the place looked the same.

By daylight a number of feeders had been re-established, and the area of no electric service was East of Abilene, South into Mexico, West to well into Phoenix, and North to Pueblo. A big slice of the Southwest at night was looking like North Korea normally does if viewed from a satellite.

The sad part was that the outages could last several months. A number of the generating stations scattered throughout the southwest had failed when the station vanished. All forty-four lines had registered an instantaneous and dead short circuit. The reflected wave back to the generating stations simply stopped the generators dead. Nearly all had damage, two just South of Phoenix on I-10 had twisted so quickly they had ripped out of the floor of the generator room and literally destroyed the plant. Fourteen workers were killed in the high-pressure steam explosion and the pure hydrogen atmospheres bursting and igniting from the generator enclosures which followed.

Explaining to the others in the room, Kough said, "You have to realize a modern generator has a rotor weighing 10 to 30 tons, it has to precisely rotate at 1,800 or 3,600 RPM's, and it's directly connected to a steam turbine with steam going through at over 1,200 pounds of pressure, at 1,000 plus degrees. The area inside the generator which is solid connected to the turbine is flooded with pure hydrogen so there are no valence electrons available to begin an arc. Imagine what happens if that stops instantly! A short circuit in New York in the 70's caused all seven generators at Niagara Falls to spin their bearings. That was the biggest power outage before this one, remember? Most of the Northeast was dark for well over 14 hours, and, remember all the babies born nine months later?"

There was not a fully functioning generating station that was connected to the western grid that had not suffered some damage. All of the power conditioning apparatus was destroyed or severely damaged. Components are not available from the new Amazon Prime and would need to be imported, many built from scratch, months at least some of the larger transformers and auto-formers a year to 18 months to build and another six months to transport and install. The western sections of the power grid would not be up to previous capacity for months at the best, years at the worst.

In the desert, daylight also presented the missing switching sub-station to the helicopter occupants. The Police chopper had re-fueled twice, and now was idling beside a bizarre disk cut out of the wiring, framework and fence of the station. Jay was walking around the circle with a camcorder, the TV camera woman had been dropped off earlier during a fuel stop.

James George, dazed and confused, wandered around the scorched disk of bare earth. Cell phone in hand. Every few steps he would pull the phone up, look at the blank screen, and push some buttons. Bart walked up to him. "Give up buddy, if you were here when this happened, the phone battery is shot."

George looked at Bart, "You know what happened here? Then you know there's a hell of a lot of people without power. What DID happen here?"

Bart looked around, "I don't wanna be a wise ass, but all I, or anyone for that matter, can say is that we don't know what happened, but it's happened before, and it happened here, again." He pointed around the clearing.

He walked away from the bewildered man, back to where Jaylee and Rand were standing.

Rand said, "Well, this one is the biggest yet, and I guess we now can speculate on what causes the discharges to pick a particular location. It's obvious this place had the biggest energy footprint. The X-pole apparently can't project anywhere it wants, it apparently gets energy, stores it somehow, then can project further for its next energy fix."

Bart looked at the wires laying on the sand. From the air the place looked like a strange spider web, with the rows of electric line towers converging on the hole in the desert, the imaginary spider being the grey circle of gravel in the center of the web, he said, "Maybe we actually got lucky this time, I mean Jay says there's no other place within a thousand miles with this much energy either in or moving through its location."

Rand considered this, "I hope you're right Bart, I've got Kough on trying to figure why the college, and the intersection." Referring to the other event locations. She sorts of stumbled, her face took on a look of something close to terror. She then felt the hair on her neck rise as a thought came into her mind. She nearly shouted to Jaylee, "Jay! Bart! Get back in the chopper, we need to go…now!"

Soon they were in the twin engine Euro-copter SA365N1 Dauphin and were heading back to Kirkland and E-R-Mag Labs on Sandia Base. She was on the phone with Jefferies, but speaking in soft tones, her hand protecting the phone. The cell system would be failing in a day or so as the back-up power supplies died, but for now they were still up and working.

She punched off her phone. "I know where the next strike will be! It may be the one that connects the dark and ordinary energy…it may be the end."

CHAPTER 18

Okay, it's over!

A few minutes after landing, into the Crown Vic and over to the lab building, then running into the meeting room, the team was looking at the pull-down map. The plots of the events had been placed on the map with round red post-it-note dots. Jefferies walked to the center of the table, leaned in and pushed the button on a small round plastic device, a soft hiss came up. He looked around the room, "For anyone not familiar with this, it's a 'white noise generator' and should keep anyone outside the room from listening in. You may have noticed the AP at the door. Our 'friend,' John Milton is still in Washington, D.C. and hopefully stays there…I will remind you all that we are discussing Top Secret information, and not to speak about any of this outside of here, or with anyone not authorized to hear it. Doctor Rand, please present your hypothesis." He looked around the room again as he walked the three steps back to the head of the table seat, and sat down.

Rand, normally the picture of composure, looked like she was made of marble, either that or a vampire had drained a good bit of her blood. She pushed her glasses higher on her nose with a manicured finger. "Like Doctor Peters, and his dark-energy theory, I hope I'm wrong. We are now working on the proposition that this anomaly is an attempt of nature to achieve a balance of dark energy and the energy we are accustomed to, the Earth's magnetic and our electrical energy. If this is the case, then the disappearance of the substation only partially explains the event. It's true it was the biggest concentration of electrical energy available. I need to qualify that. Energy commercially available." She looked at Jefferies, who nodded.

"There is another source, actually several sources of energy, and some of it we don't really have a functional understanding as to what they are and how they operate, and exactly what they do. The best guesses revolved around propulsion systems of some kind, but that was never verified. Given the geometric progression of the sequence of events, I think I can include these and other energy sources near those items as a logical 'target' of the X-pole."

"You know we provide assistance to a variety of Government operations in the area of physics, chemistry and atomic sciences. In conjunction with this support, we also support some…activities… at Groom Lake." Heads snapped up, then brows wrinkled. Some around the room had mouths moving silently. Prayers?

Bart leaned over to Jaylee and whispered, "Groom Lake? What the fuck is Groom Lake?"

Jaylee's eyes were open to circles. "Bart, that's government speak for Area 51!"

Rand continued, "I've worked on several of the items over there, but I'd like to turn the rest of the presentation of the thesis to Doctor Sanchez." She motioned to one of the men who had been at all the meetings, and had postulated the dark energy Tesla information.

Sanchez, the Latino complexioned man who appeared to be in his late 50's stood, it was obvious he was worried. Mostly grey hair kept slightly long, half over his ears. His round ruddy face was now strained, glasses free, he held himself erect, and appeared to be in great physical condition. As before he had the typical lab coat over a light blue polo shirt, with a few pens and pencils in the left front pocket, black Wrangler Jeans and dark brown plain cowboy boots. His slightly accented English - Ricardo Montauban announcing Fantasy Island? There was a difference, and it showed, he was scared.

"Thank you, Doctor Rand. Doctor Jefferies has told me that everyone here has either the proper clearances or the need to know." He looked to Jefferies who nodded. "Some years ago a team of people from here and Groom Lake were assembled to examine nine different power generators, or that's what we called them. One from here, E-R-Mag Labs Base, two spirited out of the Soviet Union, five from a place and source we were not given, and one, the most interesting in that it was made from Mason jars, hearing aid batteries and what was termed "magic wire", from a man's garage in Waycross Georgia."

In spite of the seriousness of the moment, a few giggles permeated the quiet.

"Let me discuss one of the five that we were presented from parts unknown. As we began to reverse engineer that one, we found a feature that we never figured out. Although different in size and physical appearance, most of the them would produce a magnetic field so strong that when activated, they would pull metal towards them, iron at ballistic speeds, but other metals as well. Two of the support people were injured from screws and nails pulled from the walls and ceiling that became shrapnel when we activated the second unit. Yes, all metals. While not as magnetically as responsive as iron, all metals react to a strong magnetic field, that's how the metal detectors in Airports and coin acceptors in vending machines work."

"Anyway, more germane to this discussion is unit number three. We found what we thought were connections for wires or power buss connections, and hooked some test leads, we found instantly all power from the meters, oscilloscopes and various other test instruments would disappear. Even 1,000 meg ohms of insulation on the Texas Instruments stuff was not enough to keep them isolated. Then it happened. One of the guys suggested we hook it to one of our hi-amperage power supplies."

"We no sooner touched the leads to the contact points, which were the size of a pencil eraser, than the entire facility was blacked out. The point is that energy went in, but where? The thing was the size of a pony beer keg, less than a meter tall. No heat was produced, and the estimated 14,000 to 18,000 amps that went through the contact should have melted everything in the room, we were expecting something like striking an arc with a welding rod. Not even a flash, the leads got hot, but not the connections on the 'beer keg.' Not even a spark. We had apparently kick-started the thing. Later we found it also didn't matter what form the energy was presented, if you put something hot near the connector points, it got cold. If you got a light bulb near them the light got dark, it did not go out, I mean there was still amperage being used, but the bulb just ceased to produce photons. People standing near the thing would be okay, but if got near the lead connectors, would get tired, one even collapsed and slept for fourteen hours when pulled away."

"A complete scan of the 'sponge' as it was termed showed rare stuff was also being attracted. Quarks, what appeared to be solar wind particles, naturally occurring x-rays, gamma rays and the like. After the blackout on the base, there was a very bright aurora borealis for several nights, but rather than flickering across the night sky, it seemed to be moving downward. In short, some in the group felt we had a container holding a black hole." Sanchez paused, then ran his hand over his face, as with an imaginary wash-cloth.

"Finally, we were able to get energy back out. We were not exactly sure how, well we know what we did, but not what happened, because one of the scientists decided to use a cryogenically cooled probe, a length of nickel cooled to near absolute zero, to short circuit the terminals on the device. As you know cryogenically cooling a conductor, and for some still unknown reason, nickel works best, will allow it to theoretically carry infinite current, or power."

"Apparently it did. The entire building was destroyed when a magnetic pulse so strong… well it pulled in the roof beams, exterior steel wall sheathing, a 5 ton 6X6 Army truck and three automobiles. Reinforcing rods were pulled right out of the concrete floor. An abandoned railroad track alongside the building was bent and pulled apart. Two people were killed, a husband-and-wife team sent on loan from here, the Longfeathers. They were close and dear friends." He looked down.

Bart looked at Jay remembering the story of Ivey's parents dying. Jay saw Bart looking at him and nodded, then went back to staring at the floor.

"The decision was made not to try to 're-charge' the device after it was removed, undamaged, I might add, from the wreckage of the building. The similarities of the X- pole and the sponge are frightening. How this might help us is up for discussion. The point is, and I agree with Doctor Rand, we do think it might be a source of energy for attracting a hit from the X-pole. Imagine what would happen if all the stored energy in the X-pole, if it is indeed being stored, was focused into that sponge? A nuclear bomb would be a firecracker in comparison."

Sanchez sat down.

Discussions continued, no good information coming forth.

Jefferies cell phone went off, only one side of the conversation was heard, and he made no effort to keep it private, "Mister Milton, what can I do for you?... I don't care what you think.... I don't give a fuck what he thinks either....no sir you may not use our portion of Kirkland as a base of your operations, I will order my air force Police to shoot anyone trying to appropriate this facility or at least my part of it. Where?... Well, I suggest you use the big open circle of what you think was movie magic where the switching sub-station used to be... No, Milton, that's a human physical impossibility, but in your case, having your head up your ass may make me re-think what's physically possible... I'd like to try to educate you on these events, but I have to try to stop the end of the god-damned world...good by sir." He stabbed the disconnect button on his phone, tossed it onto the table where it spun to a stop, shook his head and returned to his stack of paper.

Bart and Jaylee were in the corner, talking to Rand. Bart spoke, "Doctor Rand, what if we could re-charge the thing Sanchez was talking about, I dunno, figure how to charge it backwards to the

X-pole, then throw it into the hole on the mountain, maybe they would cancel each other out."

Rand looked at the balding, obviously tired, sad-eyed detective, "Bart, are you sure you don't have an advanced degree from someplace? That's a brilliant idea!" She literally ran from the men, caught Jefferies by the sleeve, pulled him around in his chair, where he was reading a sheet of paper, moving the finished document to one of three stacks in front of him, the turning chair stopped his reaching to select another paper from a pile on the table in front of him. She started talking, a hand shot out with a finger pointed to Bart, then returned back to Jeffries's shoulder.

Jaylee looked at his friend, "Bud, you prove everyday what I've always said, someplace, a homicide detective will save the world, if they ever listen to him."

Bart grinned, "I need more coffee." Off down the hall they walked.

CHAPTER 19

What the Hell is THAT?

It was well after dark when the boom and flash of light faded, this one the biggest and brightest of any the desert survivors had seen. The noise seemed to be a full minute of rolling thunder. In the campsite where they had just left a few hours earlier, a massive tangle of metal, wiring and large dark shapes had appeared. The mess of twisted galvanized iron creaked and groaned as it settled into the sand.

Eleven-year-old Chris said, "What in the fuck is that!"

Arthur and Gus looked at the boy, who realized what he'd said. "Sorry, I mean what the hell is that."

The women hugged each other in a circle a few feet away.

The Honda was running providing lights for the new campsite work, Art turned the car toward the new arrival, drove ½ way to it, got out. He walked cautiously toward the metal. He noticed the insulators and transformers. He called back "I think it's a power sub-station. Well, most of one anyway."

Gus looked at Chris, "Poopies, I was hoping for a McDonalds."

Mort said, "I was hoping for a topless bar, complete with beer coolers."

A dark shape came from the metal, not human, nearly crawling on the sand. Art jumped back in the car, and yelled, "Notch an arrow, we got something here, I don't know what it is!"

Mort had a bow and arrow at the ready, he was trotting fifty yards to the car.

A shell-shocked German Sheppard crawled toward the car lights, turned and sat, looking back at the wreckage of the sub-station. Art opened the door a crack, "Come here Boy, common." The dog looked at Art, and shuffled toward him, head and tail low, tail slowly wagging. Art held a hand out, the dog sniffed it, and then licked it.

"Well, looks like we have a guard dog." Mort returned the arrow to the quiver and put the bow across his back.

He mumbled to Art as he met the dog, scratching his head behind the pointed ears. "And another friggin' mouth to feed."

Back at the campsite, Art said, "I don't know how you did it, but you saved our lives, all of us. If we had been where that mess landed...you're a remarkable man, Mort.

Gus nodded and patted Mort's back. "Like Art said a few hours ago, we're lucky to have you here."

Mort looked uncomfortable with the heartfelt praise. "Thanks, really, but I'm just an observer of stuff...and people around me. I've always felt most people, especially Americans, are clueless about stuff they should take the time to know about."

"They believe all of what the right-wing nuts say, or drink the left's cool-aid. They will drive past their turn while discussing hair color with someone on the other end of the cell phone who they will be seeing in three minutes, if they had not missed the turn. They will listen to Michael Moore or Spike Lee, but discount a commission of experts. They will make stupid statements like the attacks on the World Trade Towers were an inside job because steel doesn't burn, and discount the films of the airliners crashing into them. They argue and the towers should have stood, and it was an inside job because I beams were bent, and have no idea what happens to an "I" beam when it gets hot and loses its temper."

"For heaven's sake guys! They will abort babies by the millions and condemn the death penalty. They will either believe everything the President says, or nothing. They are on a diet continuously, but somehow the rear seat of their car gets filled with McDonald and fast-food wrappers. Hell, I heard the other day that the deficit was quadrupled in the 2000 to 2006 timeframe and we have to get out of that problem by spending three times as much. What the hell kind of idiotic logic is that? Pour Gasoline on the fire to try to put it out?"

"People actually listen to the certifiable idiots on that new show, 'The View' and discount what they see with their own eyes, or forego common sense. A wind turbine is renewable energy, but a wind farm in California killed 5,000 birds of prey. 5,000! Show me 100 dead ones and I'll believe you. Where the hell did 5,000 hawks come from in a ten-mile area of mountain in the high desert of California? I guess we all overlooked the 5 million rats that 5000 raptors would eat a year. That's nuts!"

"Freon, kills the precious ozone layer, so we need a new more expensive replacement, but not as good at cooling stuff. How does the heaviest gas man ever made get from down here to the ionosphere? Why doesn't it kill the nasty ozone cars put out as pollution? I guess it just wants to kill us all, I guess Freon molecules are Al Qaeda, or ISIS terrorists and have brains."

"Global warming is going to kill us all because Polar Bears are drowning, but the number of bears is higher than in recorded bear counting history, hell the damned things have killed so many seals, the seals are going on the endangered species list! When I left the modern world a few days ago not one, ONE, of the 440 predictions of the warmists had come true, or even close to true. Shit, isn't it hotter here in this God forsaken sand-box than it will be 8,000 years from now where we left with that charlatan Al Gore and the buffoon John Kerry spouting the end of the world unless we send him money to stop it? By the way, both of them have multi-million dollar houses on the Atlantic shore where they say the ocean will rise and kill us all. Someone's lying to us."

Shaking his head and looking at the ground he continued, "I've listened to people's problems for 30 years as a psychologist, and frankly, here, in this God-forsaken desert, some place in the past, with you people, is the first time anyone, I mean anyone has listened to what I thought, and acted on what I said. Most of my patients, Native Americans, listened, and disregarded damned near everything I advised." He paused, took a breath, "I actually, should be thanking you." He turned and headed for the truck.

Art looked at Gus and Chris, "Ain't life strange?" He had backed the Honda, and followed Mort back to the trailer. Art picked up the dog, and placed him in the back of the vehicle, still in use as the bedroom as the tents were still being erected, due to be finished the next day. All were asleep except for the four men, the SWAT officer still on a cot set up along a trailer wall, and young Chris.

Chris was petting the dog, "Now stay here and let us know if anything comes by." The dog licked his hand.

Sleep was always hard to accomplish in this place. Most of the time it came prodded by shear exhaustion, and when night here was done, and the red sun had brightened the violet sky to the "normal" red-pink, sleep had never delivered the sought after refreshment. Every one of the survivors had that little apprehension that comes from being in a strange place, much less compounded with being in a strange time. There was danger here, the clear implication that something was interested in meat as evidenced by the buried remains being dug up. Then there were the 'shadow shapes' that nearly everyone had seen, the actual danger as yet unseen, clearly seen at least, and by definition, then, unknown. Everyone had an instinctual fear of these others here in the desert, and the fear was ever present. The consensus was that all this stuff appearing from the sky with the flashes of light and tremendous BOOMs was the only reason there had not been more 'direct' contact with whatever life forms were out there.

Then there was the sense of loss. The more continuous lead blanket of loss, laying on everyone's chest like a dentist office x-ray cover. The loss of family and friends. Now several days into this hell or at least this sandy red purgatory, all had the real beginnings of the loss of hope. As the days had continued it was becoming more and more obvious that they were stuck. Stuck here in the past. Stuck in an inhospitable desert. And for some, stuck with little hope. Anyway one looked at it…stuck. When would the connection through the portal, rift or whatever the hell it was, close, leaving them here, with only the food and water that someone had managed to send through?

Here, somewhere, in some unknown time, the 10 sweaty, dirty, stinking survivors of the first recorded time travel lay, praying for rescue, and when none came, just praying for sleep, then when sleep failed, just praying.

Finally, after several hours of looking at the barely visible aluminum and fiberglass ceiling of the trailer, Art did fall asleep. What seemed a few seconds, actually a few hours later, Art was awakened by a low growl, it was the dog. A red half-moon had him silhouetted against the sandy hills in the distance, near the back of the trailer. He was standing, braced near the corner, hackles raised, ears pricked. Tail straight out behind him. The dog was not poised for a jump out of the safety of the trailer, but was taking a defensive posture for sure. In some amazing way he had "adopted" the people in the trailer, and was now their guardian.

A weak voice came from the sand below, "Help me, please…help me."

Art and Gus, also awakened, crawled to the place beside the dog, who had not relaxed his posture. "Who are you?" Art asked.

"S-s-s-Sam, from the exploration party…I'm hurt…God…" His voice trailed away. Art looked out of the trailer, nothing. He called to the man, nothing. Mort had joined them.

Mort said, "I'll climb down and see what's going on." He took one of the knives and tucked it into his belt, then gingerly climbed out, stumbling to one knee as he got his bearings. Before he had the chance to stand, a shape jumped from under the trailer and flattened him. The attacker raised a hand with something in it to strike at Mort, who had grunted something and was trying to roll away. Quicker than the time it took to perceive what was happening, the dog leapt from the back of the trailer, caught the arm of the attacker and took him down and off Mort. Gus and Art were close behind.

Mort was up, knife in hand. The dog was in guard position over the attacker. Art rolled him over, pulled his hands behind him and locked the hand cuffs from the Swat man's gear around the wrists. Why he had been carrying them in his cargo pants pocket for the past three days he really didn't know, but hey. Mort and Art stood him up, then Mort got down on one knee and hugged the dog, who looked like he was actually grinning, tail wagging, kicking up a little cloud of dust.

The women were looking out the back of the trailer. Art said, "Be careful, he may not be alone."

Mary Pert, the Denny's waitress on her way to work when she had 'turned to glass and ended up in hell' as she put it, showed a knife, "Art, give us an update as soon as you figure it out."

"Will do Mary, we're gonna take 'Sam' here over by the Honda where we can shed some light on the subject."

Half-way around the truck, Sam tried to make a run for it, the dog cut him off and brought him down again, he screamed. Art got the dog by the collar and said "Guard." The dog sat, looking intently at Sam. "If you try that again I won't take him off you, do you understand?" Head nod.

In the light, Sam presented a rather scary sight. He was scratched and torn, clothes nearly ripped off. Examination in the light showed bites from the dog, but practically no blood. De-hydration? Some of the cuts and scratches had a pattern. Animal scratches? Then there was the face, a Charles Manson stare from dark circled eyes, a mouth open, a line of white foam from one side, running nearly to his chin.

Suddenly Sam tried to turn to Art, who side stepped his attempt to bite his arm. He hooked a leg and dropped the man to the dirt.

"If you try anything like that again, I'm going to thoroughly whip your ass, that's a god-damned promise, now sit there until we figure what we're going to do with you." Another nod. "This son-of-a-bitch is more than a few fries short of a happy meal." Art said to the other two men, "I don't remember anyone looking as messed up as this sorry assed loser going with the first guys, do you?"

Head shakes no.

Mort, walked back to the trailer, and returned with a bottle of water, unscrewing the top, he moved to give the man some. Art looked at Mort like he had lost his mind, "Jees, Mort, Ya think giving this guy a drink might be a few pegs down from the top priority here?"

Mort shook his head, and extended the water to Sam, who yelled like he had been hit with boiling acid, and rolled away. Mort looked at Art, "He'll be dead in a day or two. I think he's got rabies, or whatever the hell this place has for viruses like that. Hell, in 8,000 years God knows what mutations that virus went through."

Gus said, "Damned, if you're right the dog's infected, he's bitten the guy several times."

Art replied, "He's probably the only one protected, he's got a rabies tag on his collar."

Mort went back to the trailer again, returning with a towel and a bottle of alcohol, he poured some on it, wiped his face and hands, then gave the towel to Art, who rubbed his hands and arms.

Looking up from the towel he was holding, "Okay, Mort, what the hell gave you a clue as to what we had here?"

Mort looked at the man, now lying on his side, sobbing and retching, a thin line of foamy yellow fluid dropping off his chin onto the sand. "If you had been in the desert for three plus days and had returned, wouldn't your first need be water? This guy didn't ask for anything, just help. He didn't even say how he was hurt. I figured something strange was going on, but I tell ya hydrophobia was pretty far down the list, shit, it wasn't even on the page until I saw the foam on his mouth. Those cuts are several days old, the scabs are peeling near the edges. He may have been hurt when he arrived here."

Art looked at the man, "Poor bastard, what could have given it to him? Look at those scratches. They look like a bear or something, four in a row, probably not a cat, and I agree, they're several days old."

Gus said, "Art, you're comparing animals we are used to, heaven knows what's here, now. I mean, other than the grave site, there are no tracks anywhere. I don't think we have any animal worries out here, there's absolutely no reason for animals to come out here, no water, no food, no place to make a home, nest or den."

Art wondered, he had not mentioned the 'grave robbers', better check out that later.

Mort said, "Well, Gus, that was true until we got here. Now there's water, and for carnivores, food."

He looked to the horizon and the faint outline of the mountains, which seemed to glow a dark ruby in the moonlight. "I wonder if it isn't time to leave this place, if there are animals which attacked this guy, then there are animals to be attacked for food. Waiting until there are no more care packages could be dangerous, we might be too short of food and water to make the trip out of here."

"Then there's the fuel in the vehicles, every day we wait here more evaporates, our range decreases."

Mary, the young Mexican girl, and a Native American, Perl, had joined the group. Mary started to go to Sam. "Wait, he may be infectious, we think he's got rabies!" She stopped a few meters from the man.

Perl said, "I say we stay here, they will surely try to rescue us." The young girl had glued herself to Perl's waist, now looking up into her eyes.

With a groan and cry, Sam stiffened in a convulsion, arching his back. The light from the Honda headlights caught him square in the face.

Blood ran from his terrified eyes, and out of the ear on the low side of his head, he relaxed.

He was dead.

CHAPTER 20

The Milton Problem Solution

They didn't have time for this. Not now, and not with a meeting that nearly all felt could not possibly produce anything to help.

Rand had raced home, showered, and was in a crisp pleated blue skirt, cream silk blouse and light weight darker blue silk jacket, low heel blue leather pumps completed the outfit. Jaylee went to Rand and said in a low voice, "Pardon me saying so, but you are a VERY attractive doctor."

She blushed, looking at the 6'6" cop in a well-tailored $500 suit. "Not bad yourself Detective."

Jefferies was in his best dark suit, which still looked like it was hanging on a manikin waiting to be pinned for tailoring. Bart and Jaylee were, well, in dress-up-cop court-day suits, Jaylee pulling it off, Bart looking like an old cop in a dated suit. Kough, Peters and Sanchez were in clean crisp lab coats. The media tech was in a denim shirt and jeans, but they were clean. Andrew looked like his mother had dressed him for the first day of school, obviously new Wal-Mart clothes from head to foot.

Wal-Mart does not sell clothing for 6'10"-165-pound people.

Three places were left open at the head of the table, the end and one chair on either side. A neat summary paper, and water glass was in front of each, the sweating pitcher, which was becoming normal as somehow humidity was now a daily occurrence in the 20 miles around the X-pole, sat on a folded towel in the center.

The door opened, and Rand could see the AP guard at attention, with a crisp salute at his forehead. The rooms occupants stood, as they were informed was custom when the President came into a room. As the salute dropped, in strode John J. Armetich in Dockers, a light gold golf shirt with the Presidential seal, and brown loafers. Behind him was Paul Crain, the head of Homeland Security in a dark $1,000-dollar suit, and last, the Assistant to Crain, John Milton also in a high dollar blue suit. Two men in dark suits, dark copper ties, and ear-buds came in and stationed themselves on either side of the door, several feet away along the wall.

The ever-present Presidential press corps was held well outside the building, near the main gate of the E-R-Mag Labs Base and were straining to get something on the "death ray" roaming the southwest. The lack of any information and the cooperation of the news chick Hippy Peg had left them in absolute fits of speculation that made the

9-11 misinformation look like the kid with chocolate all over his face making up a story where the chip-cookies had disappeared to.

Armetich was already in the Southwest, doing the obligatory fly-over of disaster areas, this visit to E-R-Mag Labs was an afterthought, prompted and lobbied for by the one and only John Milton. The blue and white 747-800 had landed at Kirkland, helicopters from there to the various powerless areas and the scorched place in the desert where the sub-station had been.

The President sat at the end chair, Milton to the left. No hand-shakes, no small talk. Milton was enjoying this – it was going to be an ass-chewing like no one had ever seen, and all at his direction! How good can it get? This friggin' good…that's how!

The President folded his hands in front of him after sliding the summary paper to the side. "I read this document in the chopper over here. Paul says he doesn't believe much of what it contains, and John Milton has been on top of this since…what… it started a few days ago? Since there are still several dozen large cities and a whole lot of real estate without power, I thought I drop in and see if I can arrive at my own conclusions."

Consulting a small card with names, "Doctor Jefferies, please help me understand what we have here. You need to know the back-up generators in many of the airports, hospitals and God knows where else will be running out of fuel within a few days. After that, God knows what will happen. Already dozens dead from the un-air-conditioned heat." The tone was congenial, but the posture and facial expressions of the men were not. They were clearly skeptical, as stated based upon Milton's reports.

Jefferies stood, obviously nervous, but other than a glistening brow, seemed to have a handle on his nerves, he proceeded. "Mister President, several days ago we activated the ENet antenna. As stated in the briefing paper, ENet was the long sought after global communication link that would not rely on satellites for the military communication networks operation, satellites which in hostilities are vulnerable to enemy destruction. The antenna took the charge, but then simply ran away, reflected power and any controlled frequency went through the roof, numbers we couldn't even measure, the transmitter, and the power supplies here on the base literally blew up. Then, suddenly, the antenna seemed to die. We found out an incident involving a large tree and two teenagers simply disappearing, happened at the same instant the antenna field collapsed."

Milton was smirking, shaking his head.

"Soon we saw power returning to the antenna, even though we had not connected any power source to it, and had in fact isolated all wires to the antenna with the exception of sensor leads left so we could monitor what was happening in the antenna array. About 26.5 hours later, the intersection, automobiles, and some estimated twenty people, again as described in the summary, simply vanished. Later that day, actually in the evening, before it could recharge and discharged again, we tried to destroy the antenna with all the ordinance we could get on the aircraft assigned and stationed here on Kirkland. The explosives only added energy to whatever we have out there, 2 aircraft were destroyed, and 7 Airforce people died, those being the crew of the C130 noted in the briefing papers. Then 21.4 hours later the incident at the Native American Community College happened, in that incident, quite by accident, we got video from wherever the corner of the building and a SWAT officer were sent, and yes, Mr. President, sent, not blown to bits. And 30.6 hours later the Sub-station switch yard vanished, all seeming to try to align the discharges to midnight Sandia Base Labs time, which is G+9. That's where we are now." He looked at Rand, "Doctor Rand will brief you on the simultaneous events which were happening at the antenna, located on Sandia Mountain."

Rand stood, faced the end of the table, "Mister President," then nodded to the media tech, who illuminated the end wall screen, "At the time of the intersection and college incidents, we had an idea something was happening at the antenna location, but not what eventually took place." She took him through the film of the C-130 and the bombing, then the helicopter being pulled back into the X pole. "The events at the antenna site were still unknown to us. We knew of some connection, but not the symbiotic nature of their relationship."

Milton said, "Well there it is, you people really screwed up, big time. You don't even have the sense to try to blame it on someone else!" The President looked at him, obviously not amused. Milton quickly clipped his comments, then quickly looked down at the summary sheet.

Rand continued, "Mister Milton, in order to admit to a mistake, one must have the definition of what was done, so that it can be defined as what that mistake was. We do not have that definition, and you have been considerably less than no help. If there was a mistake made here, it's because there are physics in play that have never been seen before, at least on this planet in recorded time. Furthermore, there are now over 1,250 of the best minds in the United States working on this phenomenon, so far with little to report."

Milton said, "1,250! Why haven't I heard about this? Why haven't I been included in this?"

With a dead straight face Rand responded, "Because, Mister Milton, as I said, this problem needs the best minds." She looked back at her papers, then to the screen.

It clearly looked like he didn't want to, but the President smiled, but cut it short. "Doctor Rand, is the antenna 're-charging' as we speak? If so, when do we expect the next discharge or whatever you call it?"

Milton's face was red, sheer anger, he fidgeted in his chair, looking around. Jaylee began watching him closely. He noticed the Secret Service agent on the side of the door closest to Milton had slowly moved along the wall, closer to Milton. Apparently he had noticed the body language as well. Jaylee and the agent locked eyes, Jaylee a slight head shake toward Milton, the agent a slight head bob back. The man's arms were straight at his sides, not in a natural posture. Milton knew everyone in the room was laughing at him, if even to themselves. He had kissed too much ass for too long to get to the number three slot at Homeland, too much to sit and be laughed at by a bunch of pansy assed geeks. He was pissed that his hooker/coke weekend was cut short by this nonsense and was still nearly shitfaced from the coming down process, and a few shots of Hennessy on Air Force 1, and yes, a mental break was pressing at his psyche.

Rand continues, "The short answer is yes, but a little more information is required. We think the incidents are related to electromagnetic energy available at the various locations where the incidents took place. The switching sub-station being the best example of this hypothesis. The events took place in roughly a North - South path in an approximate alignment with the earth's magnetic flux lines. With the last event hitting the sub-station, all the available high energy sources available within a distance of several hundred miles have been exhausted, we're hopeful the next discharge will be put off."

She stopped, looked around the room, then focused back on the President. "There is a place we think the next event may take place, and that's Area 51, where, as you may be aware, Mister President, there are some 'interesting' power supplies, housed and being experimented upon at that location. We have contacted our fellow scientists there, and they are disbursing the ones that can be moved as we speak, along a direct East-West axis to the X-pole."

"That said, if there is no place for it to discharge, we frankly do not know what will happen."

The President looked at Jefferies, "What about the cyclotron at 51? That thing can't be moved, isn't it powered by an atomic pile reactor? How about all that nuclear material stored in Yucca Mountain? Is there any chance that might be a source of energy for this thing?"

Jefferies looked surprised at these statements. "Good points all Mister President, we had the people at the cyclotron drop the rods, the pile is cooling, and should be dormant in a few hours. We have no data on which to calculate the spent material in Yucca as storage has just started there, and then only for testing purposes. We just don't know what kind of energy, what limitations on the kind of energy that's being hoarded in the X-pole, I wish I could give you some concrete information, but…"

Milton exploded, "That's bullshit, it's all bullshit! This is a money and power grab, done by amateurs willing to take risks way out of their league! Mister President, they need to be stopped and stopped now!"

Bart stood, one of the men near the door moved a step, the President waved him still. Bart pointed at the screen where the faintly glowing hole was presented from a live feed camera on the X pole, "Mister President, I'm a police Lieutenant detective 1st class, and I have been witness to each and every one of the events presented in the briefing, with the exception of the first one, the tree. I don't know what happened, but I do know these people have done everything in their power to track, limit and stop this thing."

"You should know there are a hell of a lot of these PhDs who think this thing might run away and end it all. Some connection of known electrical and 'dark energy'. Milton here, has done everything to shut them down, and absolutely nothing to help. If we have any chance here, he's got to go!"

Milton started to stand, the President pointed to his seat, and he collapsed back into it. "Detective, I have a Masters in applied physics from Cal. Tech. So I can appreciate their concern. Doctor Jefferies, is the detective accurate in his comment?"

Jefferies dropped his notes to the table, "Yes sir. He is, the 'dark energy' hypothesis is just a working one but, unfortunately, it looks like it has some merit. Our problem is we are working completely from theoretical models of this energy, with no units of measure to populate the formulae, more X's than the Boolean calculations can work or manipulate."

"Bart, and his partner, Detective Jaylee Washington, next to him, have been a big help, that's why they are here with us. They have been able to get some resources we haven't had the time or connections to get. Milton here, has stopped any support from the Government, our calls for even a helicopter go unanswered." Jefferies, obviously irritated, stuck a finger in his collar and tried to create some space, finally he loosened his tie, and popped the top button on his white starched shirt.

Looking up at Andrew's clock, which read 13 hours 13 minutes, Armetich said, "Is that the clock tied to the re-charge of the antenna?" Head nod from Jefferies, wheeling to his right, "Mister Milton, you're excused, your lack of understanding on this matter, and the deficiencies in your reporting are inexcusable." Then to the homeland chief, "Paul, we better get ready for something like a small asteroid hitting. I don't know what will happen if those energy masses connect, but based on the past few days, it's not going to be pretty."

Milton was still sitting, shell shocked, looking around like a caged animal. "They're all laughing at me, all those bastards are laughing at me!" he thought. The President pointed to the man on the left side of the door, who had been getting closer too Milton and made a little gesture with his fingers toward him. The man walked to Milton, who shook his hand off his shoulder, started to object. Wrong move. A strong nerve pinch on the clavicle had him collapsing toward the floor, the man scooped him up under the armpits and, with what seemed no effort at all, walked him on tip-toed ox blood wingtips to the door, wiggling and waving his arms, squeaking like a compressed rubber dog toy.

At the door, Milton reached for the door jam, kicked up a leg and placed his shoe on the other side of the frame, he then shoved the Secret Service agent aside, the man cracked his head hard on the steel edge of the door frame, releasing Milton. Hearing the commotion, the Air Force guard rounded on the men and stumbled on their tangled legs and feet, Milton grabbed the AP's 9mm Beretta, ripping it out of his holster, and shouted what seemed to be something about everyone losing their minds. The arm with the pistol wheeled, toward either Jefferies or the President, as they were nearly in line at the ends of the table, the second agent wheeled and jumped into the line of fire, between the men, wrapping his arms around the President who had begun turning toward the commotion, the agents back to the gun as he pushed the President toward the floor.

Jaylee shot Milton directly between the eyes, the back of his head exploded in a red haze of blood and tissue. Every muscle in his body was energized as the inner-cranial pressure shot up from the hydrostatic pressure of the bullet hitting. His dying brain energized all nerve paths, the .40 cal 480 grain bullet's 400 pounds of energy causing him to fall backwards.

Milton did get off a reflex shot, from the full body seizure pulling all fingers toward a fist, even the one on the trigger. This shot went high as he fell backward to the floor. The 9mm bullet went into a deck of four fluorescent lights over the center of the conference table, taking out 2 tubes and the fixture. Glass and white powder dropped onto the table.

Jay cleared the next round from his custom made Glock 21s' chamber, ejected the magazine and laid his weapon on the table, then raised his hands. The first agent, recovering from the push, kicked the weapon from Milton's twitching hand. With his MP-5 drawn he surveyed the scene as two more agents ran into the room, MP-5s drawn as well. The man protecting the President yelled "Clear, all clear" and released Armetich, who the agent had helped back to his seat and seemed remarkably unshaken.

Another perspective in slow motion. Rand watched with everyone the feckless Milton being led out of the room, suddenly the agent holding his arms hit the door frame with a painful sounding crack of his head, staggered, on the verge of collapse. The second agent started toward the door, then froze for the shortest moment, wheeled and dove headlong for the President. Grabbing him, he wrapped his big arms around Armetich, pushing him toward the floor as a defending BOOM shook the room, Rand pushed Andrew to the floor, as she did she saw Jaylee with a gun pointed at what looked like the President. Another BOOM and the lights over the table exploded in a shower of glass and sparks.

Had Jaylee, the man she was beginning to trust and really like, the first man in a long time that she was thinking she might like to spend some time with, this man she couldn't wait to see outside the nuthouse E-R-Mag Labs had become…had this man just taken a shot at the President of the United States? She was halfway to the floor with Andrew and the others, but stopped. Jay was looking at her, a serious, pensive look on his face. After the second BOOM and glass exploding overhead, she began to turn from Jaylee back to Andrew, but Jaylee was doing something. She then saw him eject a bullet, and remove the magazine from his pistol, place it on the table and raise his hands.

A third perspective. Andrew was looking at his clock, something was wrong but he didn't know what. Rand was next to him. Suddenly, the first woman Doctor he had ever met, the only one who seemed to like him, the woman who always tried to help him was pushing him off his chair! In the middle of a friggin' meeting? What the…BOOM … as he was literally falling off the chair to the floor he was looking at a man clearly outlined in the doorway to the room. A man with a gun - Milton! His face became distorted, and the back of his head was coming apart. The adrenaline coursing through his long thin body had slowed everything to a millisecond by millisecond experience. A gun in his hand flashed…BOOM, some lights over the middle of the table exploded. The man in the door, Milton, was falling backwards from the room. A red cloud was behind him. Andrew knew from a primordial place that cloud was the contents of his head. He saw pinkish shards. Bone? Then he was on the floor. The table blocked his sight.

The room was completely silent except for some tinkling glass still falling. Seconds ticked by… three… four… people panting, and some shuffling sounds. More people under the table? Someone yelling, "Clear, all clear!"

Then someone spoke. Bart said, "Damned Jay! That was a very good shot!"

Jay said, "Asshole shouldn't have called Rand a liar."

Armetich said as he returned to standing from the floor, turning his gaze back to the room from the agents kneeling beside the former John Milton, "Jay is it? Yes, a very good shot, I think I almost felt the bullet go by near my ear. I take it you are the second detective on this thing?"

"Yes Mr. President, I am, and like my partner, I've seen all the chaos this thing has caused."

The President turned his head and said, "Thank you Agent Wilson", to the man brushing glass from the President's shirt, then from his own navy-blue suit. Then to Jay, "Please, sir, put your hands down. Paul, get the hell out from under the table, it's over." Armetich did what leaders do, they lead. "Everyone, please stand and take a break, over there by the wall. The Secret Service people will need photographs and interviews." Then to Wilson, "Mister Wilson, we do not have time for a full- scale thing here, so get it done in ten minutes, clear? We can get follow-up from the FBI people and Air Police here on the base later."

"Aye sir." Wilson replied, obviously an ex-navy man.

Andrew was dazed, and in mild shock, he suddenly grabbed a trashcan and threw up. Rand leaned over and placed a hand on his heaving shoulder, "Andy, it's okay, the detective saved several lives here. Common, we need you."

Andrew looked up, she handed him a paper towel from the stack on the tray by the white board. "Here."

He took it and wiped his face. "Doctor Rand, this sure ain't like a video game, what a mess!" Tears streaked his face.

Everyone in the room had a different reaction, ranging from Andrew's physical sickness to Sanchez and Bart exchanging high fives.

Paul Crain wouldn't come out from under the table, a puddle of water under where he sat. Good thing he was wearing a dark suit.

Another man, very effeminate mannerisms, had entered the room picking his way across the body and blood like a barefoot kid retrieving a ball which had gone over the fence, avoiding the dog shit in the neighbor's yard, the neighbor with the five Great Danes. He was clearly shaken. "Mr. Presi…"

"I'm fine Jerry, you'll get details later, I need to be back in Washington before the time the next 'discharge' takes place, get AF-1 informed and make arrangements. I want to see the leaders of the congress as soon as I land at the White House. Tell them no politics and no bullshit, I want them there. Schedule a press conference for…" He looked at Andrew's clock, now at 12 hours 59 minutes, then to his wristwatch, "8:00 PM EST, got it?"

"Tell the press that there's been an accident, and someone was injured, and Jerry, I need you not to let the press get any more idiot ideas about their 'death ray'. Oh, and for now and awhile nothing about the body you stepped over, Milton. Make it so."

"Yes sir, it will be done."

Secret service people, and an AP Sergeant began short, pointed interviews with the people, as they finished with each, the interviewees went back to work, the FBI could catch up later if they needed to.

The President spoke into his cell phone, slipped it into its holster, stood, walked around the room, and shook hands. Pausing in front of Jaylee. "Detective, you're a credit to lawmen everywhere, thank you so very much."

Jaylee looked sheepish, "Uh-well, thank you sir, it was an honor to have helped your people, your man Wilson is a top-notch agent." Head nod from the President. Wilson turned his head from the interview he was conducting with Andrew, gave Jay a quick nod and a discrete thumbs up. Then, "Mister President, if this thing can be stopped, these people here and in the task force are our best hope."

"Jay, I hope you're correct. I don't think there's much time left to figure this thing out." He shook Bart's hand, the last one in line, saluted the people in the room, and left.

PART 5

Strange Things?

CHAPTER 21

Clocks are no damned good

Evidence began to arrive in E-R-Mag Labs headquarters of some strange events happening sporadically across the United States, and elsewhere. Pilots were reporting their GPS navigation was off, sometimes by several dozen miles. Air Traffic radar was losing targets, which would re-appear seconds later, off course and on a slightly different heading.

The United States Coast Guard reported to NASA, who relayed the information to E-R-Mag Labs that the Atomic clock in Colorado had lost 3.1416 seconds, but that no error could be found in its program. This clock, and 11 others across the USA and its territories were installed as the backbone of the now defunct Loran navigation system, the clocks remain, still in use and still counting the vibrations of Argon atoms, all twelve identical clocks across the globe had experienced the same error, at the same instant.

Nearly everywhere in the country Newscasts, commercials, and network activities were missing their marks and hard breaks by a few seconds. The struggling commercial power people were also suffering with the dropped time issues. The few remaining undamaged power generators were dropping phase, kicking off-line, some shorting disconnects. In each case the whole plant needed to be taken offline, re-synchronized to the network grid and re-connected. This only adding to the already suffering power grid.

The conclusion was un-escapable, to the people at E-R-Mag Labs at least. It was time, the noun, time, the nebulous, unknown and undefined theoretical connecting fabric of time, was shifting.

Jaylee, Bart and Rand were in the cafeteria all three contemplating paper cups of pale brown fluid sold as 'fresh freeze-dried coffee'. Jaylee said, "Doctor, can you explain to me how we can still be here, but time is shifting? I mean why aren't we, I dunno, someplace else, or some of us anyway?"

Rand, sat her cup down, "All I can tell you is that something like this time shift thing has happened many times, pardon the pun, in the past. The early astronauts had very expensive and accurate watches with them. After a few orbits at the high speeds they travel, their clocks registered a few tenths of a second difference, shifted toward lagging behind, or slow. People on the original space station for a month or so are actually several seconds younger than the rest of us. That Russian guy who was in Soyuz for a year is maybe hours younger." She stood, tried the tea button on the machine and got a cup of clear hot water, removing the cup, the powdered tea fluffed onto the cup tray. Un-ruffled, she tossed it into the trash, dropped coins and went for the coffee button, two creams, one sugar, and continued, "I've not read any papers on this phenomenon, but my guess is that physical objects simply are someplace, and the place in time is irrelevant. I suppose the question here is how much of a shift the time stream will tolerate before indeed the object or person does, in fact, disappear." The machine made a perfect cup of coffee.

Bart said, "If I give you money, will you buy me coffee?" Then, "So, those people who disappeared are actually here, just not in the same time-place." Listening to what he had just said, "Man that's messed up! I mean if those astronauts are traveling with us in time, even though the mechanical devices we created to measure that time and other clocks on earth disagree. Like I always told my bosses over the years, clocks, especially time clocks, are meaningless."

Jaylee leaned over and dropped his latest dishwater into the trashcan with a 'thump' of un-definable liquid hitting the bottom of the nearly empty can. "If what the continental plates Andrew was talking about, you know what caused the movement or shift of the Pinal range? If the Pinal's were actually here and having moved over time, then those folks are actually right where the X-pole is located, just shifted in time, anyway, those mountains in the distance were a great way out there, maybe hundred miles, or more, that puts them kind of close to us, doesn't it? I just never figured the whole thing could be manipulated, like we could walk through a waterfall and come out someplace else in time on the other side."

He paused collecting his thoughts, "I've read a guy's postulations, I think his name is Bearden or something like that, he says we have it all wrong, Tesla was close but couldn't explain it. He says that the fabric of reality is all made of energy, all of it and that electricity, light, even gravity and inertia even matter are different forms of this energy. Atoms and molecules are connected and comprised of this energy…look I'm way off on what he says because I'm a basic electronics guy, but it's looking like the energy ideas might be what's going on here." He paused again, watched as his beautiful fantasy reached for Bart's proffered coins.

Rand stood, coins in hand from Bart, pushed the coffee button, "I've heard of Bearden, read some stuff about his earth-quake detection system…I dunno… It's not that easy, of course, I mean the rift was opened with literally all the electromagnetic energy on earth, if you count the magnetic flux that's now in play." She watched the cup for Bart drop to the platform and start filling, sat back down. She played with the left cuff on her blouse with her right hand, Jaylee watched those beautiful, slender fingers undo a button, and put a two-roll cuff to mid arm, then started on the other arm, and damned she smells good, "What has us all stuck is the relationship of energy to time. No one has ever postulated on a direct relationship. We can measure energy, well up until this thing anyway, and we can measure time. But the measurement units, even the names for the units are apples and oranges, like, amperes and volts, hours, seconds and speed, miles-per-hour, light years. Even if what you say, and if Bearden is correct, what unit of measurement do we populate the formula with?"

Bart took another sip, then gave up on the horse piss, and dropped the cup into the trashcan with another ominous 'thud' as it hit the bottom of the empty plus 1 cup of horse piss pail, reaching for the cup Rand had conjured from the machine, the plastic door guarding the cup would not open, a painful pop as he broke a fingernail. "Ouch! Shit! My gut tells me there is a measurement in some unit that is common, and when that's found, all this will make sense." Looking at his watch for the end of the agreed to coffee break, he froze, alarm on his face. "Guys...look at this!"

Rand and Jay jumped to his side. His watch was adding a second, then subtracting one, then adding two. Rand grabbed Jaylee and Bart by the arm. "Let's get the hell back to the conference room!"

Bart pulled his .380 Glock and pointed it at the coffee machine, Jaylee laughed and with his two hands over Bart's gun hand moved it with the pistol slowly back toward the back-belt holster.

A 9-1-1 page to all the team members had them back in the meeting room within five minutes. In the room everyone was watching Andrews clock. Andrew was standing under it, whacked it on the side, nearly sending it off the wall with his hand. Top science still had the universal reaction to something not working, haul off and whack the shit out of it.

Jefferies was worried, real worried. "Jesus, the time-line is coming apart! What do we have here anyway? Any suggestions?"

Sanchez said, "Doctor, we need to know if this is everywhere, or just here, near the friggin' X pole." He grabbed his cell phone and dialed a number, "Hello, Sammy this is Sanchez…Yes, that's why I'm calling, what do you have there…you're losing a second every minute or so, no time being added? Okay…okay, I'll call you later…yes…I promise." Punching the disconnect on the I-phone, "Houston Space flight is…shit you heard."

Rand said, "Anyone know someone in Europe we can call?"

Kough said, "I have some colleagues in Japan, at the earthquake sciences center in Kobe." He pulled a desk phone over, and, reading from a card he had in his wallet punched in a long series of numbers, when someone answered, began to speak in Japanese, then converted to English. "'Karrie San! How goes? Kough here, quick question…yes it has to do with clocks screwing up…yours are okay? Okay, take this number…U.S. country phone code then…" he read the number from the conference room phone, "if your time pieces' start acting up, call me right away…sorry, I honestly don't know, but look for an e-mail from me in a few days with all the details I can get…You too… say hi to Kikee and the kids… bye for now.' They are still good. How the hell can time screw up here and not there? We have a hell of a lot to learn about this time thing."

Quite the understatement.

Jaylee said, "I have my cell phone connected to my HAM radio, I can command my transmitter from the Ham Net Program App, let me call a few people on the net." Soon he had actually joined a discussion world-wide, he placed his cell phone on speaker and plugged it into the conference room teleconference desk phone so all could hear. He spoke, "Emergency...emergency...emergency... KNSB4373...I am speaking from a scientific base in the USA, please give me location and quick description of any time anomaly in your location, over."

Within another few minutes it was confirmed. The flow of time was erratic, and it was nearly worldwide. But not Japan?

Jaylee – "All on the net, I am with people working on the theory and issues discussed on this broadcast, I will give updates if I can, have to sign off for now... KNSB4373 out."

"Okay people," Jefferies stood, "Get back to your computers, if their clocks aren't screwing the run sequences of their programs and get to work. I want some answers, okay – okay, at least best guesses in..." Instinctively he looked at his watch, shook his head, his watch was not reliable. "Be available in about two hours, I'll page you."

Rand walked the short distance to her office, Jaylee and Bart followed, not having anywhere they could think of to go. Rand sat at her terminal and entered her passwords. "Please don't think I'm ignoring you, but right now I'm ignoring you. I have a few things to run through this box here." Jay and Bart nodded.

Jaylee tapped Bart on the shoulder, pointed to his cell phone. The display was adding and subtracting time. He whispered, "Bet that fucks up their billing!"

Bart said, "That would almost be worth the end of the world."

Jay looked through a recent copy of Scientific American, Bart closed his eyes and was asleep in seconds. Jay always admired Bart's ability to catch rest nearly anywhere and at any time, waking instantly, himself needing twenty minutes to unwind from even a ten-minute nap. Jay estimated not quite an hour had passed.

Rand looked over the top of her flat screen monitor. "Guys, I need to run something by you, and your common sense makes you two the best for this."

Bart was wide awake by the end of 'guys.' "I've been working toward flushing out the idea Bart had about the opposite charge of one of the power supplies from 51. My assumptions went with the X-pole being positive, and the 51-power supply Sanchez spoke of being Negative. Those pole names are arbitrary, the point is, what if they are opposite? Next, what if it doesn't matter to the power supply? If energy is just energy, then dumping it into the X-pole will suck energy out of it."

"Next, I have plugged in all the data into one of Andrews programs he wrote for the random movements of players on a war simulation game. Each person's player will react to stimulus, they are like little amoebas in that they move from threats and toward programmed goals. This is the same type of program used in recent movies like Lord of the Rings where the thousands of Uruk-hai Orcs looked like they were trying to get out from under a rock or something dropped on them. Each little monster was running a program in the digital scene. What I got back was that each of the places where the X- Pole has struck is at least a place where there is something 'programmed' in that area caused it to attract a hit."

"A field team from here found the silver tree was in line with several ATT microwave lanes going to and from repeaters on top of a few dozen peaks near Sandia Mountain. There must have been an attractive amount of reflected energy there. Building on that finding they looked at the other locations."

"The intersection was bordered by the local TV station transmitting facility, a two-million-watt UHF transmitter, PBS channel 21, the transmitter is on the top floor of the building on the north-east corner, the tower is just behind the building, and we saw the commercial power lines running down the side of the street."

"The College has a main transformer vault under the sidewalk near the Native American statue, that was the black hole opened under the sidewalk after the discharge took the Indian's hand off and all the other damage, and the switching yard is obvious."

"I think all this energy is being collected by a self-serving freak of nature that builds on itself until it consumes everything in its sphere of influence. We see the thing can now reach what, over fifty miles into the desert, want next?"

Bart said, "Please excuse me Doctor, but another thought built on the other one. If the device at 51 was an energy sponge, maybe just having, well throwing it in would stop the X-Pole. As it is you seem to be describing a black hole."

Rand smiled, "It's true, great minds do think alike. Yes Bart, the beginnings of a black hole. Doesn't that explain the time shift?"

Bart and Jaylee shook their heads. She continued, "Einstein postulated that as mass and energy nears the speed of light, time slows. What if it simply ceases to exist? What if all time connects there, in that place where time has stopped? And what if objects just step into whatever place the time-line is when they come to its threshold?"

"Since I had no datum to enter regarding the charges, I just looked at the power supply as a constant. Getting the Groom Lake generator into the X-pole is our best hope. It either all turns to shit, IE time stops, or the X-pole ceases to exist."

Jay nodded, "I agree, but where is the thing, and how do we get the '51 people to get off their prize chunk of alien spacecraft propulsion equipment?"

"Detective, you do have a way of seeing through government double-speak and bullshit, don't you?"

Her 9-1-1 page soon had the team back in the conference room.

Rand went through her ideas to the team. Andrew was the only one who thought the idea made perfect sense. The rest of the team ranged from Kough being neutral to Sanchez and Jefferies heartfelt rejection of the idea, Maurine waffled, sometimes supporting, then, a one-eighty nearly in mid-sentence. The detractors for the idea pointed out that the chances of the opposites canceling were equally in line with both energies adding.

Sanchez said, "Look, Doctor Rand, we're all looking for an easy way out of this thing, but I don't think the number three generator I worked on years ago is the answer. We still have no idea what it is or how it works. Like Doctor Jefferies says, it just as well might double the problem we have here as end it. I have to tell you people, I'm still afraid of that thing. In my view having it in Barksdale for safekeeping… Okay… shit folks, I don't even like it that close…Louisiana…Jesus, the moon would be too close."

Jefferies concluded the meeting with a thanks to Rand, and another meeting in one hour.

Rand, Bart and Jaylee walked down the hallway. She rounded on the men, "Guys, we need to get that thing and drop it in the hole."

Bart said, "Louisiana is beautiful this time of year."

Jaylee was more introspective, "Joan, if this thing works, we'll have to fly it in, and you know what happens to aircraft that get near the hole."

"Yeah, but I see no other option, maybe we can figure a way to keep the plasma from forming…we have to try. If the anomaly isn't stopped, the entire time-line will disintegrate, and everything we know with it. It really might be the end of time."

Rand and the two men went back to her office. She got into the classified "secret" phone directory. Using the scrambled lines and her best charm, which Jay noticed was considerable, she pulled in every chit she had. Using the "it may be the end of the world, or at least the end of stable time, and this is a real emergency", she methodically constructed the information needed to form a plan.

The "Sponge" had been transported in a Honda HA-420 jet, chosen because it had a composite fuselage and wings nearly devoid of steel, made from single sheets of aluminum glued to and braced with a high strength carbon fiber web. At Barksdale, it was being "tended" by two men from the Area 51 security staff. She found from one of her mentors at Groom Lake that the location of the aircraft was in the F-18 engine overhaul maintenance hangar on Barksdale

She went to the Mission style wooden locker at the corner of her office, opened it and got out field clothing, seemingly oblivious to the two detectives in the office, she unzipped the skirt and stepped out of it, half-slip followed. In panties, and unbuttoned blouse, she stepped into kaki cargo pants. "I suggest you two get some more practical clothes on instead of watching me change, get what you need and meet me back here in 30 minutes."

The detectives looked at each other, laughed and stood. Jay said, "Well, I'd rather look at you changing, but I guess you're right. We have tactical clothes in the Crown Vic." The men left, Jay poking his head around the door for one last look at Rand as she pulled on a lightweight sweater. She grinned and threw a shiny blue low heel pump at the door. "Jay, I'm going to pack an overnight bag, can I crash at your place when we get back?"

"Hell yes, but pack a hair dryer, us black guys don't have much need for one."

Thirty-eight minutes later the three were in an Air Force G-6 with wing tanks loaded ready for take-off, she had told Jefferies she wanted to be airborne when the next event happened, he had agreed. As he nodded his agreement, Joan got the distinct impression he knew what she had planned...maybe he too was completely out of options.

The aircraft was wheels up with fifty-eight minutes left on Andrew's clock. Level at 12,000 in clear sky, a Visual Flight Plan to Barksdale. Rand handed an official looking sealed envelope to the pilot, a graying Air Force Major. He opened the seal, removed a file composed of several pages, one blank, one typed, and another blank, all stamped, and sandwiched between two yellow card stock sheets that had in large font TOP SECRET CRYPTO and the attendant need to know – eyes only caution. The paper inside read…

TOP SECRET CRYPTO

You are to fly at top aircraft speed, transponder off and in radio silence to Barksdale AFB

GPS Coordinate 32° 30' 7" N, 93° 39' 46" W

Decimal 32.501944°, -93.662778°

UTM 3596268 437740 15S.

Squawk transponder channel 47 at 1000 KM from Barksdale runway.

Regular tower approaches but announce this is a top priority mission and request expedited landing.

The mission label is Time-end.

Request taxi clearance Maintenance Hanger H-18 to join aircraft in from Groom Lake.

This mission for this aircraft and crew is terminated on delivery of passengers. Aircraft crew to layover in BOQ Barksdale for re-assignment in AM. Aircraft to pool.

TOP SECRET CRYPTO

The pilot gave the message to his co-pilot, set in the coordinates in the flight GPS, and entered the data. The co-pilot, a young Captain, looked at the orders, gave a shrug, and checked the flight path maps. Made a few adjustments to the GPS flight computer, entering a waypoint route adjustment, "Major, highest land is 6,500, we can go North 30k and fly at 4,000." Then, tapping on his avionics calculator, "we will have about 680 lbs.

of JP-4 at touchdown. The distance with the jog to the waypoint for missing Pollard Mountain is 860 Nautical Miles, .8 mach."

The pilot read off the GPS, then, turning to Rand, in the doorway said, "ETA one hour twenty-eight minutes." The plane dipped toward the ground and picked up speed. Kirkland control called the plane. Rand said, "Major, answer them this once, and tell them I asked for the lower altitude, then turn off the transponder. Monitor the radio, but do not respond unless it's an emergency, your call on that."

The pilot did as asked. This was dangerous. They were in general aviation space, and flying at 550 mph. As noted fuel consumption was high, but there was no headwind. Both men watched the sky around them intently, collision avoidance radar set for 10 K.

Andrews Clock stumbled, lurched and made it to 0 hours 0 minutes.

CHAPTER 22

Join the Crowd

Jefferies and everyone in the room sat frozen as the clock hit 0 – 0. He dropped his gaze to the feed from the X-pole cameras.

Slowly, a glow started to come from the hole. Then, rays of energy like glowing, moving, multicolored tentacles of a hundred, no…a thousand armed octopus living in the depths of the mountain came forth, and kept coming. Bright laser-like rays shot into the sky. Red, green, blue and most of all bright white. They reached for the sky and arched in all directions from the pit. Jefferies imagined an intelligence at work, then threw that notion out. There was no evidence in the events, or the data to suggest that. But…

A scream from the end of the room, Jeffries wheeled in his chair, saw his colleagues made of water, the room made of glass, looking he saw his hand, then through his hand. No pain. Light - lots of light - bright white light. No pain to look at it. Time as he perceived it was slowing, slower and slower. With this came the feeling of being the shadows imprinted on a reel of film going ever slower. Then the definite feeling he was being drawn into a tube, fluid spinning into a bright, clear, glowing bathtub drain, but… smaller, much smaller, a straw. Now even smaller, a pipette, and still the compression continued… smaller. A 20-gauge clear hypodermic needle. How can this be? Alive, sentient, but stretched to a thread thickness, what, a hundred miles long? No panic, no pain. No loss of consciousness, no diminished thought.

Twisting through…what? A kaleidoscope? The unwinding frames of a movie? Shots of nearly recognizable forms, places. Sun-up, sun-down. Over and over. It was a beautiful, scary, interesting perception of being strained through a sieve… beauty? Yes, a real unknown beauty.

Moving toward a red lighted hole in the sky… not sky, but seemed to be above. A thunderous, long boom…then it was over.

The room was in shambles, ceiling tiles scattered like tossed playing cards, chairs tipped over, one wall and part of another of the room was gone, bricks were dropping from the ceiling space where that wall had been. People were getting up, dazed…some hurt, oh God, many seriously injured. The table was cut across the end from Jefferies. No artificial light, just a kind of reddish sunlight, but from the wrong direction. It seemed to be streaming in from what had been the north.

All people have an internal compass, calibrated by decades of seeing things from a 'normal' perspective. This was all wrong. The sun was coming in from where the north side of the room had been

Kough was the first to speak, "Chris, we are wherever the cameras have been sending pictures from." Turning, Jefferies saw the bottom half of Andrew, cut diagonally from below his ribs to across his pelvis. The young man had wide open eyes that were looking directly at him. Jefferies hand instinctively went to his mouth, a gasp of air intake, fingers in a fist as he stumbled back. Andrew was alive, trying to speak, a scared kid looks on his face, then, his dark eyes closed and did not move.

Some others were in similar condition. Maurine was also alive but fading fast, most of her right side was gone. Tears streamed down her face. She nodded at the desert; she knew where she…they were. A painful moan escaped her lips, then she too was silent.

She did not move again.

With Kough and Sanchez, he pushed open the door, walked out into the remains of the hallway, it ended twenty feet to the left, 60 feet to the right, nothing half way across the tiled hallway floor. The feet and legs of the AP guard lay just outside the door. The men shuffled through debris the several few feet to where the hall ended and looked out. A long desolate plain was in front of them, with… what?

A FLASH IN TIME

Overall, an unnatural red sun-bathed the scene from a reddish cloudless sky.

Jefferies thought but did not say, 'I pray to God Rand can get us out of this.'

A hundred million plus years ahead and a few thousand miles away, the reports came into President Armetich. Within thirty minutes of the event an overview was coming in focus.

In all there were over a hundred reported incidents of sections of the New Mexico desert area disappearing, some populated, most not. Video, streamed from the X-pole, directly to the situation room in the basement of 1600 Pennsylvania Ave, showed flashes of energy in rapid succession. Slowed by super high speed cameras played back at normal speed, distinctly different matter streams could be seen going into the X-pole. Then, as the E-R-Mag Labs room disappeared, so too did the video, which had been switched through that facility.

Armetich read the report from the damaged Kirkland Air Force Base Commander. He turned to his administrative aide, "Jerry, the team leaders for counteracting this thing are gone. We need someone else out there and damned quick to take over. I want the best and sharpest names on this desk in two hours. Start with the 1,200 people Jefferies had on his team. I need the Speaker, Minority leader, and the Senate Leaders here, send an Army car for each, and do it now!" He wheeled to John Crane, "Tell me you have supplies, people and resources in place out there like I ordered in the plane coming back here."

Crane looked at the table, "I...We...Mr. President we just had time to alert the sector people. It's moving, but there wasn't much of a terrorist risk for the New Mexico desert. It's going to take time..."

Armetich banged the table, wheeled to the Chairmen of The Joint Chiefs of Staff, "General, I want 10,000 troops on the ground in that area in twelve hours. I'll take care of the Posse Comitatus concerns. Their orders are to maintain order, and aid the local authorities in any way they can. Make it clear I do not see this as Marital Law." Wheeling back to Jerry, "Get a press release out. Troops on the way, not martial law, ya-yd-ya-yd-ya..."

General Al French nodded, stood, saluted, then got a nod from the Colonel on his right who was reading from a Blackberry. He handed it to the general, who read, stopped, turned back to the President "We will have 2,100 troops in the area and on patrol in less than two hours, the rest as ordered." He wheeled back, and left the room with his aids.

"Mr. Crane, please take a lesson from the General. His response was the one I was looking for. I believe you will need to consider another position when this is over."

CHAPTER 23

New Arrivals

The world was coming apart. Art said to Mort, "Just when ya thought it couldn't get any worse, this!"

The point of their concern was bright arcs of lightning coming from a point five hundred meters in the sky, arching in what seemed random paths to the desert floor. Each 'lightning bolt' hit with a blinding flash and a thunderous BOOM. Dust, rocks, sand and maybe smoke erupted at each strike. As the dust cleared microcosms of the future lay scattered in a random pattern throughout this portion of the red desert.

Placed randomly across a quarter mile of the desert were little scenes of life, like scenes from a model railroad that were built separately but not yet assembled into an entire layout. A semi-high-rise building, maybe ten stories, well over half buried in the sandy dune where it had ended. Then to the right, what appeared to be several suburban homes.

To the left, a playground with dazed kids standing near damaged equipment.

A massive tangle of twisted iron which defied recognition, a bridge of some kind?

Four locomotives and a dozen cars of a freight train had appeared running out of a spot on the red sand, still moving at 30 miles per hour. In a few seconds they ran off the end of the track they had arrived on, ploughed into the sand, jack-knifed the locomotives stayed upright, the cars flipping on their sides in a defining roar, just what they needed, 1,000 tons of scrap metal. Well, they damned well had lumber, coal and whatever was in the box cars that had crashed. Mort thought 'Thank God no chlorine or propane came through!'

They watched in horror, helpless, as the rear half of an airliner spiraled from the sky, disintegrating as if fell, landing past a line of dunes some miles away.

So many mini-scenes of destruction and horror.

The previous residents of the desert watched from the underside of the trailer, women and men alike huddled and shaking. Way too much sensory input to process at one time. Finally, the echoes died across the sand, and a deathly quiet took its place.

The original survivors crawled out from under the trailer and looked around. Sounds began to come from the new arrivals, crying, a dog barking, creaks and groans of the various structures settling into their new place in the sticky red sand. The top several floors of the high-rise cracked and fell off as people nearby ran for their lives.

Art, Gus, Mort, and with Fang collected first aid supplies, water, then began walking to the various locations, collecting people and helping injured. The with the women stayed back at the trailer to coordinate with the new arrivals. Soon it became obvious to the men that they should return and wait for the new arrivals to come to them. Soon the new kids in the sandbox began streaming back to the trailer truck, most still in shock.

Jefferies, Sanchez, and Kough decided to lay back for a while. What would be the reaction to people finding out they were the ones who pushed the "let's see the old west" button.

An hour later, Art stood on the back of the trailer, first aid triage was completed, and those who could be helped were. The dead were moved to a sturdy small house and secured inside - will need to take care of them tomorrow.

Art spoke to the roughly forty people in front of him, he outlined where they were and what the notes from the future had said. Continuing he said, "Folks, we have been here about a week. We have some supplies but not much, I suggest we need to get everything from the houses and that building," he pointed to the slice of high rise in the sand several hundred yards away, "everything that will spoil, or go bad. Raid the refrigerators. I suggest we bring it all here, eat the perishable stuff first, even if it isn't the best diet. Tomorrow we can get all the drinks, canned food and such."

A tattooed man from the crowd said, "And just who the fuck made you the King?" Everyone looked around nervously.

Art looked down, shook his head, and said, "Absolutely no one. Please come up here and take over." With that he simply jumped off the trailer and walked to his tent.

The crowd became distressed, some downright angry. At first, the punk, like ANTIFA losers, seemed to revel in the attention, snarling at those around him. When a very large rough looking Mexican man asked him to tell everyone what to do, his attitude changed, he now looked real worried, shrinking back and trying for a get away from the group. The Mexican grabbed his hoodie sweatshirt, yanked him up nearly off the ground and slapped the punk hard across the face, "Eef you don' have nothing to help, shut the fuck up...asshole." He slapped him from the backswing even harder, and threw the punk down...hard.

The Goth woman next to the tattoo freak said, hands on hips and glaring down, "Excellent Bobbie K. Just fucking excellent." The crowd continued giving "Bobby K" very bad looks.

A man in a McDonald's uniform spoke up, "I think the guy from the trailer had a very good idea. There's no sense in letting good food go to waste. We may be here, wherever here is, a long time." His voice trailed away on the last words.

The crowd dispersed, going to the various places where food might be found. The Goth girl, very pretty, but working hard to be ugly, with black hair, white skin, black eye make-up, and of course a drizzle of piercings, ears, nose and lip. And tattoos. She had a black fluffy mini-skirt, striped red and white socks and black combat boots. Her black tube top showed ample firm breasts, a flat belly with belly-button skull jewelry, small rubies for eyes. Small diameter silver chains dangled from unlikely places pinned to her clothing at what seemed random attachment points. She walked to the tent where she saw Art disappear, the tent which he shared with Mort, Randy, young Chris and, according to his tag, "Fang", the dog.

From outside the tent she said, "Mister, I'm really sorry about Bobby K, you had really good ideas out there. My name's Kristy, can I come in for a minute?"

Art said to come in. The girl pulled the flap aside, bending to enter.

She extended a hand with black-lacquered finger tips.

Art looked up from the cot on which he was sitting, shook the hand. The dog under the cot also looked up as she came in. Art was dirty, looked tired, "Miss…Kristy, we all have the really good possibility of dying out here, some time before we were ever born, some people think thousands of years before. I'm tired, and I'm frustrated. Everything keeps getting worse than it was just a day ago. I do not have the energy, will, or even the desire to argue with your friend, or anyone else for that matter. The people I arrived with have listened to me, and this man here, Mort. He actually has saved our lives, more than once...I am not a king."

She flopped, sat cross legged in the sand, white thighs showing up to candy striped red and white panties, scratched the dog behind a floppy ear, Fang had obviously found a lifelong friend. Who says love at first sight can't happen? Fang put his head in her lap, eyes closed and looking like he'd found heaven, another grin from the 'guard dog'.

Art considered that he was even too tired and too worried to more than just notice the attractive legs, attached to an equally attractive girl. A flash of 'wish my head was in her lap' instead of Fang popped in and out of his mind in a milli-second.

Randy, the cop, seemed a bit quiet, but was studying Kristy with more than casual interest. Randy had finally been able to shuffle around some on crutches from the medical supplies sent, he was now on his cot, and had also noticed the pretty legs, and there was something nagging him about Kristy...something...maybe it was the name Bobby K?

The sun was dropping into the sand some hours later. Kough, Jefferies and Sanchez were talking to Art, Mort and Gus, Chris was standing nearby, quietly listening. Randy had returned to his cot nearby. Mort recalled how he had suggested moving the camp just before the sub-station appeared. Art briefed them on the tracks, and the man dying of what appeared to be rabies. The three men said they were scientists from E-R-Mag Labs, but not that they had stumbled on the time warping monster from hell.

Kough said, "Well, I doubt if it was rabies, at least not the same kind we have…uh well, had, I guess. Jesus, how do you conjugate a verb that was yesterday but in the future?" They laughed, he continued, "Rabies takes at least five days for a human to be as nuts as your guy was, unless he was bitten on the spinal column, or brain stem. This suggests that he may have been ill when he arrived here."

Sanchez wanted more information on the tracks, Art answered, "Well I can't give you much more than they looked like bird tracks, but much bigger, I'd say a little over a 18" end to end. Three "toes" on one end, and one…a larger one on the back. The sand was real soft, that's why we chose down there to bury them, make it easier to dig and all. Back then, before the 'care' packages we didn't have any tools."

Sanchez looked around, then back to Art, "Have you folks seen any elephant looking things? Like maybe a Mammoth or something?" Yes, Sanchez was disoriented, upset, scared, and confused, but his scientific training trumped all those emotions and feelings.

The others looked at each other, then back to Sanchez, "Naw, we think we've seen something just over the ridge of those dunes there, but nothing like an elephant."

Mort said, "Mister…Doctor Sanchez, life's been a little boring out here in the distant past, but I think a few elephants would have made an impression on us."

Sanchez shook his head, "No...I know that, it's just we saw...uh, I have asked about them, what a guy from the museum in Phoenix said were early versions of Mammoths in the...uh what we saw as we came here. Now I'm wondering where 'here' actually is."

Mort had some sudden insights into these new arrivals, but kept quiet.

Randy said, "Look, it was really busy when I arrived with the remains of the parking garage, but I saw a flash of several things, dinosaurs, hairless mammoths, hell I thought they were a figment of my imagination. It was like I was watching channels being selected and changed again on a TV. Like maybe there were other destinations, but this one is where my ticket took me."

Sanchez continued to turn in a circle, looking up, and then to the skyline. "Have any of you seen the moon?"

Art said, "Well yes. It uh... rises from...over there and, well, I never really saw it set, always been asleep."

Kough put his hand on Sanchez's arm, "Sanny, what you getting at? What's on your mind?"

Sanchez looked at his sports watch, battery dead but which had a magnetic compass, "Okay, if the sun is going down there." He pointed to the red ball ready to sink into the sand. "And Art here says the moon comes up from there." Pointing again, "Then we are either on earth well over 300,000 years ago, or we are not on earth at all. Geologic evidence points to the sun coming up from the west about that long ago, how and why the earth's rotation changed is a mystery. I know quite a few of the landmarks on the moon, if there's enough of it to see, like not a new moon, I can tell if it's ours."

He shrugged, asked for and got a bottle of water, "I'm a pretty good astronomer, it's a lifelong hobby. Let's see what the star map looks like in an hour or so when the sun goes down."

Mort got Art, Gus and the new scientists aside. "Gentlemen, I think we better post a guard on the supplies in the trailer. We don't know who arrived here in paradise with us. That wack job Bobby K makes me nervous. I can take the first watch, let's say about 3 hours? I'll have a knife and Randy's pistol."

Gus started to say something, Mort cut him off with a wave of his arm "Yeah, I know it's only got thirteen more shots left, but that should do."

Gus caught on to the bluff. "I'll take the second watch, just wake me up when you get tired since we don't have a working clock."

They didn't get the chance.

Some new arrivals had started sort of a campfire near the trailer. Makeshift grill material was suspended between some metal chairs looted from the apartment building. What appeared to be wooden remains of building material salvaged from the train wreck stacked nearby for fuel. A variety of meat, breakfast sausage and even steaks were cooking, grease nosily popping into little explosions of flaring fire as they dropped into the coals. People were subdued but surprisingly did not seem unduly morose.

Sanchez was working on some drawings of the sky behind the trailer in the near darkness. He moved into the firelight and made a few additional notes. The "leaders" waited in front of their tent, now with Randy, Art, Mort, Chris, Jefferies, Kough, and Sanchez planning on sharing the 12-person squad tent.

"Gentlemen, working on the notion that the earth is rotating opposite from what we see in the 21st century, which is supported by the sunrise as compared with the moon rise, and yes it is the same moon, we are indeed still on earth. I guess that's the good news. The bad news is that as far as I can tell from the new 'south star' where the north star should be, one star on what I think is Orion's belt being brighter, and some clusters of stars I can make out through what I think is the reddish haze from either volcanic activity, or some other phenomena, we are at least 110.5 and maybe up to 140 million years in the past."

The men were struck wordless. Art said, "Gee, 2 'fucked up bad day' benchmarks in the same day! In 12 hours even. That's a dubious first. Anyone have any idea when the last dinosaurs played volleyball in this sandpit?"

Kough looked nervously around, "I'm thinking like 90 million years or so."

Art - "Make that 3 fucked up bad day benchmarks."

Sanchez - "Sorry but I have no way to calibrate the star positions, I have no charts, and no telescope. I did notice that Orion's belt is different, one star is markedly lighter than…uh…back home, that means it's moving away from us toward the other stars in the 21st century belt. That's really interesting."

Then the noise came from the valley nearby.

Not a growl, or a whine, not a bark or a yelp. A strange, half cat, half what? Human? No, a bigger, deeper and, after the dinosaur comment really scary. Every head at the campsite turned toward the sound. Fang stood and pricked up his ears. As the implications of the sound began to sink in, another sound, slightly higher in pitch came from the other side of the camp site, now full of people. Then two more seemed to answer from farther away.

Art and Mort looked at each other. "I think we have finally aroused the natives with the sweet smell of cooking meat."

"The native what?" Jefferies said as he nervously stood up from the cross-legged sand position he had finally found comfortable, dabbed his sweating forehead with a handkerchief.

Mort continued, "Damned if we know, but I sure hope they wear smaller shoes than the things that dug up the remains we buried!"

Chris arrived with the bows and arrows in their quivers. Art took one, notched an arrow, Mort did the same. Sanchez joined them, "I was a bow hunter, bagged two or three Javelinas a year."

Mort handed a bow and quiver to him. "My arthritis kicks my ass whenever I pull the string, and I really barely hit what I've been practicing shooting at."

The men split up, one on each side of the campsite. Several of the new arrivals got 2x4 'clubs' from the fire pit wood supplies and joined the bow guys on the other two sides of the camp. Bobby K, the Goth came up to Sanchez. "And just what the fuck is that toy bow supposed to do?"

Mort had walked up quietly behind Bobby. Sanchez said, "Man what do you want? This is all we have, and if it isn't good enough, then I guess those things out there will take the food, and maybe a few of us too."

Bobby reached for the bow. Mort said, "Go back with the women, if you don't have anything to add here."

Bobby swung around and tried to hit Mort, who ducked, pulled up a can of foam mace he had removed from the cop's tactical vest, and sprayed Bobby full in the face. As Bobby grabbed his eyes, Mort nailed him directly on the top of the head with the baton, also borrowed from the SWAT officer. Bobby K went down like a bag of wet cement. Looking up at Sanchez, Mort said, "Sanny is it? We really don't have time for this shit." Leaning over, he placed a wire zip-tie on Bobby K's wrists.

Movement caught Sanchez's eye. Something was sneaking toward them from the darkness. He pulled the bowstring and took aim. Mort said, "Let me make some noise, maybe it thinks we don't see it." As Fang started to slowly advance, Mort said in a command voice, "Fang, sit!" the dog sat, still attention to the approaching figure. Mort stood and waved his arms and shouted nothing in particular. The dark shadow stopped, then advanced again, now just fifteen meters away. Sanchez had a clear shot and took it. The arrow hit center mass. The thing jumped straight in the air, a blood curdling scream as it did so.

On the other side of the camp, Art took a shot at a creeping shadow as well. His arrow hit, but apparently not a significant hit. Chris handed him another arrow as the shape rose up full height and charged. Art's second arrow also was not mortal, this one hitting what may have been a leg. This, however slowed the attacker and the third arrow hit what turned out to be the head, directly in a "nose" opening just as the Fang, racing across the campsite hit and knocked the thing down.

There was total and complete silence. Then, running feet or hooves? Art took a flare from Chris and briskly struck the cap across the flare's primer powder. Slowly, like it was trying hard not to light, like the earlier one Chris had tried, and like the finally caught. The light revealed a large, 8-foot-tall, gangly, skinny, ape-shaped animal, no hair, but with a distinct difference.

It had scales.

No one slept until the dawns early light. Then people could be seen huddled together, most with someone sitting, watching. Many had armed themselves with clubs, or pieces of metal.

Kristy ran into Art's tent, "Bobby K's gone!" Mort stood, and with Art went to the place they had left Bobby K, shackled by the wire-tie. Claw-like footprints came to where he had been, then two rows went back into the sand, obviously dragging Bobby K with them.

Armed with knives, another flare, and a bow, Art and Sanchez followed the drag marks until they went around a dune. There, they found Bobby K. All large muscles had been removed. A rag torn from his tee shirt had been stuffed in his mouth. He had been harvested like a deer too heavy to drag out of the woods. All the best parts removed by something that knew what it wanted, and what to leave. And worst of all, had sharp tools.

Art, a firefighter, was used to scenes of carnage, Sanchez was not. Art took Sanchez by the arm, "Let's get the hell back to the camp. There's nothing we can do for him. This answers the question as to what happened to the exploration party, and those people I buried."

Kristy was told of the finding of Bobby K, the mace and shackling part left out. She hung her head. "Fucker was always looking for trouble. Guess he never thought it would come in a place like this. He was out of crack anyway." She turned and went back to a group of young people still standing near the dying fire. Fang started to follow, sat for a few seconds, then turned and came back to Art.

Mort, Sanchez, Art, Kough, and Jefferies had the attackers' bodies near the trailer. "Well, this corks the millions of years' theory, and kind of knocks the 8,000-year thing dead in the ass." Sanchez was saying.

Art said, "Please explain, doctor."

"Well, there is no fossil evidence of anything like these things. Their evolutionary path stayed with the dinosaur linage. These beings have some version of opposable thumbs too, see, this back 'finger' can move sideways…sort of anyway. What I'm still wondering about is the size of the eyes, they are quite large, and no eyelids that I can see, and the coloring, almost grey, no other natural scale coloring like one would expect from hunter-gathering species that would have to hide in the wild. Makes me think they probably live underground, if they were surface dwellers, then they would have better coloring, maybe even clothes."

Kough said, "Wonder if this is the genesis of the 'Grey alien' mythology?"

Chris walked up to the men, "Hey, look what I found out where Mister…Uh Dr. Sanchez shot the gator thing." He produced a club, fashioned from a hard wood-like substance. Clearly, the handle had been made to fit the three 'fingers' of the hand.

Jefferies exclaimed, "This changes everything!"

Art said "Yeah, we're being attacked by humanoid lizards."

Jeffries - "No...No. That's not it. Don't you see? Only two possibilities, either, in spite of what Sanny says, we're not on earth. Or if we are, we're definitely not in or on the same timeline! Like Sanchez says, there is no evidence that dinosaurs ever made it this far in the evolutionary chain. Look, these beings are intelligent. They planned an attack on us. They have weapons and probably tools, all made for a purpose."

Kough said, "Maybe more than that. Look here." He rolled the club toward the others. "This looks like rudimentary or elementary writing to me, and it's all the way around the business end of this club."

Sanchez said, "I think this would be the logical path if the asteroid failed to hit and wipe out the dinosaurs, look, those things were too big to be effective populates of this planet. They ate too much food, may have been cold blooded, laid eggs which is not an effective form of continuing a species."

Art, the EMT/Paramedic said, "The women I've helped in child-birth would argue that point."

They all laughed.

Sanchez continued, "Well eggs have the disadvantage of allowing the full nutrition of the fetus, and thus do not provide the time and nutrients for a complex brain to develop. Eggs only have sufficient nutrition for the growth of the body. That's why most egg-layers have tiny brains. All academic anyway, we have no idea how these gator things reproduce."

Mort, standing back from the others finally opined, "Well, this clearly changes the situation, doesn't it? I mean we are now someplace we can't even begin to figure out in terms long-term survival. We now have, what, in the best of terms is an evolutionary war between competing mammal and reptilian paths. Oh, by the way, what do they eat? Were they coming here for the steaks on the 'barbie, or us? The situation with Bobby K kind of makes that obvious, doesn't it?"

Art said, "Thanks Mort, you just, once again, proved my ongoing opinion of this place, just when I thought it couldn't get any worse, it does and this cannibal iguana theory makes an astounding new 'more fucked up than in the recent past, times four'."

Sanchez added, "I have a few 'good news and bad news', couple of thoughts. First the good news. These things, even if they have lizard like metabolisms, need a rather robust food source, which we don't see here…OK, other than us."

Art – "And that's the good news?"

"Well we know they have a food supply somewhere, I mean they ate before the Manna from Heaven started popping out of the sky," Sanchez continued.

Art continued the thought, "Yeah, but where is it, and can humans eat it?"

Sanchez looked at the ground, "And the really bad news is, I'll bet they are planning an attack for tonight, and I'll bet that after tonight this timeline's history will know if reptilian species or mammals is dominate here. Shit, people, we have food for what? A week, maybe two? Within a few days we are going to need to take out across this desert in search of a place to get more food, water, build shelter. And, incidentally defeat the lizard people."

Art said, "Well, one thing, those locomotives have enough fuel to get this truck and trailer a long damned way from here, maybe even to water, plants and what-the-hell ever is here."

Indeed.

Jefferies looked up from the club he had taken from Mort and was examining, "There may be a ray of sunshine, like Dr. Sanchez says, if these things eat meat, then there's meat to be eaten. I mean we are apparently easier than whatever they normally hunt, but they hunt something."

Sanchez replied, "That's a mystery too. I mean they ventured out here in the middle of a friggin' desert for something, and we know how uncomfortable the dry heat is to amphibians, and that is clearly what they appear to be. They must have a source of water, food, or are carrying everything they need with them, something." He took the club, "I can't see anything even remotely looking like a living tree, bush or plant to make stuff out of, as far as I've been able to see anyway." He took one of the knives and cut a chip from the club, sniffed it, and looked closely at the new wood he had exposed. "Smells like some kind of fungus, and there is apparently no grain, like a really hard giant mushroom stalk."

At first light several men had gone out to the various remains of the buildings, and collected the rest of the food. They returned also with 2 more pistols, a shotgun, and 2 rifles, a Ruger 10-22 and an Inter-arms AR-15 clone, with ammunition for each. Sanchez and Randy attempted to fire each, the only one that fired was the old single shot 12 gauge. They had carefully looked around each building for tracks of the 'Gators' as Chris had named them. None were present. "I think they are afraid of those buildings, they would certainly have gone inside if not," Jefferies said, "I can only imagine what buildings appearing out of thin air must feel to them."

Sanchez looked up from the larger of the body he was examining, making notes in his pad, which he religiously was never without. "You might be right. This thing has some tattoo like markings, made from what look like the snipped ends of some of its scales, and 'his' musculature is about a tenth again as large as the other. I'd say either this one's a male, the other a female, perhaps a male adolescent. When I pulled the arrow out, there was no blood on it, and nothing came from the wound, this would indicate a very dense anatomy with little viscus material, and little blood if any. I see no obvious genitalia, no signs of breasts, and I'm reluctant to try any kind of autopsy, God only knows what kind of germs this place has. I suppose germs, bacteria and viruses, have been on a mutation time-line like these Gators here, on the other hand, they might not have sexes, each might be a uni-sex, like some frogs and snails back on Earth." He stopped, the others looking at him. It was his phrasing, "Back on Earth" that had hit them.

Mort said, "I think we should not desecrate these things any more than we have already done. They have a primitive society, and as such probably have a ritual for their dead. I say we drag these two out there," pointing to the dune where Bobby was filleted, "and just leave them up high where the others can see them. I see nothing to be gained from keeping these bodies, and maybe our returning them will change the way they look at our presence. Okay... okay...I doubt it, but there's nothing to lose."

Art and Sanchez and two new guys dragged the corpses out, guarded by Jefferies and Mort with bows, Kough, with the single shot 12 gauge and Fang.

One of the new human arrivals came up to the men as they returned, "I found this in the remains of the blue house." He handed Art a multi-powered spotting scope.

Art literally sprung to the top of the trailer off the tractor's roof, and surveyed the desert. "Guys! Over in a direct line with the place we just left the Gators' bodies! Maybe a mile. There must be a dozen or so of them, they're in the shade of an overhang! Wait, I see a cave opening, some going in and out. They have what look like spears and more clubs lined along the side of the cliff. No bows, and no knives that I can see, but something sliced the muscle off Bobbie."

Sanchez called up, "Do you see any sign of smoke or fire? Are they sleeping or what?"

Art replied, "No, but there is not one of them in the sunlight. I think they are either afraid of the sun, or it damages them somehow. Adjusting the focus on the scope, wait a minute! The bodies we just dragged out to the dune! They're...their scales...looks like...like they're curling up."

"That's it then. We're safe in the daylight, but this sundown, we could be in for it." Mort said.

In what may have been considered good news, the newcomers had found a real compound bow and 30 arrows in one of the apartments. A few now had machetes, and a few of the men had swords from a military memorabilia collection.

The men readied their camp for an attack from all sides, but it was looking more like a lost cause by the minute. Seven kids, twelve men, some hurt and healing from amputations. Fourteen women, same scenario.

The sun dropping, lengthening the shadow of the cliff saw the gators following it out a little from the rock face. "Looks to me like they're doing a war dance." Art said from the top of the trailer.

War about describes it.

The sun sank into the desert, in spite of all the humans praying for it to stop and stay hung in the air. That ominous cry heard last night came again, this time answered by cries from all sides, followed by clicking like speech, answered and repeated. Yes, these creatures appeared to have a sort of spoken language.

Seven of the women had joined the men, two ex-militaries and 5 that said they were not about to end it before it began to a bunch of lizards. The men in Art's tent, somehow taking the role of leaders, did not argue and supplied them with makeshift weapons like the rest of the human army. The other women and kids were in the trailer, the "army" posted a second, closer row of four people around it. These with amputations but able to hold weapons, Randy was posted just inside the trailer with Fang, and 'Mollie', a mixed sort of collie dog. Randy had a sword, and his pepper spray, a very last line of defense.

Art yelled, "Here they come!"

CHAPTER 24

Get it and Run

The plane was making long turns to keep from getting close to any other aircraft. The young Captain - First Officer was intently watching the collision avoidance radar, Jaylee was sitting between the men in the jump seat, helping look for traffic.

Bart was asleep.

Doctor Joan Rand finished re-reading the quickly typed plans for the mission and tucked the papers away in the lower vest pocket, over her shirt. Leaning back, she watched the land run by, just a few thousand feet below. Her eyes got heavy, it had been nearly three days since she'd had any sleep.

Suddenly she was on the back of her first real boyfriend's restored metal flake cherry red Harley Davidson Fat Boy, with a sparkling chrome extended springer front end, her cheek against his back looking at the road going by at seventy miles an hour, the engine rumbling in her ears and the seat pleasantly vibrating beneath her.

It was just a few years earlier she remembered that she was a lanky, awkward high school girl who thought to herself that there were slim-and-no chances of improvement, and maybe slim had left town. That feeling was coupled with apparently no interest from the testosterone laden Y chromosomes buzzing all around her, but never stopping by her particular flower in high school. So, with little else in the social date-book she had buried herself in her schoolwork, boys could wait, then, in the summer between high school graduation and fall freshman college, BAM! A beautiful young woman happened. Even though she had to admit, looking in the bathroom mirror after a shower, some profound shape changes had happened that summer. Still thinking of herself as an ugly duckling, she avoided dating until her college Junior year.

The reason was a little more complicated than what her mother thought – that she's something of a "tom-boy." She had never learned from all the many hoops that many young girls by instinct, maturing, with peer connections and conflicts had gone through to find out how to be as pretty as she could be. She never experimented with different hair styles, and a change in hair color was out of the question. She seldom if ever applied any make-up. Her "planeness," simply put, was a self-fulfilling prophecy.

In college, even though becoming a striking young woman, she stayed on the study path. She was in tough no-nonsense high-level calculus and electronic engineering, not much time for thinking of dating. A little later in that Junior year Harold had persisted until she relented and tentatively, slowly started dating him. Their first "overnight" trip was underway

Where were they going? A place called Sturgis? Now as a Junior, she had moved to a Theoretical Physics major with dual minors in atomic energy and electrical engineering, it had taken everything she had to leave the campus for a day, much less four days.

What was even more amazing was to then get on the back of a bike, a big bike actually – which Harold had corrected was a motorcycle, "Not a Huffy or Schwinn, those are bikes." Weren't those things dangerous? And ride 500 miles to be with a couple thousand other bikers? No wait, she wasn't a biker, for that matter Harold wasn't either, a Political Science major with Izod shirts and sock-less loafers or Birkenstocks? Okay, he did have the Harley, but it had been left to him by his dad. No, Harold was not a biker. Harold had jeans on, but they were obviously new, and "engineer" boots, new too. She thought of the Texas people's saying as they pointed to city folk like her and Harold– all hat and no cow, wonder what the biker version was?

She had a blouse under a windproof nylon jacket, tight (for her anyway) jeans and hiking boots. Not quite making the biker couple image, yet here they were, 'blasting into the great wide open', Tom Petty and the Heartbreakers would be proud. Her mind's eye watched the road, scenery, sorgos cactus pop by, blurred snapshots viewed through cotton candy cobwebs in the camera shutters blink of her dreaming memories' eye.

And what would a pretty geek girl and a raging liberal long hair do in the middle of three thousand strangers? Strange strangers at that? When they arrived, it turned out to be 13,000 pretty damned well strange-strangers. Her first step into a different and new part of the real world. From Hell's Angles to 'Mr. Trucking' hippies, all having a great time and getting along spectacularly. She smiled in the sleep from the memories, even as the present world was coming apart time wise, and she; deep asleep in the G-6 aircraft.

Then there she was. A performer in a surreal circus. What a variety of people! And what had she done! A smile again on her sleeping face at the memory, she even chuckled under dream-memories breath. She was on a stage with twenty other women and girls. What the hell? She was topless, actually damned near bottomless, well not exactly, with a tiny tight elastic thong panty as a bottom. She had been painted with a really well-done American flag; it was painted like the wind had wrapped it around her. Standing there, a José Cuervo in a plastic cup, lime slice on the rim in hand. A voice saying, "This star here is for Alaska, my home state." As a little blast of cold air and white paint from an airbrush hit her right nipple. The last white star on the flag's blue field of stars appeared. Another laugh. This was FUN! What was she going to tell her parents about the two-foot-high Sturgis Painted Lady trophy she later had won? How will we get it back on the motorcycle? Who was the painter? Some tattooed guy with questionable dental work named Snake? He was fun, too, laughing and painting, he made her feel comfortable with her body, like being topless was the most natural thing. Never touched her trying to cop a feel, and he was very good with an airbrush. She had said, smiling at Snake, "I'll always remember Alaska's star." Yep, she had really liked the neat tingle of getting that Alaska's star.

Harold was pissed. When he had tried to pull her away, Snake had airbrushed a little circle squiggle on his forehead, "There, see, an asshole." Then turning to her, "And you have proved a point us artists have suspected for a long time, many good-looking women, like you sweetie, have two assholes," as he pointed a thumb with the airbrush ring on it at Harold, who stomped out of the tent full of people in the middle of roaring laughter. Screw him, this was fun! Yep, that was the beginning of the end of Harold…

Looking out from a stage, in a hot dry desert tent, holding a trophy, 500 people looking at her, at her body! Wild cheering and hooting at near deafening levels. Fuck those dweebs back in high school, eat your god-damned hearts out! There with her American flag, Tequila, trophy, $500.00 prize, a drop-dead gorgeous body, and one dynamite Alaska star. All this and John Kay backed by Steppenwolf at rock volume singing "Fire all of your guns at once and explode into space!" She had given a smiling Snake $250.00 of the prize money.

A few weeks later she had a permeant tattoo of the star on her nipple.

A muffled 'bump' and the sound changed. The landing gear had been lowered, flaps were extending. Damned, was she really out for over an hour?

The G-6 taxied to the hanger following instructions from ground control. Stopping 20 meters from a smaller corporate jet. The stairs lowered and the three people clambered out, backpacks on, weapons in hand. The pilot said to them as they went to the cabin door, "Radio from homeland security, says the X-pole looks like it has "fired" again and has re-charged to 80%, it's just a guess but maybe two hours or less until another discharge!"

She said, "Shit…Bart, Jaylee, this thing has gone full apeshit, it's now cutting discharge times in what? Half!" That covered it, nuff said.

Rand walked up to the door of the hanger after the G-6's engines spooled to stop. She tried the door, no go. Jaylee banged on the tin side of the hanger. A sleepy voice said through the door, "Who the hell wants to wake us up at…02:25 in the morning?"

"I'm Doctor Joan Rand from the E-R-Mag Labs Physics Center and I'm here to examine the power supply you have there; the mission code is Time-end. This device may hold the missing parameters we need to stop the events on Sandia Mountain, code named X-Pole. I'm sure you've heard of that mess, haven't you?"

"Lady, I don't know anything about any mission Time-end. The X-Pole thing, yes, that's why we brought this thing all the way out here."

"I'm not surprised about you not knowing about Time-end, this thing has been one SNAFU after another. Please, just take a look at the orders."

The voice said, "Okay, but I'll need to call this in."

Rand shot a quick look at Jaylee and Bart, "Of course, but you'll need the authentication code on the orders." She was thinking fast. That call could end the plan.

The lock clanked, and the bolt on the man-door in the larger hanger roll-up door started to open. Jaylee hit the door on a three step run, Bart right behind him. The man opening the door was sprawled on the floor, blood across his face from a broken nose. Jaylee lost his balance and rolled on the floor beside the door guy. A second man was bending for an M-16 propped against the desk. Bart said, "Stop! Now! Don't move!" He had his Glock leveled at the man. "Anyone else in here? No bullshit!"

The desk man said, "NNNo... No one else."

Never trust a guy you just woke up at 02:30, especially one reaching for a M-16.

"Drop it, both of you!" A man in pilot's coveralls had appeared from the darkness at the end of the hanger door. He had a .22 caliber survival rifle pointed at Bart.

Bart looked at Jaylee as the man advanced, he still had his pistol pointed at the M-16 guy. The pilot repeated his threat. Jay was not in position. Rand said in a loud commanding voice, "Don't do anything stupid, I have you covered." As the pilot walked in front of the open door, lights from several flood lights behind her in the doorway threw shadows across the floor. He looked out of the door, the rifle moved. Bart did also. CRACK! The pilot fired from seeing the movement in his peripheral vision. The small caliber bullet hit Bart in the right eye. He dropped instantly. Jaylee knocked the rifle from the pilot's hand, the M-16 guy went for his rifle. Jay shot twice, the man dropped.

Rand raced over and slid on the concrete to Bart.

"Jay, he's dead. I'm so sorry, Jay, he's dead." She wheeled to the pilot who was fumbling with the survival rifle, Bart's pistol now in her hand. "Drop that gun and listen you imbecile, this is actually an authorized emergency operation, and now because of your interference, two people are dead!" She shook her head, "Now hear me and hear me well. We can't wait for investigations of the shooting of these people. We just don't have time! The X-Pole has gone completely berserk. Hundreds are dead and more will follow. This may be a portal to a black hole starting right in the middle of New Fucking Mexico, and that thing in the airplane is our only hope of stopping it!"

Jay had dragged the still unconscious man to one of the air pipes coming out of the concrete near a workbench. He was handcuffing the door guy, tears streaming down his face. He was shuddering as he was racked with uncontrollable sobs.

Rand wanted to go to him more than anything she had ever wanted to do. But she replayed what he had said to her as the came down the steps of the G-6, "Joan, remember the mission. We…all of us…are expendable. No matter what happens keep moving. Complete the mission."

She continued, "Is the device still in the plane?" Nod. "Is the plane filled with fuel?" Another nod. "Then sir, you will fly us back to Sandia Mountain, you will fly full bore and at no more than 4,000 feet. Is that understood?"

"I…We can't. It's restricted space, they'll shoot us down!"

Rand punched a number on her phone, "This is Doctor Joan Rand and I have to speak to the President, it is an emergency and it's in regard to the X-Pole."

In less than twenty seconds "Doctor, this is Armetich."

She pushed the speaker button on her phone, "Mister President, I'm on a desperation mission to try to cancel out the energy in the X-Pole with a Groom Lake device. I need clearance from Barksdale Air Force Base in Louisiana to the X-Pole for a small jet, and you to order anyone who can to assist in that mission, including," she read the name tag on the jumpsuit, "Major Wacken, the pilot."

"Doctor Rand, what are the odds you give your plan?"

"Right now, 50/50. I have to tell you, some of the others at E-R-Mag do not agree, but they have no alternative plan. I'm running this one using my best instincts. We, Detective Washington, Detective Williams and I have had some problems here."

"There are problems everywhere. I'm sorry, Doctor Rand, but there are no others left at E-R-Mag. The last discharge was enormous and took two hundred meter slices across fifty miles of the desert. Your base was one, and the operations center you guys had…well, it's gone." Armetich heard a sudden intake of breath from Rand.

She said through clenched teeth in a determined cadence, "Then I am the ranking member of the team, and this is my call."

Armetich said, "Have the pilot pre-flight the aircraft. You will have clearance by the time he's ready. Major Wacken is it?"

Rand turned the phone toward the pilot, which was on speaker.

"I..uh, yes sir this is Wacken."

"You may not believe I'm the President, but the Barksdale Tower will have your clearances when you are ready to call for the runway, will that be sufficient for your cooperation? If possible, some fighters will be on your wings as far as they can go."

"I…Yes sir that will do."

"Then you are to follow Doctor Rand's orders to the letter. Doctor Rand, Detective Washington, Detective Williams, good luck."

Rand did not discuss the deaths in the hanger.

The power supply was in fact not still in the plane. Rand said with a growl that sent chills down Jaylee's spine, "Wacken you will NOT LIE TO ME AGAIN, is that understood?" Wacken nodded. The pilot carried the object of their mission to the cabin under Jaylee's watchful stare and gun pointed at his back. He had Bart over his shoulder, and the Glock in his right hand. The object the pilot was carrying appeared to be solid polished metal, but weighed only a few pounds.

Soon Rand was in the cabin of the little jet with several straps, re-tying the pony beer-keg sized device to the seat facing her. The aircraft was small compared to the G-6, the cabin only seated five. Jaylee was in the right officer's seat. The intercom was held open so Rand could hear the radio, and conversations between Jay and the pilot, and the tower and ATC. Jay looked at his watch, then yelled at the pilot, "Get this thing in the air, we don't have enough time, maybe 90 minutes!"

Bart was lying on the floor at the rear of the airplane.

Wheels up and on the way, time seemed to slow. "Doesn't it always when something needs to be done at the end of the trip." She said to herself.

Rand was thankful that Jaylee had put the killing of his longtime partner and close personal friend aside, at least for now. The tears wiped away with the back of his huge hand, then back to the mission. God, how she had wanted to hug him, let him wipe the tears from her cheek as well…she had grown to really like the gravely Bart. Later. Now it was back to the mission. Within five minutes three F18 Super Hornets came to the sides and one above and forward of the Honda. Wacken made contact and opened the throttles to 95% full, the maximum safe sustained flying setting

Was it an illusion? Was the device making noise? A hum? Was there a faint glow? It was metal, how could it be glowing, but still be cool to the touch? The pilots name was Larry Wacken. Ex-Air Force regular now in the reserves and working as a contract pilot for Groom Lake. He still wore his Air Force uniform when flying for 'Air Services Incorporated' the flight services supplier for Groom Lake, Sandia Labs, even E-R-Mag Labs and other government "off or at least under" the book operations.

Into the flight nearly an hour the Super Hornet flying above the Honda radioed a loss of power, not a stall but something not right, and peeled off to starboard.

She asked, "Larry, Major, how far to Sandia Mountain?"

"Honestly don't know. Nothings working right on the display. If your orders were any different, I'd ground this thing."

"Give me a fix from Houston center radar, it's important."

She heard the reply from Houston center, "Honda Xray 423, your return is flickering and weak, but we have you 130 miles from your announced flight plan end."

"Roger 130 miles from Sandia. Honda Xray 423." The remaining two Super-Hornets, refueled twice along the way and then catching back up to the Honda, said goodbye and wished them good luck. The fighter planes and pilots were after-burner blue dots as they peeled off.

"ETA Larry?"

"Twelve minutes, Doctor, what do you want me to do when I get there, and where exactly is there?"

"Larry, we will circle the location and determine the best way to deliver this beer keg here into a hole in the mountain."

"What! You can't open a door on this aircraft! The composite will come apart, at the very least the door will tear off!"

Jaylee leaned over to the pilot, put his pistol under the man's ear, "Larry, shut the fuck up and fly this thing. If we lose a door, or this whole airplane, it's for a good cause. Understood? What do you think would happen if time as a constant ceased to exist? We really are trying to save the planet."

Larry nodded, sweat running down his cheek. It was not warm in the cockpit.

Rand re-read the tag attached to the jumper across what appeared to be two terminals on the device. The tag attached to what appeared to be a silver bar read 'DANGER do not remove! Input-output dangerous and un-regulated DANGER' in large red letters.

The aircraft began to shake, like turbulence, but with a rhythm. The lights in the cabin flickered. As seconds ticked by, adrenaline was adding to frayed nerves.

Larry said, voice shaking, "The controls are resisting me turning to get a line on the valley, if we continue straight in, we will only have two hundred yards to clear the peak!"

They saw a sister to Sandia Mountain ahead, the east side, and down a few dozen miles from the "target," a full moon lighting it so it looked like it was made of snow. A giant iceberg in the middle of the early June New Mexico desert with a tiny Honda Airplane Titanic going straight for it. There was dancing green and blue ribbon lights in the sky ahead, Northern Lights?

Jaylee said, "Don't fight it, a miss is as good as a mile."

They cleared the peak by what looked to Jay like feet, not yards. On the other side, the plane nosed down and picked up speed, banking, the pilot brought the craft on a line with the valley between the mountain and the rolling foothills to the west. "ETA less than seven minutes Doctor."

"Thanks Larry, just trust me here. This is either going to work, or we'll be the first humans to drop into an actual black hole, the rest of earth right behind us!"

Rand considered the plight of the plane, shrugged. She took a screwdriver from the backpack tools she had carried, placed it between the side of the device and the buss bar-jumper, and pried. Nothing. She braced her leg against the seat anchors and pried again. With a flash of energy that lit the entire cabin, the jumper popped off. The device emitted a moan, her screwdriver shot from her hand and clanked to the side of the object.

Larry said in a loud, almost scream, "We're toast! Everything died, engines, controls, everything." He was trying to pull back and turn the yoke. Jaylee grabbed his steering yoke and tried to help. Both positions, Captain and Co-Pilot, were frozen in place.

Rand stood and came forward to the area of the jump-seat. The engines had become completely silent. The console was dark. She looked at her watch, why she had no idea, like she was concerned what time they were going to die. It too was dead. It then occurred to her that the device in the front cabin seat had sucked all energy from the aircraft, from the batteries, even the igniters on the two small GE turbo-fan engines.

But the craft was not slowing, or falling. The men fought the controls, with no movement, yet the craft took an angle upward. Jaylee let go of the yoke. "Larry, let go, look!" The craft was flying sideways.

Rand said, "Look…look at me!" The men turned to see her beside them, floating just above the console. The port wing dipped, no sensation of movement to those inside the plane, but the horizon turned ninety degrees.

There was a distinct yellow light coming from the device in the seat. Rand touched it with her hand and instantly saw – felt a flash of…what? It was like an entire PDF instruction book was imprinted in her mind, a foreign language, but completely understood by her, every tiny component. Rows of circuitry that were not like anything she had ever seen in all the physics or electronics labs she had been in. Not clean rows of circuit lines, but what seemed random nests of crystal wires with glowing connections to others. She knew the name of each wire cluster. She thought, in that same language 'fly straight and level.' The aircraft righted itself and the nose came around forward. She thought 'stop'. The airplane instantly stopped in midair. They, nor anything in the craft crashed to the front, although their ground speed had dropped from 300 MPH to 0 in less than a foot.

Rand said to the two faces looking back at her from the cockpit, "This thing does to the plane what I ask it to do! All I did was put my hand on it and, Jesus, I know everything about it! It's a thought-energy amplifier. All I need to do is think a command! Damned! If I didn't have to save the world, this would be a hell of a lot of fun to play with! We don't feel any push or pull, didn't go through the windshield, because we are just like the aircraft, weightless, we have no mass! Like an ant falling from a tree, no mass, just hit the picnic table, grab a birthday cake crumb and walk away."

Larry had turned to look out the front of the plane. "Someone's shooting at us!" Jaylee and Rand snapped heads to look out of the windshield

Lights, much like glowing rocket trails were coming toward the airplane from the side of the mountain. Rand lay her hand on the device, thought go in the hole, dodge the energy coming at us. The aircraft shot from side to side, and advanced to the X-pole. "Jay, this is it. The X-Pole has found this energy source and is coming for it! We were right, the generator is opposite! It's being attracted to it!"

They were moving now, being pulled or flying by the action of the 'keg' toward the energy bolts coming for them. Rand leaned over, Jaylee turned to look at her. The bolts hit the aircraft, white light inside and out of the plane. She kissed him.

CHAPTER 25

A spoken story

The old one had his young "master rank trainees" in a circle around his rock, on which he had sat cross legged, the long four toed feet relaxed to the sides. This story had been told a thousand times and each time it was important not to add to the story, otherwise it would lose all meaning to the future generations. It was and had remained alarming enough as it is.

His old dark almond grey eyes cast about the glowing phosphorescent algae covered walls of the cave and, the four adolescent disciples on the sand in front of him. "We had lived in these mountains and caves for thousands of years, and the earth and caves were, and are, good to us, plenty of food, and clean water, but many before, many family times before, some wanted to see what was above and found a way to what they called the super-light. The first ones died a terrible death as their skin scales peeled up and their life water ran out of them. Then it was found that the light went away, and stayed away for a time, returning again from the other side of the mother mountain."

"A few days after the rest of the clan had followed and arrived at the dry sand, in the dark, a bright light opened in the sky and some prey arrived in the sand. The prey was easy to hunt, and the meat was plentiful. The next dark time more arrived, these ran and hid, some were left not moving, and were covered in the dry dirt. Some had walked away from the others, and those covered with dirt and the walkers too were easy prey."

"Every dark period more things arrived from the sky, and all were amazed, this was easy hunting! A few dark periods later some young ones went to where the prey was and were killed by something coming through the air, not spears, but smaller spears. The next dark period a full clan attack was planned, as it got started, everything in the sand, all the prey fought them, nearly all the clan were killed. Then, in front of the clan survivors, all the things that had arrived from the sky vanished! None here in the deep caves believed the story, until a few sleep times later all who had gone to the light and eaten the easy prey died a painful death, bodies hot like the smoke rocks, and with much pain. The others, who did not eat the prey from the sky were not sick, and since that time no others have ever gone again to the light."

"Take this legend forward and do not add to it. It is the truth as told for generations and must be told exactly as I have told you, so no others try to go to the light. We live here, safe and supplied with everything we need, so go now, tell this to all you meet, and remember now to keep your young friends from trying to go to climb the long caves to the light."

PART 6

The Last Part of The Story

CHAPTER 26

The End of Time

Detective First class Jaylee Washington bolted upright from what he thought had been a deep but dream troubled sleep. He was covered in sweat...and...sand? Disoriented, he looked around, and realized he was in his bed, in his one-bedroom condominium apartment.

Washington was not a light sleeper, well, unless he was working a case, which did not seem to be the problem here. In fact, he and his partner, Bart Williams were just about out of work. The New Mexico Homicide and Gang Special Task Force, a group of detectives, undercover people and selected special operations officers, each some of the best in the Southwest, had been very successful. But, in terms of the survival of the task force, too successful. They had ended an ongoing spat of gang related homicides, in fact all but ended the gangs. He remembered the last action, the killing of "Tiny" Vasquez happening...when...just this morning? The criminal gang members had been flung nationwide in nearly every Federal Prison in America. Even there, strict orders were to keep members separated.

Now the funding was running out, and the lack of new murder cases meant the end of a two-year effort. The Task Force would be history in a few more weeks according to Captain Walker, the administrative command officer. Jaylee tried to focus, when was the killing of the major Las Germen kingpin, "Tiny" Vasquez…when? Yesterday morning? This morning? What happened to the day after the warehouse incident? Walker had said this probably would be the last operation in the pre-op briefing.

Jaylee was also not a sleepwalker, the sand clinging to his muscular, now somehow sweaty body even in the air-conditioned apartment/condo was also a mystery. He gave up on that one for a minute, went to the bathroom, peed, and ran cool water over his face. A bad dream? A hangover? Where had he been last night? Where had he been yesterday? In fact, what day is it anyway? His mind was in a dense fog of shapes and sounds, little he could focus on, nothing that made sense, much less in line with his routine…a round of really weird dreams? What was his routine? Had he been drinking? No hangover, but he felt like he'd been riding in a giant industrial clothes dryer and had been banged around for a while. He did his panther waking stretch, and found a few pains in some sore muscles, returning from bathroom he realized he was thirsty, and decided not to return to the bed just yet.

This was not good. He went to the kitchen of the efficiency, turned on the under cabinet lights. It was still dark, or was it yet dark? Looking to the walk-in closet/equipment room/office, he saw the red, green and a few yellow pilot lights on his HAM radio equipment, the transmission leads going up the wall and into the trap door leading to the attic of the four over four condo apartment building. His mortgage holder, the buildings' old retired owner, was a good guy, and tolerated the radios and various antenna on the roof. A good exchange for having a 6'6" solid Police Detective living there, hell, anything helping security in this peeling and fading area of town was worth it. Okay, he needed the kitchen light, but what time was it? Why had he not looked at the glowing blue numbers on the bedside clock? The only clock visible here, on the microwave said, '44 seconds, hit start.' 'That's a big help,' he thought.

'It doesn't matter what time it is, it never will again,' a clear voice in his head said.

He stabbed a glass retrieved from the dish drainer into the front of the refrigerator, ice cubes clanked into it, the obligatory one crescent block escaping and racing across the floor, it skittered into one of his dusty tactical boots, the left one standing, right one on its side. The cube banged into the boot, recovered like a kid skipping class who had run headlong into the principal in the hallway, and stopped. Jaylee picked the ice up, blew on it (the 5 second germ rule) then noticed sand on the cube, it went into the sink, germs, okay, no matter but no sand in his glass, he straightened.

Damned, he was sore, he reached for a soda on the light blue speckled Formica counter, his arm hurt, like he had just climbed 30 feet of rope, and the old bullet wounded shoulder, which was always sore when waking up – a shadow passed his memory, him pulling real hard on a steering wheel, a small steering wheel, lights flashing then going out, someone, a man yelling. He unscrewed the top on the three quarter full two-liter keg of Diet Dr. Pepper, it hissed like a startled cat, he poured. Going back toward the bedroom/bathroom end of the unit, he stopped. What are my boots doing under the table? The voice again from somewhere between subconscious and conscious inside, 'You were playing in the desert, wake her up, she needs to go to work.'

Wake who up? What the hell is going on? He thought as he turned and started shuffling back toward the bed. He noticed a lump under a sheet on the couch. The hair on his neck began to tingle, like the feeling he had when entering a store with a burglar hiding someplace inside, or this morning… was it this morning – when he was facing "Tiny", the Las Germen boss?

Cautiously, he moved around the end of the couch. A spray of dark hair cascaded over the couch pillow toward the floor. He bent, and gently shook the part of the lump he thought was a shoulder. The woman jumped, looked up at him with wide, but not terrified, eyes. The look was more like complete disorientation. Jaylee stepped back from the couch. "Mam' this may sound strange to you, but I'm detective Jaylee Washington, this is my little condo, and I do not, for the life of me know..." He paused, then said "That's not true, Doctor, I do know you, but...I can't remember..." again trailing off.

She said, "Okay then, I'm in a handsome, very large black man's apartment," looking under the sheet, "in my underpants, and..." She trailed off too. "I know you too, but how...and for how long." Shaking her head, "I can't seem to get my thoughts in a line, were we out drinking or something? If so, it must have been one hell of a party..."

Jaylee said, "Are you covered in sand?"

The question was so out of place she almost laughed, the little giggle caught in her throat, then, as she brushed her hand over her left breast as she drew her arm from the sheet, the right hand holding the sheet in place, she cut off the laugh, "Uh, yes, detective, I am!" A clear confident voice in her mind said, 'trust him, he's good for, and good to you, now get up and get ready for work'. She reached out, took the Dr. Pepper glass from his hand, took a drink, then handed the glass back to him, "Jaylee, I think when we figure this out, it's gonna be one hell of a memory." She swung her feet to the floor, pulled the sheet off her, not feeling even a little self-conscious about being nearly nude, and walked toward the bathroom. Speaking of voices, where was the voice of modesty, or fear, or propriety? Where's a voice when you need one? Maybe the voice where she was when she got her "Alaska Star?" She shrugged and continued to the bathroom.

Jaylee stood there, holding the glass as a beautiful woman got off his couch, wearing only pink thong panties, brushing past him toward the bathroom. A few seconds later, he heard water running.

He went to the door of the bath, still wide open. Setting the glass on a safe place near the back of the toilet tank, he stepped out of his customary sleeping attire, underpants, and entered the shower. After all, it was HIS shower, and he did have sand all over his 6'6" body too.

They washed each other like a couple married for years. He became aroused, she of course noticed, he was not at all a small man, there or anywhere. She gave him a gentle pat, but said, "Not now, I have to get to work and figure out this thing, like who you are, and why I'm here."

Jay said, cupping a very nice breast, "Mind if I ask what a little star is doing tattooed over your nipple? I mean it seems strange for an applied atomic physics doctor, you know, a scientist to…" The thought hung in the shower's steam, how did he know…? He retrieved his hand, "sorry, I just had to…well, you now…"

She laughed a short burst, "Oh, That's Alaska's star."

Jay looked confused. "I'll tell ya all about it sometime." She started to open the shower door, then kissed the tips of her fingers and patted his erection again. "Yeah, I'll be back." Now the voice of propriety went off, 'Joan, what the hell are you saying?'

Drying, she noticed a familiar overnight bag by the end of the sofa, looking inside, she had a change of clothes, a few basic toiletries, even a hairdryer. That clear mind voice replayed, like a good quality recording of a voice saying, 'bring a hairdryer, us black guys don't need one.'

What the hell was going on?

Jay cranked off the shower leaned, then stepped out and got a towel.

She was bending to get something out of a bag, Jaylee saw the most perfect ass he had ever seen, well, seen in person, well okay, seen in his apartment in person. Just for an instant he got a shot of adrenalin, she was getting something out of a black bag, "What you doing?"

"Getting a hair dryer, you black guys don't need one, so I brought one, and some underwear."

Relief washed over him, he felt silly, "I'm so embarrassed to ask this, really I am, but what's your name?"

Stepping into the clean, but also pink panties, she said, "Jay, I don't know why, but that question doesn't bother me at all." Then, "In fact for some reason I really don't know why, but, so far none of this bothers me. I gotta tell you though, this is the strangest situation I can ever remember being in since Sturgis. I'm Doctor Joan Rand, and I work at E-R-Mag Labs on Sandia Base." She hooked a little light-colored bra, then pulled the catches around to the back, the cups came from the other side to the front. Bending over, she wiggled so her just a bit larger than average breasts were properly seated inside, arms went through the shoulder straps. "Excuse me, but I have to dry my hair."

While the whine of the hairdryer was going, he dressed in Dockers and a polo shirt, oversized to conceal a side holster for his Titanium custom Glock .40, dark brown suede ankle high desert boots, wool socks. Back in the kitchenette he opened the fridge, got an apple, holding it out to Rand, she nodded, he tossed it to her, she caught it with her right hand, never slowing the hairdryer. Jay got another. Pointing to the coffee maker he signed 'Want coffee?'

The hairdryer wound down to silence. "Yes, the coffee at the base is…" a memory of dropping several cups into the trash can popped into her head.

Jay saw a shadow of coffee machine disasters from someplace in his mind, Bart pointing his pistol at it, he said, "Have I had any of that coffee? I don't know…"

Clean and dressed, he said, "Doctor, work or no work, I think we have to do a little 'mind work' here to figure out why our heads are so screwed up about how you got here, and how we know each other." He crunched another block of apple and studied her. "I'm a cop, and I don't like stuff happening around, or to me that I can't follow. I must say, too, that I've never given up so easily on sex with a beautiful woman, especially a nude one with me in a shower."

Rand smiled, said, "The shower thing happens a lot, does it?"

"Okay...well...shit...Okay, It's never happened, at least not here and not anywhere for ten years, but that's not the point. If it had happened here I wouldn't have given up so...Christ! You know what I mean."

She laughed out loud, "I did leave a promise hanging, even if you weren't, didn't I?" She then thought, jees Joan, cock jokes? That's really not your style. "Look, Jay, I don't think we have done 'it' yet, but I really trust you...and...I really like you. Somehow and someway. A rain-check for sex with a guy who...well...who I can't really remember, that's not like me, not like me at all. My training leaves me a skeptic, albeit a scientific skeptic. Yes, we definitely need to figure this and a bunch of stuff out."

Rand sat cross-legged in a kitchen chair, in a light beige bra and another pair of those nice little pink underpants, waiting for the coffee to drop. The machine gurgled like a cat barfing, and fumed little clouds of steam. She continued, "So, what's the last thing you remember before waking up here a few minutes ago?"

Jay thought about that, a look of real concern crossed his face, he actually ran his hand over it like he had an imaginary washcloth. "I don't know if it's the last thing, but I have my pistol pointed at a pilot in some kind of aircraft. I don't remember what kind. Wait, there's a Honda insignia in the center of the wheel, there's no co-pilot. Jesus, does Honda make airplanes? How about you."

She screwed up her face like she'd bit into a crabapple instead of a Grimes Golden. "I'm in an airplane too, with a beer keg sized thing between my legs that I'm tying down to the seat in front of me with some kind of ratcheting straps. I see your back, you have on black pants, black boots, some kind of military looking vest and you're yelling at the man, pilot I guess, to 'get the fuck in the air, we only have ninety-eight minutes!'"

Jay remembered too, "Yeah, like later he's saying that the instruments are not working, and the flight computer is giving him bullshit numbers…I said we're all going to be dead if he can't get in the air!" He looked at her, she was standing now, an odd look on her face. "Doctor, I was scared, I don't remember ever being that scared. And Bart…my very best friend Bart…he's…god, I hope it was just a dream."

The words crumbled at the end of the sentence, he shook his head, turned to the coffee pot, now silent, poured a cup for himself, one for her, turning. Rand, remembering someone she cared for a great deal shot…Bart? She went to him as his shoulders shook, patted his back. Sighing, what came out as a very, very sad sound, he got two little creamer thimbles from the dairy door in the refrigerator, poured them in, put in one barely rounded teaspoon of sugar, then, stirring it, handed the coffee to her.

They both stopped as she reached and took the cup. Then taking it from him, "Two creams, one sugar, detective, you're quite the mind-reader, or…"

Suddenly Jaylee staggered back, "This has to be a dream, Rand! But it seems so real. It's later, like an hour …no more…I'm saying, yelling like in a panic, 'we now have two minutes'. Out the front of the plane is a weird light, flashing, blue, white, red, all colors. Not lightening, but looks like it, someone's saying 'They're shooting at us!'"

"He's yelling, 'we have to pull up!' Then…oh God! Rand, he says the controls aren't working! He's sweating, it's running down his face as he struggles to pull up the aircraft! He pulls the throttles wide-open, the engines are quiet…dead! Nothings working!" He was in a trance as deep as any Chris Angle ever put anyone under. "I'm not paying any attention to the instruments, they are flashing and all over the place, then die completely anyway and go dark. "

"We're going directly toward a mountain. You're giving me instructions, 'a little to the left, down now' but it doesn't matter, it's like we're being pulled toward the mountain, then down the valley just over the top! The plane misses the crest by a few feet! My memory, the order of the events seems messed up like time is scrambled." As the dream, or was it a memory, played, a tear ran down his cheek, the panic was back in his voice and on his face, "I… I see the target, it's a hole in a mountain! Then…I instinctively try to help the pilot pull up, the controls are frozen…solid, they are like welded in place, I'm pulling so hard the wheel is bending – but the plane is dropping toward the hole." One of his hands then extended, pointing, at some remembered thing out an invisible windshield, the extended finger shaking.

"Rand you are saying, 'It's ok Jay, trust me', the plane is doing what-ever I want it to."

Doctor Rand nodded her head. "Yes, yes. I remember." She stopped, eyes wide, "I remember the whole explanation of a mind-controlled energy amplifier…I'm not trained in the details of that type of electronics, but I see circuits and components, and I thoroughly understand every connection, every tiny component and their function!" Then looking back to Jay, "Go on I'm right with you. If it's a dream, we had the exact same one…Jay this is important we… go on…Jay, we both need to remember!"

He continued, voice shaking, more emotion and feeling than he'd ever remembered, certainly much more than the rough-edged homicide detective he had become ever spoke of, "You're on the console, you pull yourself in between the seats, real near me. You're floating! Rand, you lean over and kiss me as we seem to be moving slower and slower. The mountain and hole are all we can see out of the windshield. It's like a monster's mouth, like gagged teeth-looking-rock on all sides…then, we are inside the hole, but not flying at 500 knots, we are…like…falling. The engines are silent. Everything's silent, I try to speak, no sound. I'm thinking, 'the wings should have been torn off.' The thing in the cabin, the round thing you were tying to the seat is giving off a high pitched whine, it's now bright white, like it's going to melt, but there's no heat!"

Jaylee is sweating, a panic look on his face. His hand is shaking. Rand took his coffee and set it on the counter. She took both his hands and looked directly into his eyes. He stuttered, then continued. "The scene is...like the plane, walls of the hole, even you, are made of glass, liquid glass. I've seen this somewhere before." He was struggling to continue, "The light is getting brighter, both inside the plane and from outside. Way bright now, hard to look at... suddenly there's a flash, heat, I feel like concussion hit me, hot heat, but no burn! Then..."

She took his hand interrupting, "Then we are laying in the desert, under a big tree, with something flashing in its branches. We hear voices and some kids are giggling, a teenage girl, she's pulling a tank top down, and a long-haired boy, maybe a Native American kid, he's turned away, like he's zipping his pants. We struggle to our feet. The kid asks if we were hiding in the tree and fell out! We tell him to mind his own business. Then we all laugh, and like...we can't stop!"

Jay continued, "Yes, I got it now, we walk down a sandy path, to the road, and start to walk toward the lights of town, a young Sheriff's Deputy, stops and gives us a ride, says he thought someone would be walking toward town, in fact gave us a ride all the way here." He paused, washed his face with the invisible cloth again, "Then...we're here...I don't remember how long ago that was, or what we did when we got here. If it was anything physical with you...and I don't remember, that would really piss me off!"

Rand laughed, "Well, I don't have a whole lot of 'physical' about you in my memory, and, big fella, well some in fantasy…from a few days ago? And then what I know from the shower." She finally blushed, "But nothing more than that with you, I mean I did wake up on the couch, right?" She laughed again, another blush.

Jaylee laughed, "Doctor, you have healed a wounded, lonely soul."

They reminisced, and talked of the events of the night, and disconnected incidents of…what? The past several days? Nearly another hour went by in a blur, that one time, in Jay's apartment.

As the remaining night and early morning dragged on, the memory seemed to fade, details so troubling and vivid just a few minutes prior dimmed. Soon it was a shared dream, then a distant echo.

Forty-five minutes later, Jaylee and Rand got out of the taxi which had left them beside his Crown Vic. He then drove from the Kirkland air base parking area and dropped her off in front of her building at the E-R-Mag Labs main building – funny, after the guard let them into Sandia, he drove straight to the building, one of dozens scattered around the center of the base proper without any prompting from Dr. Rand. Putting the car in park, he was going to try to think of something catchy but as he looked at her, Jay leaned over and as she turned to him, they came together over the console for a very nice and 'warm to the heels' kiss. Breaking the smooch she said, "Wow. Detective, I need more investigation of this!" Brushing her hand across his cheek she turned and left the car, walking into the building.

CHAPTER 27

The Details

Inside the building Rand walked down the hallway leading to her office, Doctor Chris Jefferies was puffing, nearly running, down the hall from her office where apparently he had been looking into for her, he was red faced and really upset. "Joan, where the hell you been, I last saw you hours ago when we threw the switch?" Then not waiting for an answer, "We're done, toast...the ENet antenna is completely fucked up!"

Joan said, "Woah, what the hell do you mean? How does an antenna made of 1000-MCM copper cable, 19,000 meters long, buried nine feet in the ground get messed up?"

"Jesus, I don't know, but there is no continuity in any of the Yagi radiators, no sampling leads either. Nothing. If I didn't know better, I'd say it vanished! Poof! Shit, glad you're in field clothes, we need to get out there. We energized it a few hours ago like the plan, you remember? Then poof! Nothing!" He wheeled, made another full turn, and grabbed her arm. "Joan, the damned thing took the load then BAM, it dropped like we had opened the breakers, the load from the transmitter went poof, apparently some reflected power fried the whole transmitter, the inverters, the modulator…all of it, some melted, some with holes blown in the sides like they were shot with a pulsed high-energy laser-beam! We're done! Thirteen years of work, gone!"

Rand looked at Jefferies, in her mind she saw him in a bus type thing in handcuffs? As she shook her head, he was 'normal'. "Jeff, maybe some thieves got a machine, hooked it to one end of the cable and pulled it out. I dunno, it's either there or someone stole it. What other possibility is there?"

By noon of the day for Jaylee, Rand and the others the events, like the airplane, the monsters mouth hole, even the weirdness of the previous several days and nights were quickly turning into faded shadows. Yes, for her and the others they would return in dreams, and fragments of thought, but, for the most part, all but gone.

Were the events fading to somewhere else, sometime else, a divergent path to a different place? Or the same place but not accessible? Try as they would, she and Jaylee never again came to their full consciousness with the detail of that early morning discussion over coffee, 2 creams 1 sugar, an apple and a hair dryer.

Arthur Cheete was on the way home from a completely calm evening shift of the Albuquerque Station 45 Fire and EMS service. There were no calls in his whole 24-hour shift, quite unusual. He was absolutely fighting to stay awake, and was in no particular hurry, driving the 6 miles to his apartment, where he lived alone with his cat, wives were hard pressed to stay with a firefighter, the schedule, the effects of the stressful job. Why was he so tired, and come to think of it, dirty? He stopped at the intersection, noticed a very attractive young woman standing, waiting to cross the street, she raised a foot to step off the curb. Suddenly the scene waved like he was seeing the scene reflected from underwater, looking up as a stone dropped into the middle of the intersection, a wave of dizziness swept over him, then everything was back to normal. Did he just see what he thought he did? Naw – too much coffee and not enough sleep? And where did this reddish sand stuck on his arms come from? The light changed and the world continued.

New Mexico State Police Captain Randy Potet'e detoured from his commute to the regional headquarters office building, and stopped at the Burlington Northern Santa Fe Yard police substation, used with the railroad's permission as a drug/gang task force staging location. He walked up the stairs, nodding and saying hello, a few hand-shakes. Inside he found his son, Randy Jr., completing some overnight paperwork. He walked up behind him, tapped his shoulder. "Dad! What brings you to the wrong side, well actually the middle, of the tracks?"

Captain Potet'e said, "I dunno, just wanted to be sure you were okay, silly, I know, but…" His voice broke.

Junior stood, "Hey, dad, it's okay, the bust went just as planned, no gunfire from me, but the point guy shot "Gang Tiny." It was a good shoot, no problems but the paperwork. None of the good guys hurt. I must have knocked both my shins, someplace and bruised em' and they hurt, they hurt like hell, but I don't remember anything hitting them…I'm fine other than that." He took his dad's arm and led him to an empty interview room a few feet away.

Senior said, "I know, I heard the whole thing… the radio I had on Tac 2. I just had a dream, but it seemed so…shit, Randy, this is silly." He hugged his son, a little harder and a little longer than he ever had. They broke the embrace, Jr. a little uncomfortable, but kind of warm inside. Senior opened the door, "Be sure to call your mom, you know how Ms. Betty is." Then he was gone.

Christian Halloway looked up from his game tablet, then put it down. "Hey mom, when do kids outgrow stuff like Gameboys and PlayStations?"

His mother looked at him from the rear-view mirror of the mini-van, he saw questions in her eyes. "I don't know, Chris, some people I know never do. One guy, Andrew, you know, the eight-foot-tall guy from over on the base, plays all the time he's not working. I go to the hairdresser with his mom sometimes, and she's always talking about his gaming. Anyway, why do you ask?"

He looked out the window at the intersection, Cheete was in the car next to his, their eyes met, and just for a second… "I guess if you've been stuck in the desert a few million years ago, fighting gator-lizard people, spending hours on a game box seems kind of stupid. I think I'll give mine to Wash Hutter at the school, he's poor and their family can't afford to buy him one."

Maggie Halloway now looked concerned, "Look Chris, you give that thing away and we are NOT going to buy you another, do you understand me?"

No typical comeback, no inane adolescent arguments, just a nod. The eyes of her son, looking back from the mirror had aged, seemed much wiser. Older. The boy had not grown in size, but something in the eyes. Yes, this young mother knew, that then and there, her little boy had taken some big step toward growing up. Had this boy matured somehow since getting into the van twenty-three minutes ago? Yes, she knew something, somehow had changed him, and she knew that her little boy was well on the way to a young man.

She swung her eyes back to the slow-moving traffic, then, a wave of pure mothers-worst-nightmare panic hit her. She stopped the car, swung her arm over the seat and looked at her son, eyes filling. The boy looked from Cheete, to his mom and said, "It's ok mom, I'm right here, like nothing ever happened." She reacted to a high-pitched beep-beep from behind her, a guy on a motorcycle, tapping his horn, and continued to the school in silence.

Macy was just getting out of the car where her dad had driven her to the High School just after lunch. She looked over at her dad. "Hey dad, I know how hard it's been since mom died...I just want you to know how much I love you, and that I know how much you think about me. I dunno, ...okay, I love you...really."

Art Plankerton looked at his daughter, tears sprung to his eyes. This was not the normal thing from a teenage girl. He choked out an answer, "Macy, you are worth every and any amount of effort I put in." Then, grinning "You keep me young and maybe give me a good reason to go to Wal-Mart every day. What's wrong with your arm? Is it hurting you? Looks bruised."

Macy looked at her arm, yeah, it hurts, must have hit it on something, looks like a rash, or bug bites too," she brushed some little red ants off, "Now where did they come from, and why did they bite me?"

Six-foot ten-inch Andrew Bodkin looked in his mom's bathroom mirror where he had just cleaned the spray of toothpaste dots from brushing his teeth. His face shimmered, he instinctively touched the glass to see if it had been melted by the water on the washcloth he had in his hand. Nope...solid. Nothing to contemplate and no more information to process. The 165 IQ eighteen-year-old moved on. Melting mirrors that hadn't, were in and out of his mind like water through a screen. He re-buttoned his shirt and started back to the "problem", the call from the base about the vanishing antenna on Sandia Mountain. What a dream, someone shooting a guy right behind the President? And in the blue conference room?

Wow! How did I get home anyway? I was there when the switch was thrown, or was I?

James George had been the Switch Manager for six of his twenty-one years with the AmeriSouth Power Consortium, thirteen of them right here. Nothing like this had ever happened. A few hours ago, as his shift was half-way to ending, but well before the day crew of three people arrived, every alarm in the yard had gone off. Every breaker started a disconnect sequence. Then, reversing, everything went back to normal. The data loggers had not even recorded the glitch. What was he supposed to tell the day shift? Screw it. No record, no foul.

Fang, the dog, walked across the open area in front of the switch control building, carefully cocked his leg on the barrel cactus planted there, carefully keeping the needle spikes safely away from his watering apparatus. The dog looked at James, wagged his tail and drifted back toward the guard shack. As George turned, he noticed something rather weird, the last few inches of his belt was missing, like clean-cut off. "What the hell?"

Sherriff Sam Bush was reading a report of vandalism at the Native American Community College campus. Some asshole or assholes, as yet unnamed, had melted the arm of the bronze Native American mascot. He and Mayor Jamas had decided by telephone an hour earlier to make city funds available to repair the thing. He mused, "Luna, you got any idea at all why someone would unload a torch and melt the arm off a god-damned Native American statue?"

Luna sat down her egg, sausage, bacon, home-fries (with onion) on Texas toast sandwich, careful not to tear the double layer aluminum foil, wiped her chin with a Brawny double size paper towel, added it to the forty-seven already in the wastebasket, and shrugged. "You know, that poor Native American gets painted every graduation, pigeon-shit plastered in between, rode by drunks, and in general dis-re-expected on a routeeeen basis. I guess this is the latest dis-re-expectation. Most of us thought that Native American's hand was givin' everybody the bird anyway." She lifted the foil, took another bite.

Deputy Ivey walked in, looked over to Luna, who was dressed on a sweatsuit outfit completely in pink, looking like she was made of frozen Pepto-Bismol, in the middle of a Spring thaw, then looked at the Sheriff, "Oh, I took a ALB detective and a woman down the road to his place. Flagged me down on 165, they were near the Silver tree, maybe drinking 'cause they didn't have much to say about how they got there. Very strange though, I felt like I knew them, and knew they were going to be there…one of them strange nights all around." Then to Luna, "Thirty bucks for a guy to tell me there's nothing wrong with my TV set? I'm in the wrong business."

The gentle breeze waved the board with the Amish Hex sign, dusty, rusty screw-eyes holding the board made little squeaks like baby chicks, below the flowers fighting dust, bobbing their heads to the squeaking chicks. Old man Foxlight rocked gently on his porch, the trailer perched on the dry wash dirt cliff where it had been for nearly four decades. Every storm took the edge a half inch closer to the trailer toppling into the muddy torrent that came and went in an hour with each monsoon thunderstorm. He felt he had about twenty-four inches until the disaster. He'd never live to see his house swept away.

The faded red Jeep grumbled to a stop followed by a small dust cloud and a faint screech of sandy brakes, "Hi Gran!" Willy called out. The old man waved, and pointed a bony hand to the chair beside him. The boy normally didn't want to spend much porch time with his grandad but this morning? Something about this morning. His leg and fingers on one hand hurt bad, 'what's that about' he thought as he shuffled over to the #2 Cracker Barrel rocker and sat.

"I won't keep you long, Willy, I know you're hungry. I got fry-bread, scrapple and eggs ready to go." He looked down at the porch boards. "Willy, I thought I'd lost you, had a vision, clearest one I ever had." Willy noticed a tissue clutched in the old man's hand, his unusually extra-watery eyes. "You was hurt bad and lost someplace in the desert with Macy. I also knew you'd be back somehow, the Spirits and a young Native American Deputy in the vision, said so. Welcome…home…boy…" A tear ran down the old man's cheek.

Willy got up and hugged his grandfather, now both of them tears running down their faces. "Gran,

I ain't going nowhere, you make the best fry-bread in New Mexico! – maybe the whole Southwest!" Willy somehow also knew the vision, and was himself troubled by it; now even more so troubled that his Grandfather had the vision too, that he made a decidedly adult decision and didn't mention it. A red desert? No leg? So that's where the hurt came from…but? Something coming out of the night, big, scary and stalking he and Macy…those huge black eyes! She was hurt too, and scared, so scared she couldn't even scream, just small whimpers as she hugged him…with one arm! Here on the porch an ice water shiver went down his back.

One thousand six hundred thirty-two miles away and two hours later in the time-zones, John J. Armetich had Paul Crain, the Homeland Security Secretary in front of the Resolute desk in the Oval Office. "This might seem strange to you, but I have my reasons for giving this order. I want your third in command, Milton, assigned to our counselor office in Pakistan, effective immediately. I expect him to be at that post in three days, earlier if possible. If Mister Milton does not wish to take this post, wish him good luck in the private sector."

"M… Mister President I…" The look Armetich gave Crain stopped him mid-sentence. "I'll see to it."

"Thank you Paul. I also have set it up for you to spend some time at the war-college in leadership training, I expect to have good reports when you're finished the six-week course. That's all."

A tall Secret Service Agent caught the President's eye, just a small nod and smile crossed between them as he opened the door to the Oval Office for Crain to leave.

A pretty dark hired girl walked up four flights of urine smelling stairs, walls tagged with countless layers of graffiti, turned left to the dirty, scratched apartment door, inserted a key and went in. Bobby K looked up from the faded color picture on a worn old screen TV set, "Krystal? What the hell did you do? Why you dressed square? You gonna get a job or something?"

"No, I just figured you out. You're a crack head loser, and so are damned near all our, well actually your 'friends' if you can really call them that. I'm leaving, I'm just here to get a few things. No hard feelings, Bobby K, and I wish you good luck."

He stumbled to his feet, "You ain't going nowhere less I say so!" He took a step toward her, she wheeled and pushed him back, hard, then as he came forward again cracked him on the head right between his eyes with the small T-ball bat that was always behind the door. He fell backwards on the couch. She went by and collected her things, put them in a medium duffle bag, leaving the chains, a pair of black work boots and a little pin shaped like a skull with red fake ruby eyes. Bobby was holding his head in his hands, he got up and started to block the way, anger in his eyes and blood running down his face from the two inch cut between his eyes, this time she pushed him again, hard over the bed where he crashed doubled up like a well-worn billfold between the bed and the wall as she walked out, slamming the battered door behind her. The T-ball bat swinging loosely at her side.

That evening, at Albuquerque Station 45, an older graying man walked to the firefighter leaning in a chair against the wall beside the open engine bay door. "Mister, uh Lieutenant," the man said, "this might sound strange, but you mind if I sit and talk awhile with you? I've been by this station a number of times, but today…strange, I think I know you, but from where… I just don't exactly know," Mort said.

Art looked at the man, angled his head a little to the side, "Yeah, me too Doc." Standing and pulling another chair from just inside the doorway. "Please, have a seat, let me get you some tea." They looked at each other, and laughed. A man in a tan uniform with a bunch of kids walked out, "Thanks Lieutenant Cheete, the scouts appreciated the tour of the station." Gus Wasocki took his group of seven Boy Scouts to the van waiting on the side of the building, loaded them in for the ride back to the church where Troop 1994 of the Boy Scouts of America were headquartered. He looked at the older man, then to Cheete extended his hand, "Sorry, I never got the chance to shake hands with you two…I… ahh…well…uhh…nice to meet you." Looking at the ground, he walked to the driver's passenger door of the van, and got in. Gus thought as he turned the key and started the van, 'couldn't shake hands because you had no right hand'. Where the hell did that come from? Some dream? A movie? 'Oh well'… he put the van in reverse and backed onto the fire station apron, completed the three-point turn and headed for the church.

It wasn't a fair fight. The coyote, normally docile and reclusive, had come from under the bridge and growled, then lunged for the sandwich Sam Freeman was un-wrapping, he had just taken it from the shelter van where the outreach people were distributing food fifteen minutes earlier. He batted the animal on the side of the head with his clenched fist. "Try to steal my damned sandwich! I don't goddamned think so!" The coyote, in an unusual display of ferocity, proceeded to bite him at least ten times on the arms and twice on the face, he scratched Sam with a paw deformed from being caught in a spring trap. Sam did get the sandwich back though. A rock upside the animal's head concluded the argument. A paranoid schizophrenic, even though he needed stitches, doctors were not an option! He shuffled back to his box near the dry gulch railroad bridge. He ate the battered sandwich, and drank a bottle of water provided in the box lunch.

Now, five days later he had a terrific headache and had stumbled into the free clinic. Soon he was in Mercy hospital. The staff had him strapped to a bed, IV lines going into both legs and an arm. Lying in a Quarantine room, delirious, the tests had come back with bad news. His son in Phoenix had been called, the man told them to cremate his father, and he would get the ashes sometime next week.

No one could find his ex-wife. Sam was dying of Hydrophobia. Rabies.

The same day Sam had entered the hospital Detective Bart Williams had also been delivered by ambulance to the hospital. Something had damaged his right eye, he had waked up in extreme pain, and had trouble making it to the phone for the 9-1-1 call. Soon he was in surgery and they were trying to save the eye. Jaylee had raced to the hospital eye center after dropping Doctor Rand at E-R-Mag Labs on Sandia Base, and getting the phone call from the 9-1-1 dispatcher who knew both the detectives, and that they were partners. A few hours later, in the recovery room. "What the hell did you do?" Jay said to his friend, whose head was a ball of bandages.

"Jay, I really don't know. Since the fight with gang Tiny and the Las Germen guys, it's been like a dream, it seemed so real. You and I were drawn down on some guys in a warehouse or hanger, shit I don't know, I'm pretty sure it wasn't the Las Germen warehouse, but I don't know. I think I was shot, but the doc says I would have been killed if whatever hit me had been a bullet, and the eye was damaged but not destroyed, he asked me when it happened, and said that some hours of healing was apparent. He says the eye ain't gonna look right, but I will probably be able to see okay with glasses. Man, I barely made it to the phone, I don't ever remember such pain. I'm hoping this don't mean retirement!"

Jay took his friends' hand, "Listen you-old-bastard, you gotta be careful. I can't go on being a cop if you get killed or something." He turned away, even though both of Barts' eyes were bandaged, he instinctively didn't want him to see the tears running down his face. The nurse taking Bart's blood pressure patted the big man's arm, made a note on a computer tablet, looked at the floor and walked out. Could he tell him he had a dream of him being killed by a gunshot to the eye? And where was that, in a dark big tin hanger, like Bart said, not the Las Germen building. What good would talking about what seemed a dream do? Still... he coughed and said, "Hey you got to get better, Bart. Bro, I have a girlfriend! Her names Joan and she's beautiful, you got to meet her! I think this ones' gonna work out, somehow I know it!"

Bart turned his head, the older man's mouth, practically the only thing visible on the bandaged head was smiling. "You always did like the dark haired smart ones, shit, Jay, she can even make a vending machine work!"

How did he....?

A week later, Jaylee and Bart had parked the Blue Crown Victoria unmarked cop car (like a three-year-old couldn't tell it was a cop ride!) and walked to where the tracked excavator crawled across the Bar-Nunn Ranch from the trailer on which it had just arrived. It was making its one-mph way toward where Rand and a group of people were waiting beside a row of surveyor's stakes. Rand waved at Jaylee as the detectives arrived beating the crawler by a minute. It was just seven days after she and Jaylee had awakened, covered in sand in Jay's condo, and yes, they had seen each other again for some rather fun bonding. "Hi guys, glad you could make it. Doctor Jefferies said I could invite you, and, as he said, he has no friggin' idea why. Anyway, we're about to dig across this line of stakes to see what happened to our buried wire here." She gestured to the barely scrub grass covered free-range 'pasture' across the hill. "It was supposed to be part of a communications net, but when we energized it, something went wrong."

Jay remembered something from the far distant memory of looking out from under a canopy in the hot sun, looking up the mountain at rows of disturbed earth...what was he saying in the dream? Something about enormous power to excite an antenna?

Jay and Bart, who still had an eye patch, but to the complete amazement of the doctors, the eye was practically back to how it had been before the damage and surgery.

The men followed Rand to the group of unlikely looking hi-desert hikers, and extended a hand to Jefferies who gave them a limp fish handshake. "Gentlemen, Rand says you people are somehow connected, although I have no idea why, and anyway maybe a few detectives can help us uncover what happened here to my 1000 MCM Delrin covered pure copper cable."

Jaylee did a double-take, then whispered to Bart's ear, "That's about a 1 ½" thick wire, Bart, and if it goes where the stakes are, there's tons of it buried here."

Rand, standing close also whispered to Jaylee and Bart, "Yes Jay, it's 9,055 meters here and goes all the way back to E-R-Mag Labs base near where you left me off a few days ago."

Jay's only response, "Wow."

The excavator was in place and began digging, dry sandy/clay earth being piled up outside of where the ditch would cave in if the removed dirt was stacked near the edge of the trench. The ditch was also being made wide enough to not be a concern of burying anyone if a collapse happened.

At about seven feet down the machine operator yelled and bailed out. "I got a shock, you said there was no juice down there, what the…"

Jefferies said, "Two things, first you're in a metal machine sitting on metal tracks, and second there is no power being supplied to this antenna, that's why we're here." He went to the machine, heaved his overweight bulk up into the cab, touched the controls and said, "Must be static or something, Manny, bring a meter here." A handsome dark-skinned man, answered with a slight Spanish accent and handed up a Fluke DVM. After a few probes, Jefferies said, "Yes there's about 35 volts and that might be from the electrical system of the machine. Your hands are sweaty, otherwise you would never have noticed it. Put on some gloves and please, get back to work."

The machine operator, a central casting redneck heavy machine guy in faded jeans, slight beer gut, poorly trimmed (if trimmed at all) beard, Union 633 Teamsters ball hat, and a black tee shirt on the back of which was printed "If you can read this the bitch fell off," reluctantly took some offered gloves from an Asian man's fanny-pack which stretched but fit his hands, and climbed back in the machine. Everyone was intently looking into the 8'wide, 15' long trench as the operator carefully, a few inches at a time scraped the trench.

It was obvious that he had cut across an earlier but much narrower 1' wide trench, Jay thought, likely the trench where they buried the cable. At the 8-foot line they noticed a green tint starting which became more intense green as the inches revealed more of a circle of green dirt. As the depth reached 11 feet, Jeffries signaled the operator to move the bucket aside.

Everyone walked, actually mostly slid down the end of the cut to the circle of green. The Asian man, who Jeffries addressed as Dr. Kough, started taking pictures as a 6' 10" tall young man began bagging small dirt samples as Kough instructed him to label each to align with his pictures. Manny exclaimed, "Well look at this," as Rand held the Fluke digital Volt Meter – DVM in one hand with the meter's face toward him. She stabbed the red lead into the center of the green circle, "I have an AC voltage of over 100 volts, but…" They looked at the other meter lead which was held in his hand pointed straight up in the air!

Jaylee said, "Look people, if you don't know the frequency of this AC, I suggest you get out of there until you know if it's radio or even microwave. You could be getting RF burns or worse! And…since you have one hand in the air, I think Tom Bearden, and his dead mentor Nicholai Tesla might have some of you folks reading or re-reading his version of Tesla's uni-pole theories."

Rand smiled at him, this guy IS smart!

Jefferies said, "You're correct, I haven't read Bearden since college, but…anyway I'm glad Dr. Rand invited you here, clear the trench until we get more data. It's obvious the cable is turned to copper ore, but how?"

How Indeed.

EPILOGUE

The mind...a curious place to visit, others especially. Walking through their gossamer cobweb draped mind-shadows, in places they think they forgot, remembering people they thought they may have known. Maybe just the times they lived through...or dreamt. My life is exploring those dimly lit passages, those locked doors with things behind that some do not wish ever to see again, or events to claim, or even remember...again.

Many people in the Sandia mountain range valley and the central parts of New Mexico had strange dreams and fitful memories of...what? Explosions in the night, clocks not working, 'people made of glass' and a host of other weird things. A local broadcaster even started a blog – "The mass alien abduction north and south of Albuquerque" in a somewhat sincere but off-base attempt to explain the dreams and "feelings" many locals have reported.

The collective trip down what I think is an alternative time path would fade and eventually disappear from all our consciousness, but I think, if the dreams...and some nightmares we all seem to be having are an indication, the sub-consciousness still has them. Mine was doing the fading like everyone else's, but true to my training, I wrote it down as the fits and flashes of memory were happening and filled in the details from conversations I had with those people who arrived with me in the "red-hell-desert," and more from those we "left behind." My documenting these events started with Firefighter-Paramedic Arthur Cheete and grew from there. The events back here, where my watch tells me the "correct" time, were filled in by some people I found, the lady Doctor who signed the note that came through with the supplies, Doctor Joan Rand. She put me in touch with most of the players, her husband Detective Jaylee Washington, and the others. As I summarized the events and details, most agreed to be interviewed, some even hypnotized. Jefferies was an exception, even though he was …well…forced to retire, saying everything was classified, but with everyone else, I didn't need him. Their memories had, like everyone else's faded. I think maybe the nature of the universe is to have the timeline heal itself. Many were harder to re-construct, but like I said, they came around with some hypnosis, and a little prodding.

Of all the things that were hard to explain, the total lack of any news footage, or the stories in the library morgue file papers about those several days. My first visit had some space where stories may have been, but the words were scrambled, faded, or even missing. In a few weeks the papers had no space at all where the stories had been! That, and the ever receding memories convince me that time is indeed a self-healing stream of events, with rules and laws we may never understand.

Oh, I have to admit, the part about the elder Gator instructing the young ones was complete conjecture. Before we were saved by the cancelling of the X-pole that last night, we killed or injured over 30 of them, sadly we lost 2 humans to spears, another 12 injured, a few pretty seriously. If the fight had continued, we probably would have lost it all. We were nearly out of arrows, and the old shotgun was down to 3 birdshot shells, which would not kill them unless they were close, well within their spear range. An 8-foot-tall lizard that can see in the dark can throw a spear a long way, and at night the incoming spears were all but invisible until the last second.

The real question remains, how far would we have had to travel to get out of that desert, and what would we find out there if we did? The Cretaceous period was winding down 93,000,000 years ago, so we were well within the best guess of dinosaurs being around, their last throws of their lifetime, if indeed they also were riding along that timeline. It does beg the question; why did the gators go underground? Was it too dangerous above for creatures of their size in the regular land or on the seas? Questions probably never to be answered.

I told all of those who agreed to help with the recalling of faded memories that I'd put it all together, took damned near a year…and Jaylee was a great help, and Bart who ended up retiring about a year after the "incident" in the hanger. Both helped find some of the others, but, you know, time doesn't seem so important now. The hardest to find was the unfortunate Sam, turns out he was a homeless man, poor devil, hydrophobia is a very bad way to go. He actually was traced by being one of 2 rabies cases in the area that year, the other case caught and treated with vaccine a few hours after being bitten by a coyote. Sam, not receiving treatment for what looked like a hell of a dog fight, died.

I was pleased when I visited the AmeriSouth switching facility, and the dog, Fang, nearly ran me over, tail wagging and licking my hand. Jim George said he never saw such a thing, some guard dog. I guess a dog's memories aren't stuck in the time-line thing.

When Dr. Rand agreed to be hypnotized and had her deep memories returned to where they could be examined and recorded, she also gave me some interesting information on the antenna. Obviously nearly $120,000,000 worth of cable and equipment and another $8,000,000 to bury it could not just be written off. Sixty-five excavations were done on the antenna site, and the cable was found...sort of anyway. As each ditch crossed where the cable should have been, a circular strip of copper-sulphate about a meter in diameter was found. Careful analysis also had some decayed hydro-carbons around the edges of the circle of turquoise/green dirt. The best guess is that this is what a large plastic-coated pure copper cable would look like if buried in the slightly acidic and salty Sandia Mountain dirt for 100,000,000 years...imagine that. Oh, and there are still some un-accounted for voltages and frequencies in the area.

On a really good note mentioned before, Jaylee and Rand got married, pooled their savings and bought the Bar-Nunn ranch, neither could tell me why, after the "event" they were drawn to the place, but the folks who lived there left and put the place up for sale early in 2007. Several people walked the land and some said they thought it was haunted or possessed. Jaylee and Rand felt at home there, and allowed Bart to summer his class C motorhome on the property with him in it. He never married as of this writing, but dates a Hispanic lady he "somehow knows" but from where he doesn't remember. Both love kids but like to babysit others, As Bart says, "They go home at the end of the day or weekend." Makes good sense to me.

Dr. Rand also informed me that a device was missing from the Groom Lake warehouse, which she couldn't go into for security reasons, but was probably the one in her memories of the last night flights to and from the Gulf coast.

No, I will not go on a book selling circuit or a gig on George Norrie's Coast to Coast with the story, even though, like so many alien abductees, the events are really locked in each of our minds someplace…just a little out of reach. Oh, sometimes it seems we can touch it, but never seem to get a grip on the actual memory. Of all the folks the boy, Chris, remembered the most, and had the whole thing under hypnosis, even starting the motorcycle. I give thanks here to his mom, who had some moving memories of that morning. I guess kids have all the layers of their mind much closer to the surface. His

A FLASH IN TIME

mom says he grew into a better man that day than "most any I've even met."

Funny, why I took up archery so late in life is clear now, seemed an odd thing to be driven to pursue at the time, now a few years ago.

I know, you've never heard any of this, have you? It's been a number of years, going on a few decades actually, and I'm about done here on this mortal coil, so here the story is, and yes, as the old bromide says, time can heal all things. Now we know, including itself.

Me? I'm Doctor Mort Pocker a retired Clinical Psychologist, my practice was in New Mexico, working for the Department of Native American Affairs, now the Native American Trust, in their uncaring Federal Mental Health bureaucracy. A promising career doomed to listening to people who wanted the drugs we gave out, and 80% never got better. I retired some time ago, as soon as humanly possible at 46 years of age, I'm now 67 and what's really funny is I feel better now than I have in 30 years.

Maybe time can stand still! Yes, a quiet retirement, but then a strange thing happened one morning, walking past the downtown drug store on the way to the Dunkin'-Doughnut's for my breakfast routine of hot tea and a pecan scone.

THE END

www.ingramcontent.com/pod-product-compliance
Lightning Source LLC
LaVergne TN
LVHW021755060526
838201LV00058B/3108